A Very SINGULAR GUILD

Book 3

ALSO BY
CATHERINE JINKS

The City of Orphans series
A Very Unusual Pursuit
A Very Peculiar Plague

The Paradise Trap
The Abused Werewolf Rescue Group
The Reformed Vampire Support Group
The Genius Wars
Genius Squad
Evil Genius
Living Hell

The Pagan Chronicles
Pagan's Crusade
Pagan in Exile
Pagan's Vows
Pagan's Scribe
Pagan's Daughter

www.catherinejinks.com

A VERY SINGULAR GUILD

BOOK 3

CITY of ORPHANS

CATHERINE JINKS

ALLEN&UNWIN

SYDNEY • MELBOURNE • AUCKLAND • LONDON

Australian Government

This project has been assisted by the Australian Government through the Australia Council for the Arts, its arts funding and advisory body.

First published in 2014

Allen & Unwin
83 Alexander Street
Crows Nest NSW 2065
Australia

Phone: (61 2) 8425 0100
Email: info@allenandunwin.com
Web: www.allenandunwin.com

A Cataloguing-in-Publication entry is available from the National Library of Australia
www.trove.nla.gov.au

ISBN 978 1 74331 309 1

Cover and text design by Design by Committee
Set in Stempel Garamond 11/17 pt
This book was printed in August 2014 at Griffin Press,
168 Cross Keys Road, Salisbury South SA 5106.
www.griffinpress.com.au

10 9 8 7 6 5 4 3 2

The paper in this book is FSC® certified. FSC® promotes environmentally responsible, socially beneficial and economically viable management of the world's forests.

To Reka Simonsen and
Jeannette Larson

LONDON
ENGLAND
C.1870

1

UNDERGROUND

Newgate Market was an empty, echoing shell. Doors hung askew. Windows were smashed. Iron hooks were rusting away. The market clock was no longer ticking, and the stalls were silting up with rubbish.

All of the butchers had long ago moved to Smithfield, taking their sides of beef and saddles of mutton with them.

'I don't know why this place ain't bin torn down long since,' Alfred Bunce remarked. He stood hunched in the rain with his bag on his back, gazing across an expanse of muddy cobbles towards the central pavilion. Water dripped off his wide-brimmed hat and trickled down his long, beaky nose. Even his drooping moustache was sodden. 'Ruined buildings breed every kind o' strife, from coining to murder,' he added. 'Bogles would be the least o' yer problems, round here.'

Beside him, a brown-eyed boy was scanning the shops that fronted the square. Some of them were boarded up, and those that remained in business were for the most part seedy-looking taverns or coffee houses.

'I don't see Mr Wardle,' said the boy, whose name was Ned Roach. He was dressed in a navy-blue coat with brass buttons, very worn about the elbows, and a pair of buff-coloured trousers, damp and soiled. A flat cap sat on his springy brown hair. Despite his missing tooth and scarred hands, he looked respectable enough. 'Which o' these here establishments would be Mother Okey's?'

'Ask Jem,' Alfred replied. 'He knows the neighbourhood better'n I do.'

'Jem!' Ned turned to address another boy, who was lagging behind them. 'You bin here once. Which pub is Mother Okey's?'

Jem Barbary didn't answer. He was too busy peering at the dark silhouette of someone skulking on a nearby doorstep. Ned didn't blame Jem for being nervous. This was John Gammon's territory, and Gammon was a dangerous man.

'What's that feller doing there, lurking like a cracksman's crow?' Jem hissed. He was smaller and thinner than Ned, with so much thick, black hair that his head looked too big for his body. He wore a bedraggled suit of speckled brown tweed. 'D'you think he works for Salty Jack?'

'Mebbe he's sheltering from the rain,' Ned offered.

But Jem scowled. 'I don't trust him. I don't trust *no one* hereabouts.'

'Which is why we should pick up our pace.' Alfred spoke in a gruff, impatient voice. 'Wardle said to meet at Mother Okey's. Any notion where that might be?'

Jem considered the half-dozen public houses scattered around the market square. 'T'ain't that 'un,' he announced, pointing. 'That there is the Old Coffeepot. I spoke to the barmaid last time I passed through.'

'And that?' Alfred nodded at the nearest tavern. Although it had a sign suspended above its front door, none of them could read the lettering.

'There's a cat on that sign,' Ned observed, 'so it's more likely to be the Cat and Fiddle. Or the Cat and Salutation . . .'

'Here!' Jem suddenly clutched Alfred's sleeve. 'Ain't that Mr Wardle?'

It was. Ned recognised the man who had emerged from the old-fashioned alehouse to their right. He was large and middle-aged, with fuzzy side-whiskers and a slight paunch. Though respectably dressed, he had an untidy look about him – almost as if his clothes were buttoned askew. Wisps of wiry grey hair escaped from beneath his bowler hat. His necktie was crooked. There was a crusty stain on his waistcoat lapel, and an unshaven patch on his chin.

Even when he spotted Alfred, his worried expression didn't change. The anxious lines seemed permanently engraved across his brow.

'Mr Bunce!' he exclaimed. 'You found me!'

'Aye,' said Alfred, touching his hat.

'I was afeared you might have taken a wrong turn.' Mr Wardle's small blue eyes swung towards the two boys. 'I see you brought your apprentices with you.'

Alfred gave a brusque nod. 'Can't kill a bogle without bait,' he growled.

'Yes, of course.' Mr Wardle blinked uneasily at Ned, who wondered if the Inspector of Sewers could even remember his name. They had first been introduced to each other only a week before, at the Metropolitan

Board of Works, where they had all sat down at a very large, round table to launch the Committee for the Regulation of Subterranean Anomalies.

But more than half-a-dozen people had been present at that meeting, and a lot of business had been discussed. And since neither Ned nor Jem had made much of a contribution, it seemed likely that Mr Wardle had forgotten who they were.

'This neighbourhood ain't safe for Jem,' Alfred continued. 'There's a butcher as runs all the rackets hereabouts, and he's got a grudge against the lad. We ain't bin troubled thus far, since the butcher don't know where I live. But the longer we stay, the more likely it is we'll be spotted by one of his cronies. And I don't want that.'

Mr Wardle looked alarmed. 'No, indeed,' he said.

'So you'd best tell me about this here job, and then we can set to it,' Alfred finished. 'Back at the Board o' Works you mentioned there's three young 'uns vanished, and one sighting in a sewer. Which sewer, and where was the kids last seen?'

Mr Wardle hesitated for a moment. 'Perhaps it's best I show you what was shown to me,' he finally suggested, before heading across the cobbled square towards the central pavilion. Alfred hurried after him, with the two boys in tow. As they approached the dilapidated structure that had once sheltered row upon row of hanging carcasses, Ned felt uneasy. There was no telling what might lurk in that labyrinth of dark, rotting wood. As Alfred had so truly said, bogles might be the least of their problems.

'You don't think this is an ambush, do you?' Jem whispered, as if he was reading Ned's mind. 'You don't think Mr Wardle is in John Gammon's pocket?'

'No.' Ned was sure of that. John Gammon was a 'punisher' who liked to threaten local shopkeepers with bodily harm if they didn't pay over a portion of their earnings to him. But Eugene Wardle wasn't a local shopkeeper; he was a municipal officer who hailed from Holloway. 'Ain't no reason why Mr Wardle should know Salty Jack Gammon. *I'm* just concerned them missing boys is all a hum. Mebbe Jack's bin spreading tales, to lure us into a dark, quiet corner—'

'It ain't no tale.' Jem cut him off. 'There's at least one kid gone, for I heard it from the barmaid at the Old Coffeepot when I were here last.' After a moment's pause, he added, 'She said the lad passed a bad coin at the inn, then legged it into the market cellars. No one's seen him since.'

'... chased a printer's devil into the cellars, after he passed a counterfeit coin,' Mr Wardle was saying, as he led Alfred through the gloomy depths of the central pavilion. There was a rank smell of old blood and manure. Water was pooling under leaks in the roof. Here and there a rat would skitter out of the way, frightened by the crunch of broken glass underfoot. 'The second child was a young thief who went down to look for scrap metal,' Mr Wardle continued, 'and never returned to the sister he'd left waiting above. The third was a coal merchant's son who used to play in these stalls, though no one can be certain if he found his way beneath them.'

'And the sighting?' asked Alfred.

'Ah,' said Mr Wardle. 'Well, that didn't happen up here.' He stopped suddenly, having reached a kind of wooden booth, behind which lay the entrance to a wide room with an opening in its stone floor. 'You see, the heads of four sewers meet under Newgate Market. They used to be flushed out regular from a big cistern fitted with iron doors, though it's not much used these days. I had a team of flushers down there last week, oiling the screws and checking the penstocks. They caught a glimpse of something that scared the life out of 'em. And when they alerted me, Mr Bunce,

I thought of you.' The inspector stamped his foot, as if marking a spot. 'That cistern's close by, and one of the sewers runs beneath the cellar – which used to be a slaughterhouse, or so I'm told. They had to wash down the floors—'

'And the dirty water had to go somewhere,' Alfred concluded with a nod. 'There'll be drains, then.'

'I believe so.'

Alfred dropped his sack and began to rifle through it, pulling out a box of matches, a small leather bag, and a dark lantern with a hinged metal cover. 'You boys stay up here till I call you,' he told Jem and Ned as he struck a match to light his lantern. 'I need to look downstairs, and don't want no bogles lured out ahead o' time.'

Jem grimaced. Ned couldn't help asking, 'You think there's more'n one of 'em, Mr Bunce?'

Alfred shrugged and said, 'Ain't no telling, in this part o' the world. That's why I had to risk bringing Jem.' He appealed to the inspector. 'I'd be obliged if you'd mind the lads for me, Mr Wardle. I don't favour leaving 'em up here by themselves.'

'Yes, of course, Mr Bunce.' Mr Wardle sounded more anxious than ever. 'If that's what you'd prefer . . .'

'I'll not be gone long,' Alfred assured him, before disappearing down the cellar stairs. For a minute or so the others stood mute, listening to his footsteps recede underground. Then Mr Wardle said, 'You boys can't be very old, I'm persuaded. Are you?'

Ned and Jem exchanged a sideways glance.

'I'm eleven,' Jem volunteered. 'And Ned, here – he's just gone twelve.'

To Ned's surprise, Mr Wardle shook his head in bewilderment. 'Why would any man of sound mind be nursing a fatal grudge against an eleven-year-old boy?' the inspector wanted to know. 'What kind of offence could you possibly have committed to merit such bad feelings?'

'It weren't *me* as committed the offence!' Jem spluttered. He went on to explain that John Gammon, the butcher, had tried to feed him to a bogle only a couple of weeks before – and was therefore afraid of what Jem might tell the police. 'Which I ain't about to tell 'em *nothing*, since they'll not believe me in any case,' Jem finished. 'But Gammon don't know that, and is likely not to care.'

'Villains like him don't never take no risks,' Ned murmured in agreement.

'But why *wouldn't* the police believe you?' asked Mr Wardle. 'I don't understand.'

Again the two boys exchanged a quick look. Jem

flushed; he seemed unable to speak. It was Ned who finally answered, 'It's on account o' Jem used to steal for a living, and wouldn't make a good witness in a court o' law.'

'Though I ain't prigged *nothing* since last summer,' Jem blurted out, 'and won't never hoist so much as a twist o' tobacco ever again! I'm done with all that now – ain't I, Ned?'

'You are,' Ned confirmed. Though he'd seen Jem's eyes latch onto many a passing watch-chain and snuffbox, the former pickpocket had never once given into temptation – not while Ned was around. 'Besides,' Ned added, 'most beaks don't believe in bogles, and wouldn't credit any claims to the contrary, no matter *who* made 'em.'

'I see,' said Mr Wardle. He studied Jem for a moment, as if wondering how they'd ended up on the same committee. Then he turned to Ned. 'And you? Are you a reformed thief?'

'No, sir,' Ned replied stiffly. For six years he had been supporting himself, and not once had he stolen so much as a dirty handkerchief. 'I were a mudlark until Mr Bunce took me in. I used to scavenge for scraps along the riverbank.'

'Indeed.'

"'Twas a dirty job, but it gave me a good knowledge o' the East-End sewers,' Ned went on. He'd been interested in Mr Wardle's description of the cistern under the market, and wanted to know more. 'Could you tell me what a "penstock" is, sir? For I ain't never heard the word afore this.'

Mr Wardle opened his mouth, but all at once Alfred's voice hailed them, echoing up from the chamber beneath their feet. 'Are you there, Mr Wardle?'

'I am, Mr Bunce.'

'Could you send them lads down? And I'll have me sack along with 'em.'

'Yes, of course.' As Ned picked up Alfred's sack, Mr Wardle cleared his throat and said, 'I take it you've found something of interest?'

'Oh, aye. This here is a bogle's lair, make no mistake.' Alfred appeared suddenly at the foot of the stairs, his lantern raised, his long face grim. 'What I *don't* know is how many of 'em might be a-lurking down here. For I ain't never seen no den more suited to a bogle's taste, nor better laid out for the trapping o' children. If you ask me, Mr Wardle, there's more'n three kids has met their doom in this rat's nest.'

And he motioned to Ned, who reluctantly clumped downstairs with Alfred's sack on his shoulder.

2

THE SLAUGHTERHOUSE

Ned had explored a few sewers in his time. He'd spent years digging through river mud, and had more than once been forced to sleep in a coalhole. But when he arrived at the bottom of the cellar stairs, he felt his heart sink.

It was the most unpleasant spot he'd ever seen.

The ceiling was low and slimy, the floor caked with filth. Iron hooks hung from the ribbed vaults overhead, stained black with old blood. A great wooden tank, topped by a grill of metal bars, was slowly disintegrating in one corner. The whole place stank of corruption.

'Where would you like me to stand, Mr Bunce?'

asked Mr Wardle, from the top of the stairs. He spoke a little too loudly, and Alfred immediately shushed him.

'The fewer folk is on hand, the better,' Alfred softly replied. 'One thing you *could* do is keep others from coming down here.'

'By all means,' said Mr Wardle, in a much quieter voice. 'I'd prefer to stay up here. For this stench is worse than any sewer I've ever flushed.'

His silhouette vanished as he withdrew. Alfred, meanwhile, was gesturing at the ring of salt he'd laid down near an open drain in the middle of the cellar floor. There was a gap in this circle, directly opposite the drain. But when Ned glanced from the salt to Alfred, the bogler shook his head.

'Not you. You're over there.' Alfred jerked his chin at another, smaller ring of salt positioned across the room. Ned realised that Alfred had appointed him as decoy, in case more than one bogle should appear. While Alfred polished off the first monster, Ned was supposed to distract any others that might show up unexpectedly.

It was a technique that Alfred had used only once before, as far as Ned knew, because normally bogles were solitary creatures. For most of his bogling career,

Alfred hadn't needed more than one apprentice. But a recent plague of bogles around Newgate had prompted him to change his methods. And though the source of the plague was now gone, no one yet knew whether the bogles gathered in the neighbourhood had begun to drift away since Jem's former employer, Sarah Pickles, had stopped feeding babies to them.

Ned thought about Sarah Pickles as he stepped into the smaller ring of salt. He'd met her just once, having helped to capture her while she was escaping from the police. Now she was sitting in Newgate Prison, no more than a few hundred yards from where he stood, awaiting trial for the murder of sixteen infant children.

Her good friend John Gammon was also close by – only *he* wasn't in gaol. Ned wondered if he might be circling Newgate Market at that very moment, making plans to silence Jem. It was a chilling thought. Ned felt certain that, given a choice, Alfred would have turned down the Newgate job entirely. But because Alfred was now on the municipal payroll, he'd *had* no choice. He couldn't pick and choose his jobs anymore – not when they came from a municipal officer like Eugene Wardle.

'Ssst!' Alfred had stationed himself against one side of the wooden tank. In his right hand he carried a short spear; in his left, the leather bag. He nodded at Jem, who was already waiting inside the larger ring of salt with his back to the bogler. Between them, the drain yawned like a mouth; it was the size of a manhole, but any cap that might once have rested on top of it was now gone.

Ned decided that Alfred had chosen his hiding-place well. Though the tank provided excellent cover, it also gave Alfred a clear view of the drain – and of Jem, too. Ned found himself wondering what the tank had been used for. Blood, perhaps? Had freshly slaughtered sheep been laid across its metal grill?

Suddenly Jem began to sing.

Ten or a dozen cocks o' the game
On the prigging lay to the flash house came,
Lushing blue ruin and heavy wet,
Till the darkey, when the downy set.
All toddled and began to hunt
For readers, tattlers, fogles or blunt.

Jem's husky voice sounded like a cricket's chirp in that big, hollow space. Would the bogle be able to hear it? Ned was glad that *he* didn't have to sing. It was hard enough simply breathing the foul air, let alone shaping it into a tune. Besides, Ned wasn't much of a singer. During his six months as a coster's boy – before Alfred had finally hired him for bogling work – Ned had strained his vocal cords by touting his wares on busy street corners. 'Ripe damsons!' 'Potatoes, full weight!' 'American apples, round and sound!' Ned knew all the cries, but couldn't hold a tune.

Jem could. He piped away gamely, his gaze riveted to the mirror in his hand, which framed a small, murky image of Alfred's shadowy form.

As I were crossing St James's Park,
I met a swell, a well-togg'd spark.
I stopped a bit: then toddled quicker,
For I'd prigged his reader, drawn his ticker;
Then he calls, 'Stop thief!' Thinks I, my master,
That's a hint to me to toddle faster.

Ned understood that he was quite safe inside his ring of salt. There wasn't a bogle on earth that could break through the magic circle protecting him. Yet he felt weighed down by a peculiar sense of dread, which grew stronger and stronger as he thought about John Gammon, and Sarah Pickles, and the hole in the floor. What if *two* bogles emerged from that hole? Or three?

What if a whole pack of them appeared; what was he supposed to do then?

In his entire life he'd only ever laid eyes on three bogles, and although he had personally killed one of them, he still wasn't properly trained. Compared to Jem, he was just a raw recruit. Suppose he made a mistake? Suppose something went wrong . . .?

Suddenly Ned gasped. This black despair wasn't natural. He recognised it from previous bogling jobs. And Jem must have recognised it too, because his voice began to shake as he launched into another verse.

Whatever swag we chance for to get,
All is fish as comes to net:
Mind yer eye, and draw the yokel,
Don't disturb or use the folk ill.
Keep a lookout, if the beaks is nigh,
And cut yer stick afore they're fly.

When Ned first heard the underlying noise, it was so faint that he couldn't quite make out what it was. A draught? A sigh? Gradually he identified it as a kind of whispering gurgle, and he licked his lips as he peered at the drain.

But he couldn't see any movement in its depths. Though the air seemed to thicken, no bogle emerged from the sewer. It wasn't until Ned glanced towards Alfred, seeking guidance, that he spotted something black and shiny spilling over the rim of the tank.

At least a dozen long, boneless arms were unrolling like wet streamers, clinging to whatever surface they touched. The bulk of the creature soon followed, hauled out of the tank by its own straining arms like cargo winched from a ship's hold. It was covered in jagged spines that waved about as it dropped towards the floor, dragging itself along as silently as a snail.

Horrified, Ned opened his mouth, then shut it again. He didn't know what to do. Alfred had told him, over and over again, not to speak except in an emergency. But surely this *was* an emergency? Alfred hadn't yet noticed the bogle; he was too busy staring at the drain. When Ned shot a quick glance at Jem, he saw the mirror shaking in Jem's hand. Clearly *Jem* knew what was happening.

In fact it might have been the sudden catch in Jem's voice that caused Alfred to look up. For an instant he froze, wide-eyed, as the bogle slid down the front of the tank, barely a foot away from him. Luckily, however, its wet, slithering shape passed him by.

It seemed anxious to reach Jem, who was still bravely singing.

> *B-but now the beaks is on the scene,*
> *And watched by moonlight where we went –*
> *Stagged us a-toddling into the ken*
> *And was down upon us all, and then*
> *Who should I spy but the slap-up spark*
> *What I eased of the swag in St James's P-Park?*

Slowly the creature advanced. It had a gaping maw lined with spine-like teeth, and glowing yellow eyes with no pupils in them. Alfred was edging forward, adjusting his grip on the spear. Ned could hardly breathe. Jem was faltering; his voice was now just a hoarse squeak, and nearly failed altogether when the bogle's reaching arms slipped through the gap in the ring of salt. They fastened themselves to the floor like suckers, then tightened until the rest of the bogle surged forward, leaving a slimy trail in its wake.

> *There's a time, says King Sol, to dance and sing;*
> *I know there's a time for another thing:*
> *There's a time to pipe, and a time to snivel –*
> *I wish all Charlies and beaks to the —*

'*Go!*' yelled Alfred.

He jumped out of the shadows. There was a white flash as he tossed a handful of salt. At the very same instant, Jem threw himself into a forward roll, bowling along like a hoop. Alfred raised his spear. The bogle reared up, frothing and hissing, its tentacles writhing, caught in the glittering trap—

BANG! It exploded like a giant grape, releasing a geyser of black liquid.

There was a long, shocked silence. Then Mr Wardle reappeared at the stop of the stairs.

'Mr Bunce?' he murmured. 'Are you all right?'

'Aye,' Alfred said hoarsely. He shuffled forward and stooped to retrieve his spear, which was lying in a sticky black puddle. His green coat was dripping with goo. Even his shaggy, salt-and-pepper hair was splattered with the stuff.

'That weren't so big,' Jem croaked, climbing stiffly to his feet. Ned saw that he, too, had been sprayed with slime.

'Nay,' Alfred agreed. 'I've seen bigger.' He took a handkerchief from his pocket and began to mop his face. 'You'd best get that off you,' he told Jem. 'Though it don't burn none, I doubt it's summat you'd want on yer skin.'

Meanwhile, Mr Wardle was advancing down the stairs. 'Uh – Mr Bunce?' he asked. 'Was there a bogle?'

'Aye,' said Alfred.

'And you killed it?'

'I did.'

'Um . . .' Mr Wardle hesitated. His gaze drifted towards the puddle of fluid on the floor. 'I should tell you that there may be another close by,' he said at last.

Alfred frowned. 'What do you mean?'

'Well . . .' Again the inspector seemed lost for words. Finally he cleared his throat and explained, 'I just had a young lad wander up to me, saying there was a bogle in his father's house. Somehow he knew that I was with a bogler – perhaps he'd heard me speaking to the barmaid at Mother Okey's. But when I asked him for an address, he grew very anxious. He asked why you couldn't come directly. And as soon as I pressed him, he ran off.' Seeing Alfred wince, Mr Wardle blurted out, 'He was in such a state that he made *me* nervous!'

Ned swallowed. He caught Alfred's eye, then looked away. Jem was grimacing as if he'd just caught his hand in a door.

'We need to get out of here,' Alfred declared. He thrust his spear towards Ned, who took it obediently.

(It was Ned's job to clean the spear.) 'There ain't no saying who sent that boy. Or who might decide to follow him here.'

'D'you think—?' Jem began, but Alfred cut him off.

'I don't know what to think. All I know is, I ain't taking no risks.' Alfred went to pick up his sack, which lay under his hat near the dark lantern. 'Come on,' he told the boys. 'We'll go straight home and clean up there. I'd sooner take me chances with a crusting o' bogle innards than I would with John Gammon.'

By the time he'd finished speaking, Jem and Ned were already on their way upstairs.

THEATRE FOLK

Alfred Bunce lived with his two apprentices in a garret off Drury Lane. The crowded room was six floors up – a very long climb with a bucket of water. So when they finally arrived home, Ned wasn't surprised to discover that the jug on the washstand was empty.

'I'll fetch another pail,' he offered, since he was the only one not covered in smears of dried bogle. Unfortunately, Orange Court didn't have its own water supply. It didn't have anything much; it was just a narrow alley full of costers' carts, cabbage leaves and drifts of grubby children. To reach the nearest pump, Ned had to head down Drury Lane, towards Covent Garden Market. But this didn't worry Ned, who regarded Orange Court as the height of luxury, despite its lack of water. After years spent sharing beds in cheap boarding houses, he felt very, very fortunate to have a palliasse all to himself. And he was profoundly grateful to Alfred Bunce, whose generosity had transformed his life.

Baiting bogles was a small price to pay for a roof, a fire and a full belly.

Ned was on his way back from the pump when he spotted a knife-grinder, parked outside a coal merchant's shop. Ned loved to watch knife-grinders at work. This one was bent over his machine, sharpening a pair of scissors. As he pedalled away furiously, a wooden wheel on his cart turned the circular whetstone by means of a leather belt.

Ned couldn't help admiring the smooth, efficient way the mechanical parts interacted. For a moment he stood entranced, forgetting that he had to hurry home.

'There he is! The barrow boy!' a loud voice suddenly exclaimed. 'Hi! Ned Roach! We've been looking for you *everywhere*!'

Startled, Ned spun around. He saw a knot of people surging towards him, all young and handsome and well-groomed. The oldest was a man of perhaps twenty-five, with a thick moustache and curly hair parted in the middle. He wore striped trousers, a silk cravat, and a coat with a velvet collar. Accompanying him were three girls who looked very much alike. They had huge, pale eyes under finely arched brows. Their heads were crowned by masses of brown ringlets, which tumbled out from beneath frivolous little hats sprouting knots of ribbon and tufts of lace. The youngest, who wasn't much older than Ned, wore violet taffeta. The other two were dressed in gold-braided, brass-buttoned Garibaldi coats.

'Hold up there!' cried the young man. 'Do you know me? Frederick Vokes? My sisters and I have bought fruit from your master's barrow.'

'Y-yes, of course,' Ned stammered. He knew the Vokes family very well – at least by sight. They were actors from the Theatre Royal, which lay just down the road, and they had always been highly visible. What surprised Ned was that they recognised *him*. For although he had worked as a coster's boy for several months, he hadn't exchanged a single word with the Vokes siblings during that time. 'But I ain't on a fruit barrow no more . . .'

'We know *that*!' said the youngest girl, whose name was Rosina. She had a very loud voice for such a little person. 'We were at Covent Garden Market, searching high and low, until we discovered that you were no longer to be found there!'

'That's right.' Ned found himself edging backwards as the family closed in on him. 'I'm a bogler's boy now.'

The Vokes sisters gasped, then burst into squeals of excitement. By this time they were all gathered around Ned, striking poses and waving their hands about, while rougher, dirtier, busier people swerved to avoid them. Some of these passers-by briefly slowed down, because the girls were worth a look. But none of the Vokes siblings seemed conscious of the curious stares that they were attracting. Instead they fixed their attention wholly on Ned – who felt dazzled, like a mouse caught in the glare of a miner's lamp.

'Why, what a fortunate thing!' Rosina trilled. 'We were told that you lodged with a Go-Devil man, but not that you *worked* for him!'

'We wish to engage him, you see,' Frederick explained.

'And here you are, placed in our path, just when we'd given up hope!' said the eldest sister, whose name Ned struggled to recall. The middle one was Victoria; he remembered that. He also knew that they were renowned for their dancing, and that after every show they would eat a late supper (or early breakfast) at the Tavistock Hotel, near Covent Garden Market, before picking up a handful of fresh plums or grapes on their way back home.

But they weren't on their way home now. Ned decided that they must be heading *for* the theatre.

'Who told you I lodged with a Go-Devil man?' he asked, unable to imagine why the Vokes family would be discussing him with anyone. But then Frederick briskly related how he and his sisters had been lamenting the loss of 'poor Noah' while they passed through Covent Garden Market that morning, and were overheard by a fat, bald coster with a ginger moustache. 'He said that if we wanted to hire a bogler, you were the person to find,' Frederick concluded, with a very theatrical flourish. 'And now – *voila!* We've found you!'

Ned still didn't understand. 'Who's Noah?'

'He is a boy from the ballet,' the eldest sister replied. 'He's missing.'

'And he was last seen near an underground tunnel,' Rosina said eagerly, 'so he *might* have been taken by a bogle – don't you think?'

'Unless, of course, he's tucked away in the Nell Gwynn public house, drinking himself witless,'

Victoria drawled. 'That tunnel leads straight from the theatre to Mr Cooper's tavern, does it not?'

'Oh, *Vic*!' Rosina shot her sister a reproachful glance. 'How can you be so heartless? The poor boy's only nine years old!'

'Besides, the passage to Mr Cooper's has been bricked up for years, if it ever existed,' Frederick pointed out. But Victoria didn't seem convinced.

'Has it? Truly?' Her tone was sceptical. 'I've been hearing about some very odd smells down there. And you know what the cooking is like at the Nell Gwynn.'

Her eldest sister laughed. 'That smell isn't cooking, dear, it's *drains*. I heard Mr Todd say so himself.'

Ned stiffened. A missing child was one thing. But when a child vanished near a tunnel, directly over a sewer pipe, in the presence of a mysterious stench . . .

He didn't like the sound of it.

'Of course, that smell *could* be a rotting carcass,' Frederick suddenly remarked, with a wicked glint in his eye. 'Mr Chatterton has been threatening to kill any number of theatre critics. Perhaps he's been hiding the corpses backstage.'

'Oh, do stop joking!' Rosina bristled at him. 'I *like*

Noah! And he isn't the first – why, what about that poor little lost girl?'

'What poor little lost girl?' asked her eldest sister.

'Oh, *you* know, Jessie!' Rosina cried. 'The little girl who came to watch *Tom Thumb*! She wandered off into the crowd, and her mother made *such* a fuss . . .'

'But she was found again, surely?' Frederick objected.

'I don't think she was.' Rosina glanced at Victoria, who shrugged.

By this time Ned was thoroughly confused. Listening to the Vokes family was like watching a team of jugglers tossing balls. 'So there's two missing kids?' Ned interrupted. He was trying to get things straight in his mind. 'A boy and a girl?'

'Yes, indeed. And a lot of talk about something in the tunnel beneath the theatre,' Frederick replied. 'That's why we need your bogler, Ned.'

'At *once*,' Rosina added. 'Or what will befall all the other poor children?'

'Like our darling Rosie . . .' The eldest Vokes sister flung her arms around the youngest. 'How can we risk losing our dearest and daintiest?'

Ned doubted very much that Rosina was young enough to tempt a bogle. She looked at least sixteen.

But instead of pointing this out, he said, 'Mr Bunce can't do nothing for you now, Miss. He's due at the Board o' Works in an hour.'

'The Board of Works?' Rosina echoed. 'Goodness me!'

'Are there bogles at the Board of Works?' Frederick asked, with real interest.

'No, sir, but Mr Bunce is hired by the Sewers Office, now. On a regular wage, like.' Seeing the three sisters blink in astonishment, Ned suddenly remembered that he wasn't supposed to be telling people that the Sewers Office had hired a Go-Devil man. So he quickly did his best to change the subject. 'That's why I don't know as how Mr Bunce can help you. He ain't taking on private jobs no more, see.'

'Oh, but he'll help *us*, I'm sure,' Frederick declared, in ringing tones. 'You could hardly describe us as *private* people. We're very, very public.'

'You must persuade him. For our sake.' Jessie leaned towards Ned, twining her arm through his. 'You must tell him we're in dire need, and so very frightened.'

'Ladies in distress,' Victoria confirmed stoutly.

'And think of the poor little children, Ned!' Glittering tears had welled up in Rosina's huge, pale eyes. 'Why, there are twelve in the ballet, as well as all the backstage boys! What will happen to them, if Mr Bunce refuses to help? Surely he couldn't be so *wicked* . . .?'

Ned didn't know what to say. He was cowed by the girl's emotion.

Or was it all just an act?

'M-mebbe you should talk to Mr Bunce,' he stammered. 'Mr Bunce'd listen to you.'

'Is that so?' When Ned began to nod enthusiastic-ally, Rosina said, 'Then tell him to come to theatre. Tonight. Once he's finished at the Board of Works.'

'Oh, but—'

'*Please*, Ned. *Dear* Ned. You know how wretched you'll feel if you fail us!' Rosina cried, as Jessie patted his cheek and Frederick clapped him on the shoulder.

'I defy you to refuse 'em, my lad, for they're not the least accustomed to disappointment,' Frederick warned. Then he drew his watch from his pocket and spluttered, 'Dash it, is that the time? We have lingered too long, my beauties! Come along, now. Hop to it.'

'Ask for Mr Todd at the stage door,' Jessie advised Ned, as her brother hustled her away. Rosina blew a kiss and Victoria lifted a graceful hand in farewell.

A VERY SINGULAR GUILD

'We'll be expecting you!' they said. 'Tell Mr Bunce how keen we are to meet him!'

Soon they were gone, though they left a drifting cloud of scent in their wake. And the crowded street suddenly seemed empty without them.

Ned was still reeling when he arrived back at Alfred's lodgings.

'You took yer time,' the bogler growled.

'I couldn't help it.' Ned set down his bucket. 'Someone stopped me.'

Over by the fireplace, Jem was poking at embers. He stiffened and looked up. 'Not Salty Jack?' he asked.

'No.' As Ned explained what had happened, Alfred's long face settled into even gloomier creases. 'I told 'em you don't take private jobs no more,' Ned finished, 'but they wouldn't listen.'

Alfred gave a grunt. Jem looked surprised and said, 'No private jobs? Who told you that?'

Ned hesitated. He shot a glance at Alfred before mumbling, 'Mr Bunce said as how we're all living on public money now, and should allus put official business first.'

'Truly?' Jem turned to Alfred, eyebrows raised. '*I* never heard no one warn you off yer own work.'

'Not yet, no,' said Alfred, who was pouring water

into the chipped white basin on the washstand. 'But I'll not take on no extra jobs till they're cleared with the committee. For if there's rules to follow, I'd not want to break 'em.'

'Rules?' Jem echoed. 'I didn't hear no mention o' rules at the last meeting.'

Alfred shrugged. 'We'll find out soon enough if I'm allowed to take work where I can find it. If I can, we'll go straight to the theatre from the Board o' Works. But I ain't so sure it'll be worth our while.' Having splashed his face with water, he wiped his eyes and peered at Ned. 'Them Vokes young 'uns,' he continued. 'Would they be the kind to let their fancies run away with 'em?'

Ned frowned. Then he sighed. Then he reluctantly admitted, 'I think their fancies would have a hard time *keeping up* with 'em.'

'I thought as much,' said Alfred. 'Actors is all the same. Wherever there's a choice, they'll favour a tale above the truth.'

And he started scraping bits of bogle out of his hair with a gap-toothed comb.

PLANS

Mark Harewood was a Clerk of Works at the Sewers Office. He was tall and young and vigorous, with flashing blue eyes and a broad, clean-shaven face. Everything about him was sunny: his gleaming smile, his thick blond hair – even his yellow waistcoat.

Ned had met him only once before, but had quickly decided that he was an excellent fellow. Now, seeing him on the third floor of the Board of Works building, Ned was relieved to know that they were in the right place at the right time.

'Why, here you are!' Mr Harewood exclaimed, upon catching sight of Alfred and his apprentices. 'Come in! Take a seat! I've something to show you . . .'

Obediently, Alfred led the way into a room that was lined with oak panelling. Red velvet curtains were draped across two lofty windows, and the walls were hung with oil paintings so dark that Ned couldn't tell if they were portraits or landscapes. In the centre of the room stood a large circular table surrounded by hard chairs.

Mr Harewood and Erasmus Gilfoyle, the naturalist, were leaning over this table, studying what appeared to be a map. Mr Gilfoyle was shorter and slimmer than his friend. His wispy fair hair was plastered down with oil, whereas Mr Harewood's golden fleece fell into his eyes. Though they were both about the same age, they looked very different. Mr Gilfoyle was as neat as a pin in his dove-grey suit, while Mr Harewood was wearing ink-stained shirtsleeves and an unknotted tie.

'Look at this,' Mr Harewood urged Alfred. 'D'you see what I've done here? Thanks to what you told me last week, Mr Bunce, I was able to mark up the exact location of every bogle you've killed in London during the past five years.' He began to jab at the map with one finger. 'See those red dots? Each represents a dead bogle. And this is the river, of course, with all its bridges. And this is St Paul's.' As

Ned edged closer to the map, Mr Harewood retrieved another roll of paper from one of the chairs and said, 'Now *this* is a plan of the city's sewer system, traced onto wax paper. If I put it on top of the map, you will see how our underground waterways intersect with London's bogle sightings.'

Ned stared in amazement. Before him lay an intricate network of pipes and channels and gates, superimposed upon an even *more* complex tangle of streets and squares and canals. The effect was like a three-dimensional model. He had never seen anything so exquisite – or so fascinating.

He only wished that he could read the street names.

'It's evident that there *must* be a connection between subterranean water and the incidence of bogles,' Mr Harewood went on. 'Only consider the clusters of red dots here ... and here ... and here, of course, near the Fleet Sewer—'

'Is that the Fleet?' asked Ned. He was so excited that he forgot about keeping his mouth shut. Alfred had told him, over and over again, to hold his tongue while a gentleman was talking. But the sight of London's innards, spread out before him like something dissected, had pushed everything else out of Ned's mind.

'That *is* the Fleet,' Mr Harewood confirmed. He didn't seem offended. In fact, he smiled at Ned. 'And that is the viaduct, and that is Newgate Street—'

'So *that* must be the flushing tank!' Ned exclaimed, pointing. 'The one beneath Newgate Market!'

'Perhaps.' Mr Harewood lifted his head suddenly. 'Mr Wardle – *you* would know, I'm sure.'

'Know what?' the inspector said. Despite his bulk, he had slipped into the room without attracting much attention. 'Good evening, Mr Bunce. Mr Gilfoyle. Good evening, boys,' he added, mopping his red, sweaty face with a crumpled handkerchief. Then, seeing Mr Harewood beckon to him, he moved across to the table. 'Ah!' he exclaimed. 'So my plans arrived.'

'They did indeed.' Mr Harewood tapped at the wax paper. 'This symbol here – does it represent a flushing tank?'

Mr Wardle squinted at a tiny black star like an ink-blot. 'Why, yes,' he replied. 'That's one of 'em. We have ten altogether – at Newgate, and Leadenhall—'

'If the bogles live in the sewers,' Ned interrupted, 'mebbe they could all be *flushed* out.' The idea had struck him as he traced the course of a sewer-line from one end of London to the other. 'If you was to flush the bogles from pipe to pipe, until most o' the sewers was closed off, would you be able to herd 'em all together like goats?' he asked Mr Harewood, who grinned his approval.

'An interesting notion, young Ned. I must admit, the same thought crossed my mind when I saw this pattern of red dots. But it would be a difficult task, I fear, what with the variable water pressure, and the number of flushing gates, and the unknown degrees of resistance we'd be facing from the creatures themselves . . .' Mr Harewood trailed off, his brow furrowed in concentration, before he turned to the inspector. 'What do you think, old boy? Could we blow 'em all into the Thames?'

'What for?' asked Mr Wardle. It was a good question. How were the bogles to be disposed of, once they'd been expelled from their lairs? Ned was wondering if Alfred could be positioned over a sewage outfall, where he might spear each bogle as it emerged, when all at once every man in the room snapped to attention.

'Good evening,' a familiar voice remarked. 'Forgive us for being so late. St Martin's Lane was at a standstill, and the porter seemed reluctant to admit us.'

Looking up, Ned saw that Miss Edith Eames had appeared at the door. She was wearing a mustard-coloured mantle, a matching skirt without frills or flounces, and a slightly peevish expression. Her black brows were knitted together beneath the tip-tilted brim of her modest felt hat. Her face was even paler than usual, and she pursed her lips as she impatiently peeled off her beige kid gloves.

Clearly she was annoyed about something.

But Ned barely glanced at Miss Eames. He was far more interested in the girl beside her, who seemed to glitter like cut glass. Her golden curls were even brighter than Mr Harewood's. Her blue eyes gleamed like stars and her fair skin glowed beneath a light dusting of freckles. From the ribbons on her hat to the buttons on her boots, she was dressed all in white.

Ned smiled at the girl, hoping to receive a smile in return. But she had already flung herself at Alfred.

'Mr Bunce!' she exclaimed. 'Did you go to Newgate Market?'

'We did,' he replied, holding her off. 'Mind yer pretty clothes, Birdie – I've mud on me trousers.'

'Was there a bogle?' she demanded. 'Did you kill it?'

'Aye.' Alfred turned to the Clerk of Works. 'You should make a note o' that, Mr Harewood.'

'I shall.' As Mr Harewood produced a pot of red ink, Birdie McAdam continued to question Alfred about the Newgate bogle. She was particularly curious about its size, its exact location, and the traces that it had left behind. Mr Gilfoyle was also interested; in fact, he began to take notes in a little black book. But Ned knew that Birdie's interest was more than academic.

Having once been a bogler's girl, she still felt personally involved in every job that Alfred agreed to do.

'Samples of the residue would be useful,' Mr Gilfoyle remarked, when Birdie had finished. 'Perhaps I should be present at your next encounter, Mr Bunce.'

'Perhaps,' Alfred agreed, though he didn't sound very enthusiastic. Meanwhile, Mr Harewood was carefully drying the new red dot on his map with a piece of blotting paper.

'Now that we're all here,' he said, 'I think we should commence formal proceedings. We'll start with last week's minutes, perhaps – unless anyone has any questions?'

No one did. So they all found a chair and sat down, facing each other across the table. Then Mr Gilfoyle cleared his throat, donned a pair of spectacles, and began to read from a stack of loose papers that had been placed in front of him.

First he reminded everyone that elections had been held the previous week. As a result, he said, Mr Harewood was now Chairman, Mr Wardle was Treasurer, and he himself was Secretary. He went on to relate that the committee had agreed to meet every Monday afternoon – at which time a sum of fifteen shillings would be paid to Mr Alfred Bunce, by way of a salary.

'Miss Eames then moved that our mission as a committee should be to rid London of its bogles,' Mr Gilfoyle continued in his gentle, precise voice, 'and this motion was carried without dissent. The next item on the agenda was a discussion regarding the typical characteristics of a bogle. Mr Bunce, Miss McAdam and Miss Eames all contributed to the discussion, after which the Secretary suggested that he and Miss Eames form a subcommittee entrusted with the task of finding out more about bogles as a species. Mr Gilfoyle undertook to write a report on any information gleaned, in order to classify the creatures in accordance with the standard biological taxonomy of Linnaeus . . .'

Ned strained to remember what the 'biological taxonomy of Linnaeus' meant. Mr Gilfoyle had explained it to him the previous week; it had something to do with the way plants and animals were divided into different classes and families. But the families didn't have mothers and fathers, and the classes didn't have anything to do with school. According to Mr Gilfoyle, these were simply scientific terms that gave people a better understanding of the world . . .

Ned wished that *he* had a better understanding of the world. Sometimes, when Mr Gilfoyle was speaking, he felt as if he were trying to catch soap bubbles; the meaning of each word either drifted out of Ned's reach or vanished completely just when he thought he had a grip on it. *If only I had some schooling*, he thought, shooting a glance at Birdie. Thanks to Miss Eames, Birdie was now educated. She had learned to read and write. And for that reason, perhaps, she was staring at Mr Gilfoyle with an expression on her face that wasn't blank, bored or bewildered, but intent and absorbed. She looked as if she was really *listening* to what he said.

Jem, on the other hand, was twisting restlessly in his seat, his gaze flitting around the room.

'. . . Mr Harewood then proposed that he and Mr Bunce form another subcommittee,' Mr Gilfoyle continued. 'He further suggested that this subcommittee's first task would be to circulate a memorandum among all the municipal offices, asking that they notify Mr Harewood of any unusual subterranean activity that may pertain to bogles. The motion was carried without dissent. Mr Harewood promised to alert the committee if his memorandum uncovered any evidence of bogle activity. He also asked Mr Wardle to provide him with a map of London's sewage system . . .'

Jem caught Ned's eye and grimaced. Ned immediately looked away. Though he sympathised with Jem, he didn't want to be caught yawning or wriggling. He didn't feel secure enough for that.

Of all the committee members, he was probably the least qualified. Birdie had been a bogler's girl for nearly eight years – since she was just three years old. Her voice was so fine that she could sing *any* bogle out of its den. Jem was as nimble as a monkey; he had once climbed a six-storey chimney to escape a bogle's clutches. Mr Bunce was a bogler, Mr Wardle knew the sewer system, Miss Eames was a folklorist . . .

Ned, on the other hand, had no skills to speak of. He couldn't even read. He had nothing to offer but sturdy good health, a willingness to work, and an ability to concentrate. Knowing this, he felt dispensable, and always took great care not to offend, intrude or disappoint.

Since the age of six, when his mother's death had cast him onto the street, Ned had struggled to find a place in the world. He had worked for a rag-and-bone man, who had beaten him, and for a beggar, who had starved him. He'd spent a very short time in the Whitechapel workhouse, before running away to become a mudlark. And in all that time, no one had cared whether he lived or died.

But things had changed, thanks to Alfred. And Ned wasn't about to jeopardise his new life by pulling silly faces.

'. . . and the meeting closed at six o'clock.' Suddenly Mr Gilfoyle finished reading. He raised his eyes and glanced around the table. 'Are there any objections to the contents of these minutes? Does anyone wish to amend them?' Two or three people shook their heads. No one spoke. 'Very well,' the naturalist murmured. 'Then we'll proceed to the next item on the agenda, which is, I believe . . . um . . .'

'The report of the Chairman's subcommittee,' said Mr Harewood. And he reached for the rolled-up map that was sitting nearby.

5

ALL IN FAVOUR?

Birdie was very impressed with Mr Harewood's map. She and Miss Eames both stood with their noses almost brushing against it, marvelling at its complexity, as Mr Harewood explained what the red dots meant.

'As you can see, there appears to be a link between bogles and underground water,' he said. 'In fact, it's been suggested that we try to *flush* the bogles out of our drains.' He winked at Ned, then turned to Mr Gilfoyle. 'Make a note of that, Razzy, will you? *Mr Harewood to consult the Chief Engineer about flushing the sewers.*'

Mr Gilfoyle immediately began to scribble on the paper in front of him, as Ned pondered his surprising nickname. 'Razzy' seemed much too undignified for someone so gentlemanly.

Meanwhile, Miss Eames was frowning at Mr Harewood. 'Do you propose to exterminate all of London's bogles by pushing them into the river, and thence to the sea?' she asked him. 'Will that have the desired effect?'

Every eye swivelled towards Mr Harewood, who shrugged. 'I've no idea,' he admitted. 'What's your opinion, Mr Bunce? Would salt water kill bogles?'

Alfred scratched his scrubby cheek, but said nothing.

'Salt keeps 'em at bay,' Birdie pointed out. '*And* cures their bites.'

'Aye. It does that,' Alfred agreed – at which point Ned raised his hand.

'Thames water is fresh as far as London Bridge,' he piped up, just in case no one else knew the river as well as he did. After five years spent scouring its muddy banks, he was only too familiar with its habits. 'Beyond that,' he continued, ''tis brackish until Southend.'

'Brackish?' Miss Eames echoed thoughtfully. And Jem, who was finally paying attention, said, 'What's brackish?'

'Brackish is half-salt, half-fresh,' Mr Wardle kindly informed him.

'But would brackish water kill bogles?' Mr Harewood appealed to Alfred. 'What do *you* think, Mr Bunce?'

'I don't know as how it would,' Alfred replied. 'Fact is, I don't know as how salt would. For I ain't never seen it done – nor heard of it, neither.'

Ned found himself nodding in agreement. He couldn't help thinking that if salt were toxic to bogles, people would have long ago stopped hiring Go-Devil men. Instead, they would have kept a bag of salt handy, just in case.

'Perhaps if a bogle was *completely immersed* in salt?' This suggestion came from Miss Eames. 'Or even a very highly concentrated solution?'

'Mebbe we should flush out the sewers with salt water,' Birdie added. But the inspector winced, and Mr Harewood looked pained.

'I doubt we'd get leave to do that,' the inspector remarked. 'Salt in our sewers? It would rust all the sluice-gates, *and* kill half the trees in London.'

'Ahem.' All at once Mr Gilfoyle, who had been busy taking notes, lifted his head and coughed. 'We should not be employing salt as a weapon until we determine what it would do,' he said. 'Mr Bunce uses salt to deter bogles. Is that correct, sir?'

'Aye,' Alfred conceded.

'But when you kill them, you employ your spear, which once belonged to Finn MacCool. Is *that* correct?'

'Aye.'

'How do you know?' Seeing Alfred blink, Mr Gilfoyle rephrased his question. 'That is to say, who told you about the origins of the spear?'

'Daniel Piggin. Me old master.' Alfred was looking more and more uncomfortable, Ned thought. But that wasn't surprising. The bogler had always hated discussing his past. 'Mr Piggin's bin dead these twenty years, though. And he weren't talkative at the best o' times.'

'What a pity,' Mr Gilfoyle sounded genuinely regretful. 'I'm sure we could have learned a great deal from Mr Piggin.'

'Did he happen to tell you what your spear is *made* of, Mr Bunce?' Mr Harewood broke in. 'Or if it has been treated with any kind of unusual substance?'

As Alfred shook his head, Ned gasped. The spear! Of course! If Alfred's spear could be copied, somehow . . .

'According to Irish legend, Finn MacCool's spear *was* poisoned,' Miss Eames volunteered. 'But I'm afraid nothing else was said on the subject.'

'Which doesn't mean that we couldn't find out more,' the naturalist observed. 'It so happens I know a chemical operator who works at the Apothecaries' Hall, on Water Lane. I shall ask him if he would examine Mr Bunce's spear, with a view to identifying any toxins adhering to it.' He abruptly dropped his chin, and began to scratch away so energetically that his pen sputtered. *'Mr Gilfoyle to make inquiries at the Great Laboratory on Water Lane . . .'* he muttered to himself.

Meanwhile Jem was bouncing up and down in his chair, too excited to sit still. 'If Mr Bunce's spear is poisoned, and we find out what the poison is, then we can make a thousand spears!' he cried. 'And we can send a whole *army* down the sewers, to kill every one o' them bogles!'

'We wouldn't need no army, Jem.' Birdie seemed unaware of the horrified looks that were being exchanged all around her. 'Not if we put the poison in the flushing tanks—'

'Whoa! Hold up there!' Mr Harewood raised both hands. 'We will *not* be flooding the drains with poison! *Or* armed men!' As Birdie opened her mouth to protest, he added, 'The river water is bad enough. We don't want to make it worse.'

'Oh.' Birdie stared at him for a moment, then blushed. 'No. Of course not,' she mumbled. Ned wanted to assure her that the same thought had crossed *his* mind – at least for an instant. But Mr Harewood had something else to say.

'Was Finn MacCool a real person?' he asked Miss Eames, with a crooked smile. 'I thought him a myth.'

Miss Eames hesitated. She opened her mouth, then shut it again. It was Mr Gilfoyle who answered.

'When the mists of time descend, history can sometimes become confused with mythology,' he informed Mr Harewood. 'A rhinoceros might turn into a unicorn, and an ancient king might be given a magic sword. It's my belief that by studying fantastical beasts through the lens of scientific method, we may be able to assign them a place in the natural hierarchy. A sea monster may actually be a sea creature, mis-identified. And perhaps Finn MacCool suffered a similar fate . . .'

As he trailed off, there was a brief silence. Glancing around the table, Ned saw that Mr Wardle looked impressed, Mr Harewood was nodding, and Miss

Eames had an approving smile plastered across her face. Even Mr Bunce seemed resigned.

Only Birdie and Jem hadn't been won over. Jem's attention had wandered again, and Birdie was frowning at Mr Gilfoyle.

'But bogles *are* magic,' she protested.

'Perhaps,' said Mr Gilfoyle. 'Or perhaps not. Once upon a time, people used to believe that the pelican fed its young with blood from its own breast. Now we know better, thanks to scientific observation.'

Ned didn't know what a pelican was. He wasn't sure that Birdie did, either. It hardly mattered, though, because she wasn't really listening.

'But big bogles can squeeze through the tiniest holes!' she argued. 'And they vanish like soap bubbles when you kill 'em! No *ordinary* creature does that!'

'Not all bogles do that either,' Mr Gilfoyle gently pointed out. 'Mr Bunce just told us that the bogle under Newgate Market left a great deal of itself behind.'

'But—'

'There are certain jellyfish which disintegrate when touched,' the naturalist went on. 'And even the humble rat can fit through a hole no bigger than a five-shilling piece.' As Birdie scowled and folded her arms,

Mr Gilfoyle concluded, 'We don't know enough about bogles to classify them as magical creatures. Not yet.'

'Then what *do* we know about 'em?' asked Mr Harewood. Ned wondered if he was trying to change the subject, for Birdie's sake. She looked so flustered that Ned felt sorry for her.

He also agreed with her. How could a normal, everyday creature make you feel miserable before you even laid eyes on it?

'So far we don't know much about bogles,' Mr Gilfoyle admitted, 'and what we *do* know will be covered in my report. But before we hear that, we need to make sure that the Chairman's subcommittee has nothing else to contribute.' He cocked his head, eyebrows raised. 'Did you circulate your memorandum, Mark?'

'I did,' Mr Harewood replied. 'But so far I've received only one response.' Reaching across the table, he picked up a sheet of paper. 'This letter was sent to me by the office of the Postmaster-General. It concerns the mysterious disappearance of three telegraph boys. I wrote back suggesting that Mr Bunce pay a visit as soon as possible, but I've yet to receive an answer.' To Alfred he said, 'Naturally, I shall inform you the very *instant* I have a date and a time.'

The bogler nodded. Then, to Ned's surprise, he asked Mr Gilfoyle, 'May I say summat?'

'Why, of course, Mr Bunce.'

'It so happens I've another job on. At the Theatre Royal, in Drury Lane.' He shifted uneasily. 'But I'll not do it if you'd prefer I didn't.'

Mr Harewood blinked. 'Why on earth would we want to stop you?' he asked.

'On account of it's private work, and I'm on the city payroll. I thought as how there might be rules . . .'

'Oh, I shouldn't worry about *that*,' said Mr Harewood. And his friend added, 'Every time you exterminate a bogle, Mr Bunce, the city benefits greatly. In my opinion, you have *always* been working for the common good.'

'Hear, hear!' Miss Eames exclaimed. Ned half-expected Birdie to say something similar – until he caught sight of her expression. She was gazing at Alfred the way a dog might gaze at a butcher's shop.

'Please, Mr Bunce,' she begged, 'may I go with you to the Theatre Royal?'

'Well . . .' Alfred glanced uneasily at Miss Eames, whose dark eyebrows had already snapped together.

'Oh, *please*, Mr Bunce!' Birdie's voice cracked as she wrung her hands. 'Let me do a job at Drury Lane!

For if the folk there hear me sing, they might put me in a show!'

'Aye, but ...' Alfred was no match for Birdie's pleading. Ned felt sure that he would have buckled already, if not for Miss Eames. 'I thought you wasn't keen to go bogling no more?' he rasped.

'Just this once!' cried Birdie.

Miss Eames, however, was shaking her head. 'Birdie, you can do better than a Drury Lane pantomime,' she objected. 'Why, Signora Paolini has high hopes for you. If you apply yourself, you could be a lyric soprano at the Royal Opera House.'

'But I don't want to be a lyric soprano! I want to be in a pantomime!'

'Be that as it may, I don't want you accompanying Mr Bunce.' Conscious of all the reproachful looks being levelled at her, Miss Eames said crisply, 'She wouldn't be singing – she would be bogling. And you know what my position is on *that*.'

'But it ain't down to you, no more,' Ned blurted out. The pitiable look on Birdie's face had compelled him to speak. Why *shouldn't* she sing in a pantomime? He knew that she was bound to light up the stage. 'Birdie's on the committee now, same as the rest of us,' he continued. 'So we all get to vote on what she does.'

Seeing Miss Eames's indignant expression, he subsided abruptly, cursing himself for being too bold. But Jem was already raising his hand.

'I move Birdie should go bogling at Drury Lane if she wants to!' Jem declared.

Mr Harewood winked at Mr Gilfoyle. Mr Gilfoyle shrugged. Then he said, 'All in favour?'

Ned's hand shot up. Alfred raised his more slowly, keeping his eyes lowered. When Birdie's hand joined Alfred's, and Mr Wardle's joined Birdie's, Mr Harewood offered the girl a lopsided grin and said, 'The Chairman has the deciding vote. I suppose you'd hate me forever if I ruled against you?'

'No,' Birdie stiffly replied. 'Of course not.'

'I'd rather not risk it, all the same.' Mr Harewood put his hand in the air. 'The ayes have it. Miss Birdie McAdam may go bogling at the Theatre Royal.'

As Birdie caught Ned's eye, the gratitude in her gaze sent the blood rushing to his cheeks.

6

BACKSTAGE

Though he lived very close to the Drury Lane theatre, Ned had never gone inside. He couldn't afford even the cheapest seat, which cost nearly two shillings. He was also intimidated by the grandeur of the building's fine stone portico. And he had seen boys his age being cuffed and cursed by stagehands as they lined up beneath the colonnade on Russell Street, hoping to be engaged for the Christmas pantomime. This, more than anything else, had put him off the place.

But he had formed an idea of what the interior was probably like. He assumed that it was full of gilt and plush and marble – not to mention haughty ushers in spotless evening dress. So he was surprised by the cluttered, dirty warren that greeted him when he stepped through the stage door.

'We're looking for Mr Todd,' Alfred informed the doorkeeper. 'I am Alfred Bunce, and this is Miss Edith Eames, and Miss Birdie McAdam—'

'Mr Todd is with Mr Chatterton,' the doorkeeper interrupted, without even glancing up from his newspaper. He was a glowering, unshaven, middle-aged man perched on a high stool; it was obvious from his manner that if Queen Victoria herself had appeared on the threshold, he wouldn't have been impressed.

Alfred glanced at Ned, who cleared his throat and squeaked, 'Miss Rosina Vokes sent for us. Mr Bunce is a Go-Devil man.'

The doorkeeper heaved a long-suffering sigh. 'Mr Spong!' he barked. 'Are you off to the Painting Room?'

A very young man in a dirty smock had been trying to slip past. Now he paused and said, 'I'm finished for the day, Mr Jorkins.'

'Not yet, you ain't. You can take this here crew to see Miss Rosina Vokes. She'll be getting dressed, I daresay.'

'But—'

'And if you run across Mr Beverly, you can tell 'im his parcel's arrived,' the doorkeeper concluded, rattling his newspaper as he shielded his face with it.

Mr Spong didn't look happy. But he jerked his chin at Alfred and headed back into the bowels of the theatre, which was crawling with people. Ned couldn't believe how busy the place was. At times the narrow, gaslit corridors were so crowded that Mr Spong was unable to push his way through the packs of costumed performers. Instead, with Alfred and the others close at his heels, he had to take long detours through rooms full of labouring seamstresses, racks of clothes, or gigantic pieces of painted scenery. At one point he was buttonholed by a bearded gentleman who smelled of turpentine. 'I cannot stop,' Mr Spong told him. 'I've an errand to run.'

And run he did. In fact, Ned and Jem and Birdie soon fell behind as they stopped to gawk at passing knights and princesses. Miss Eames had to keep rounding them up like stray chickens. 'Hurry, please, or we'll lose our way!' she chided.

Sure enough, it wasn't long before her party found itself adrift in the Property Room, with Mr Spong nowhere in sight. All around them were shelves laden with masks, trumpets, swords, bellows, plaster fish and wooden fruit. Silver wings dangled from the rafters. Bits of tinsel were scattered across the floor. A woman scurried past with an armful of fake pewter, as a man in an apron boiled something gluey over an open fire near a stone sink.

'I can't see Mr Spong,' said Alfred, who by this time was pouring sweat and red in the face. 'Where did he go?'

Ned shook his head. He glanced at Jem, who shrugged.

'Perhaps we should return,' Miss Eames suggested. But before she could move, a loud voice suddenly cried, 'What ho! Is that Ned Roach the bogler's boy?'

It was Frederick Vokes, all dressed up in a gold crown and a velvet doublet. He had been rushing down the corridor outside, on his way to some distant part of the theatre. But one glimpse of Ned's worried expression caused him to stop short, swing around and bellow, 'Rosie! He's here!'

'Who is?' came the high-pitched reply.

'That bogler!' Mr Vokes dodged two men in a horse suit as they shuffled past. Then he took a step forward. 'Are you Mr Bunce?' he said.

'Aye. And you are—?'

'Frederick Vokes. You'd best come with me,

for you'll do no good here.' All at once Mr Vokes caught sight of Miss Eames. 'Hello. Would you be *Mrs* Bunce?'

'Certainly not!' Miss Eames snapped. 'My name is Edith Eames. I came with Birdie.'

'And who is Birdie?'

'I am.' Birdie thrust herself towards the actor, eagerly extending her hand. She was dressed in what Jem liked to call her 'bogling outfit': a plain, dark dress and matching bowler hat. 'I'm a bogler's girl,' she announced, with a dazzling smile. Mr Vokes looked startled. He was about to take Birdie's hand when his youngest sister burst into the room, almost knocking him sideways.

'A bogler's girl! How *very* brave!' cried Rosina, who wore a great deal of fluttering gauze. Her arms were bare, and her hair tumbled down her back. 'Goodness, aren't you a pretty thing!' she exclaimed, upon catching sight of Birdie. 'Isn't she pretty, Fred?'

'Shocking waste,' Mr Vokes agreed, as he motioned to Alfred. Then Birdie, who had been staring at Rosina in mute admiration, said, 'I ain't as pretty as you.'

Ned didn't agree. Neither did Rosina. 'It's all slap, my dear. Make-up,' she confided. 'I only wish my cheeks *were* this pink.' Then she tucked her arm through Birdie's. 'Come along and I'll show you where the tunnel is. Come along, Ned! Come along – what's your name?'

'Jem Barbary.'

'Hello, Jem Barbary. I'm Rosina Vokes.' The actress began to follow Alfred, who was already following her brother. She hardly paused for breath as she bustled along. 'Bogling must be just like the theatre, these days,' she babbled. 'There are so many children involved! D'you know that our Tom Thumb is only six? Or so he says. I'm beginning to wonder if he's as young as he claims, but there can be no doubt that he *is* a prodigy . . .'

Trailing after the two girls, Ned marvelled at how silent Birdie was. He had never seen her quite so subdued. Even Jem was speechless, though he gave Ned a nudge when they passed a gaggle of fairies in short skirts.

Miss Eames was looking cross. She trudged along at the rear, eyeing everything suspiciously. 'Should not we speak to the manager?' she asked Rosina, who replied, 'Oh, Mr Chatterton doesn't believe in bogles. His secretary, Mr Todd, agreed to engage Mr Bunce. But poor Mr Todd is so busy at the moment—'

'Our Merlin has fallen ill,' Mr Vokes cut in, clattering down a set of stairs. 'And it's less than an hour until the curtain rises.'

'But never fear,' Rosina finished. '*We* shall take care of you, Miss ... er ...'

'Miss Eames. Edith Eames. I'm a folklorist.'

'Oh, yes? How lovely for you.' Rosina's tone was rather vague; her attention had shifted to Mr Vokes, who was banging through a door at the foot of the staircase. 'I'm very fond of floral arrangements.'

Miss Eames frowned. 'I am a folklorist, Miss Vokes, not a *florist*,' she said sharply. The actress, however, had already surged forward, dragging Birdie with her. 'Wait, Freddie! Slow down!' Rosina implored. 'Anyone would think you were running away from us!'

By this time Ned was completely lost. He thought that they were probably underground, but he couldn't be sure. Then he found himself in a large space full of pipes and pulleys, and he stopped caring.

'Do you have a hydraulic lift ram?' he asked Rosina, halting in front of a pressure gauge mounted at eye level. He had last seen a hydraulic lift ram beneath Smithfield Market – at Birdie's last bogling job – and he had never forgotten it.

'What? Oh. I'm not sure.' Rosina didn't even pause to look. 'I think this may be part of the sub-stage machinery. Isn't it, Fred?'

Mr Vokes, however, wasn't listening. He had already disappeared into a forest of shafts and gears and weights on chains. 'Not far now!' he yelled over his shoulder, as his sister blew a kiss at a grimy, pallid little man who was tightening a bolt on a piston. This man wore a cloth cap and braces, and his jaw dropped when he caught sight of the mismatched group scurrying past him.

But his astonishment was nothing compared to Ned's.

'Why, what kind of a wrench is that?' Ned demanded. 'I ain't never seen one like it!'

The man blinked. 'This? It's brand new, from America. They call it a ratcheting socket wrench.'

'And you don't have to move it off the bolt?' asked Ned.

'Clever, ain't it?' The man proudly demonstrated. 'Them two pawls have springs inside, which work to hold the ratchet wheel —'

'*Ned!*' Miss Eames exclaimed. 'Don't dawdle!'

Reluctantly Ned dragged himself away from the remarkable socket wrench. He followed Miss Eames through the maze of machinery, past the orchestra pit, and into a narrow cellar with a vaulted roof. One side of the cellar was lined with low, blind arches that had been turned into storage bays for bags of coal and planks of wood. Utility pipes ran along the walls.

Ned identified two water pipes, a possible boiler pipe, and a gas pipe that fed the lamp that hung from the ceiling.

'What an unpleasant smell.' Miss Eames pressed a handkerchief to her nose. 'Is it sewage?'

'Seems to be,' said Alfred. And Ned, remembering something Mr Wardle had told them earlier that afternoon as they left the Board of Works remarked, 'The Norfolk Sewer lies below.'

'If we're smelling sewer gas, there must be a hole somewhere.' Alfred dropped his sack on the floor, then proceeded to rummage through it. 'And if there's a hole,' he continued, 'it may be big enough for a bogle.'

'I can *show* you the hole!' cried Rosina. 'It's behind those crates!' She pointed at one of the blind arches, then turned to her brother. 'Help him to move them, Freddie, so we can see!'

'My dear girl, are you joking?' Mr Vokes spread his arms. 'I can't afford to tear this costume – it'll be overture and beginners, soon!'

'I'll do it,' said Alfred. As he lifted the topmost crate, Ned rushed to help him. Together they cleared the storage bay, while Rosina explained that the missing boy had last been seen practising his steps in this very room, well away from the scorn of his fellow dancers.

'He was last seen *dancing*?' Birdie interrupted, just as Jem blurted out, 'Could he have bin singing, as well?'

'Perhaps.'

Jem looked at Birdie, who looked at Ned. They all grimaced. Then Alfred dragged another crate from the top of the pile and said, 'Here it is.'

He had uncovered a deep, ragged hole in the brick wall.

'Oh dear!' Miss Eames's voice was muffled by her handkerchief. 'You seem to have found the source of that smell, Mr Bunce.'

Jem began to cough. Rosina clapped a hand across her face. Holding her nose, Birdie turned to Mr Vokes and asked, 'What *is* that?'

'I've been told it's the tunnel that once led to the Nell Gwynn tavern,' he replied, from behind his sleeve. 'It was bricked up long ago, and then this hole was made – I'm not sure why. Perhaps someone was hoping to find another corpse.' He started to explain that, some thirty years previously, a skeleton had been discovered behind a wall upstairs. But the bogler wouldn't let him finish.

'Shh!' Alfred flapped them all away from the hole, before thrusting his own head into it. Rosina gave a shriek. Ned, who was setting a heavy crate onto the floor, glanced up at her in alarm – but soon realised that she was simply overexcited.

'Don't worry, Miss,' Jem assured her. 'Mr Bunce knows what he's doing.'

'Shut yer mouth!' Alfred suddenly rounded on him, startling everyone with his ferocity. 'D'you want to lure the bogle out ahead o' time?'

Rosina gasped. Her brother struck a dramatic pose. Miss Eames whispered, 'You think there's a bogle, Mr Bunce?'

'I know there is,' Alfred replied. And he began to make his preparations.

7

THE TUNNEL

According to Alfred, the hole *did* seem to be a tunnel,
though it was badly choked with rubble and other
debris. 'Only a bogle could get through there,' he
muttered, as he began to lay a ring of salt on the floor.
He placed it at one end of the long, narrow room, while
everyone else hovered at the other end, watching him.

The ring looked very small to Ned, though it was
as wide as the available space. He wondered if there
was going to be a second circle. Alfred had often said
that most bogles were solitary creatures, but it seemed
a little risky to assume that they shared their dens only
in the neighbourhood of Newgate Market. What if
Drury Lane had become overcrowded as well?

'This is as good as a play,' Mr Vokes said in a low voice, as his sister tried to smother her excited giggles. 'I'd wager people would pay a shilling a head for this.'

'Aye, but we don't want no audience down here, getting in the way,' Alfred rejoined. 'That's why I'll be needing you at the very top o' them stairs, Mr Vokes. To stop anyone as happens by.'

The actor's face fell. 'Am I not to witness the proceedings, Mr Bunce?' he lamented. 'That seems unduly harsh . . .'

'The proceedings, Mr Vokes, might take some time,' Miss Eames weighed in. 'And you yourself are due on stage very soon, are you not?'

Before Mr Vokes could answer, Alfred looked up from his work and said, 'They both are. That's why neither of 'em can stay in this room.'

Rosina caught her breath.

'I'm sorry, Miss,' Alfred continued. 'I'll not have you slipping out suddenly when you're called, or you'll disturb the bogle.'

'Oh, but Mr *Bunce*—'

'I ain't about to argue.' Alfred stood firm. 'If you'll promise not to move or speak for the next few hours, then you can join us. Otherwise you'd best leave.'

Rosina looked heartbroken. Her eyes brimmed with tears and her bottom lip quivered. Mr Vokes, however, wasn't impressed by this display. He flicked her cheek with two careless fingers as he began to hustle her upstairs. 'Turn off the plumbing, Sarah Bernhardt,' he said breezily. 'Mr Bunce knows what he's about.' On the landing he paused for a moment to say, 'If we're gone when you finish, Mr Bunce, you must report to Mr Todd. But do try not to wander on stage while you're at it.'

He then turned a corner and vanished up the second flight of stairs – though not before throwing a sly wink at his unhappy sister. Ned caught the wink, and was puzzled, but didn't say anything. He knew that Alfred wouldn't want to hear the sound of children's voices.

Not while a bogle was listening.

'There's a deal too many ways into this cellar,' Alfred remarked. He was already laying down a second ring of salt near the foot of the staircase, where a door stood opposite the first blind arch. Made of scarred oak, this door was shut, though not bolted. The door on the landing was also shut.

A third door, at the other end of the room, was standing ajar. It led to a dingy space full of old furniture.

'You're to go in there,' Alfred told Miss Eames, nodding towards the storeroom. 'For I must leave that door open, and don't want no bogle sneaking through.'

'Then why leave it open at all?' Miss Eames wanted to know.

'So Birdie has a place to run,' said Alfred – and Ned saw at once what he was talking about. The cellar in which they stood was so narrow that, if the bogle approached Birdie from behind, she would have only one means of escape.

'Jem, you're to bolt that door and guard it.' Alfred jerked his chin at the door near the stairs, which Jem promptly secured. 'I doubt as how any bogle would try to break it down, but there ain't no telling. So if a strange noise should trouble you, throw me a signal. And Ned . . .' Alfred shifted his gaze. 'I'll want you on the landing, for I ain't easy in me mind regarding that other door, up there.'

Surprised, Ned glanced at the door in question. He couldn't imagine why a sewer-bogle would want to use such a roundabout route. But then again, the door might lead to a closet. And Ned had often heard Birdie talk about closet-bogles . . .

'That door's locked,' Jem informed Alfred. 'I tried it on me way downstairs.'

'It's still worth watching.' The bogler's dark gaze skipped from one boy to the other as he lectured them. 'You must yell if you see owt as seems untoward. And if yer way upstairs is blocked, just remember – you'll be safe inside this circle. Ain't no bogle on earth could pierce it.'

He stamped his foot, drawing Ned's attention to the second ring of salt on the floor. It was a closed circle, and looked smaller than the one across the room. But as Alfred explained, it was just a precaution.

'I'm expecting the bogle to come through that tunnel and head straight for Birdie,' he assured the two boys. 'It shouldn't trouble you – not while Birdie's singing. Just be sure to keep mum and stay still.'

He waited for a moment. When no one said anything, he went to stand beside the gaping hole, armed with his spear and his bag of salt. The others then took up their own positions. Birdie stepped into the larger magic ring. Jem stationed himself by the bolted door. Miss Eames hurried into the neighbouring room – where she had to hide herself away, since Alfred didn't want her hovering on the threshold, scaring off the bogle.

Ned trudged up to the landing. He didn't have much of a view, from there. Even when he squatted down, he couldn't see Birdie in her ring of salt. But he *could* see Jem and Alfred, as well as a tiny sliver of the hole in the wall.

He could also see Rosina Vokes, who was sitting on the second flight of stairs. When Ned caught her eye, she put a finger to her lips – and flashed him such a soft, pleading look that he couldn't bring himself to alert Alfred.

Then Birdie began to sing.

I've travelled about a bit in me time
And of troubles I've seen a few
But found it better in every clime
To paddle me own canoe.

Birdie's voice was as clear and sweet as a cascade of silver bells. In that confined space it was also very loud, cutting through the air like a razor. Ned found himself marvelling all over again at its strength and purity.

He saw Rosina's jaw drop, and her pale eyes widen. But he knew that he shouldn't be watching the actress. His job was to monitor every visible approach.

So he flicked a look at the door behind him as Birdie continued.

Me wants are few. I care not at all
If me debts are paid when due
I drive away strife in the ocean of life
When I paddle me own canoe.

A slight scuffling sound reached Ned's ears. Glancing sideways, he spotted Mr Vokes creeping towards Rosina, one step at a time. Birdie's song appeared to be drawing him back downstairs.

Ned frowned at the actor before shifting his attention to Alfred, who stood quite still, poised to pounce. Ned couldn't decide if the sewery smell was getting worse, though he *did* feel a creeping sense of unease. Did it stem from his own anxiety, or was it evidence of an approaching bogle?

Suddenly he realised that Rosina had advanced a little more. She was sitting very close to him now, on the first step of the second flight, trying to poke her head around the corner for a better view of the action downstairs. And Ned couldn't stop her because he wasn't allowed to move or speak.

Then Birdie launched into her next verse.

Love yer neighbour as yerself
As the world you go travelling through

And never sit down with a tear and a frown
But paddle yer own—

A shriek from Jem cut her off. Something had shot out of the tunnel, slamming into the wall opposite, then bouncing off and hitting the floor. It looked like a giant flea, except that it was jet-black, with a rubbery hide, huge fangs, and four pink eyes as big as dinner plates. It landed by Jem, who acted on instinct. Since the bogle was blocking his route to the ring of salt, he sprang straight up in the air, grabbed one of the water pipes on the wall, and used it to swing himself *over* the bogle, which hadn't yet jumped to its feet.

By the time it did, Jem had turned a midair somersault and landed inside the magic circle.

But water was already gushing from the pipe he'd wrenched apart at the join. Horrified, Ned saw that this water was rapidly dissolving the salt on the floor. So he lunged towards a likely-looking cut-off valve, which he'd spotted earlier.

'*Jem! Duck!*' Alfred roared, as the bogle reared up, hissing. Jem obeyed, and Alfred's spear flew over his head.

FOOMP!

Suddenly there was no bogle. Nothing remained except a rapidly deflating, crusty black thing like an oversized boil on the ground. Alfred's spear was sticking out of it.

'Jem? Are you hurt, lad?' The bogler dropped down beside Jem, who was curled up into a little ball. As he slowly uncoiled himself, shaking his head, Birdie descended on him in a flutter of petticoats – with Miss Eames close at her heels. Rosina, meanwhile, was staggering downstairs. 'Oh, my! Oh, dear! I never did!' she croaked. Even her heavy make-up couldn't conceal her pallor; she was as white as the salt that had begun to liquefy at her feet.

Luckily, Ned had been right about the cut-off valve. Water wasn't gushing from the pipe anymore.

'That pipe needs to be soldered,' Ned observed hoarsely. He was still hanging off the valve, trying to stop his hands from shaking. But Rosina didn't seem to hear. She had reached the little group clustered around Jem, who was on his feet again, looking stunned.

'Are you a *circus performer*?' she squeaked. 'Why, Freddie has the liveliest legs in the business, and *he* couldn't have done that!'

'Not to save my life,' Mr Vokes agreed, from the bottom of the stairs. He had taken off his crown to mop his damp forehead. 'You ought to be on the stage, boy.'

'And Birdie, too!' Rosina cried. 'Have you ever *heard* such a voice, Fred?'

'Never.'

'We must arrange an audition for you.' By now the colour was returning to Rosina's face, though she still sounded very shrill. 'My dear,' she exclaimed, reaching out to grasp Birdie's arm, 'you'll be the next Jenny Lind! And Jem might be the next Joe Grimaldi!'

'Who's Joe Grimaldi?' asked Jem.

'Oh, he was a *famous* acrobat,' Rosina replied. 'They say he haunts this very theatre. Don't they, Fred?'

As Mr Vokes nodded, Alfred glanced at him and growled, 'How do *you* know Jem's so fast on his feet? You was meant to be guarding the top o' the stairs.'

The actor pulled a sheepish face. Then he quickly produced some coins from the purse at his belt, by way of a distraction. 'For your trouble, Mr Bunce,' he said. 'Six shillings and sixpence, was it not?' As he surrendered the money, the sound of a distant bell made him wince. 'That's our call,' he told his sister. 'We must go.'

Rosina grabbed both of Birdie's hands. 'Come

tomorrow morning. Come for an audition. I'll arrange one for you. *Promise* me.'

Birdie beamed and nodded, her expression radiant. Ned had never seen her look so happy. When Rosina finally released her grip, and retreated towards the staircase, Birdie rounded on Miss Eames and stammered, 'I *must* go. You – you see that, don't you? I *must!*'

'Bring Jem with you!' Rosina cried from the foot of the stairs. Then she disappeared in a flurry of white gauze.

Her brother followed more slowly, executing an elaborate farewell bow before he rounded the corner on the landing.

There was a brief silence after they'd left. Finally Ned, whose gaze had drifted towards the bogle's remains, observed diffidently, 'We should keep a bit o' that for Mr Gilfoyle. Don't you think?'

OFFICIAL BUSINESS

Alfred Bunce received an unusual number of visitors the next morning.

The first of them arrived at around eight o'clock. He was an errand boy from the Theatre Royal, and he carried a message from Mr Todd, the manager's secretary – who had scribbled down Alfred's address the night before. 'Mr Todd says as how Jem Barbary is to report to Mr Chatterton's office at eleven o'clock, for an audition,' the errand boy announced, lisping slightly. He then turned and ran back downstairs, leaving Ned open-mouthed on the threshold.

Alfred's next two visitors turned up at ten, while Ned was still darning one of Jem's socks. (Jem was darning the other one.) It was Alfred who answered the door. He didn't seem very surprised to see Birdie and Miss Eames on the threshold, though Birdie's glossy appearance made him blink.

'You look a picture today, lass,' he said, ushering them into his stuffy garret. 'You're off to the theatre as well, I daresay?'

'Mr Todd sent us a telegram,' Birdie replied. She wore a dress of pale blue satin trimmed with silk braid, and seemed to glow like a gas-lamp.

Ned was dazzled.

'We thought we might take Jem along with us,' Miss Eames explained. 'Though of course we weren't sure if he had been summoned . . .'

'I have,' Jem proudly confirmed.

'And you're going?' asked Birdie.

'Of course!' Jem stared at her as if she were mad. 'Why not?'

Birdie raised her eyebrows, but said nothing. Ned could imagine how she felt. Unlike Birdie, Jem had never expressed any interest in performing. He'd always talked as if bogling was his dream job. So Ned had been very surprised, the previous evening, to hear him babble on about a stage career as they followed Alfred home from the theatre.

'Frederick Vokes is a dancer, and *he* has a watch worth at least thirty shillings!' Jem had confided to Ned, behind Alfred's back. 'I saw him pull it out!'

'But what about Mr Bunce? You *begged* him to take you on. Don't you want to be a bogler's boy no more?'

Jem had shrugged. 'Bogling's better'n prigging, or sweeping out a grocer's shop. There ain't no future in it, though. Soon as I'm too big for a bogle's stomach, I'll be out o' work. T'ain't the same for theatre folk. Them Vokes sisters – why, they bin on stage since they was babies! And can expect to earn their keep as long as they're limber.' Seeing Ned frown, Jem had quickly added, 'Besides, I don't see as how there'll be much call for boglers, now we got a committee doing the same job. Once the committee knows how to kill bogles in a scientific way, Mr Bunce'll find hisself catching rats for a living. And *you'll* be selling fruit out of a coster's cart.'

Ned couldn't help wondering if this were true – and if Alfred himself might be thinking the same thing. Certainly the bogler raised no fuss about Jem's audition. Even when Mark Harewood suddenly appeared, with the news that Alfred was urgently needed at the General Post Office, Alfred didn't change his mind about Jem. 'I'll have Ned to help me,' the bogler said. 'Besides, that post office is on a street off Newgate. So it's probably safer if Jem don't come.'

Watching everyone exchange courtesies, Ned decided that Mr Harewood was much happier to see Miss Eames than she was to see him. The engineer even asked her to take a trip to the post office. 'I couldn't persuade Razzy to come, because he had a previous engagement,' Mr Harewood revealed. 'But if you were to replace him, Miss Eames, you could take notes and write the report yourself. As a representative of our research subcommittee.'

Miss Eames, however, refused his invitation. Her first duty was to the child in her care, she said. Birdie's future was of great importance, and Miss Eames wanted to ensure that the Theatre Royal's management wouldn't exploit or misuse the girl.

'As if I'd let *that* happen,' Birdie muttered scornfully, rolling her eyes. But she didn't say anything else. Instead she waved at Alfred, smiled at Ned, and disappeared downstairs before Ned had a chance to wish her good luck.

The whole room seemed dingier without her.

'Ah, well,' said Mr Harewood, as Miss Eames hurried after Birdie, 'it seems that *I* must do the note-taking this time.' To Alfred he remarked, 'I cannot endure the shame of being the only member of our committee not to have laid eyes on a bogle, Mr Bunce. Even old Gilfoyle has the better of me there. But I'm about to remedy the situation, and will be chaffed no longer for my failings.'

'Mr Wardle ain't never seen no bogle, neither,' Ned interrupted. 'He weren't in the Newgate cellar yesterday.'

'Was he not? In that case, I shall be able to chaff *him*.' Mr Harewood was looking tidier than he had at their last meeting. He wore a soft felt hat, a pair of grey kid gloves, and a silk-lined frockcoat. Nevertheless, there was something wild about his appearance. His hair was too long, perhaps, or his manner too energetic. Was that why Miss Eames had been slightly cool with him?

'I walked here from Trafalgar Square,' Mr Harewood went on, 'but we must take a cab to the post office. If you're ready, Mr Bunce?'

'Aye.' Alfred reached for his sack.

'I shall want a full report on your job at the theatre last night. Was there a bogle? Yes? I thought as much.' Mr Harewood held the door open for Alfred and Ned, just as if they were gentlemen.

Ned could only assume that it was done in a fit of absent-mindedness. 'I've been studying our maps, and have established that Mr Wardle was correct: a sewer *does* pass beneath the Theatre Royal. It commences at the junction of Drury Lane and Long Acre, runs along the Strand, then enters the Thames via Norfolk Street.'

Ned thought about this as he made his way downstairs. It was only after a hansom cab had been hailed, and they had all piled into it, that he finally ventured to ask Mr Harewood if there was a gate on the Norfolk Street sewer outfall.

'I never bin that far west – not along the riverbank,' Ned admitted. 'It's the eastern mudflats *I* know.'

'Alas, I fear I'm no better acquainted with the outfalls than you are,' said Mr Harewood, 'though I'm sure Mr Wardle can help us. Why?'

'Well . . .' Ned took a deep breath. He always felt slightly tongue-tied in the presence of well-educated people, and couldn't help stammering as he answered Mr Harewood's question. 'I – I were puzzling as to how we might flush them bogles into the river, and then I thought to meself: what if they already live there?' When the engineer didn't scoff at this notion, Ned found the courage to suggest, 'Mebbe we should check the tide tables. If there's kids being taken when the tide is high—'

'Then we might have ourselves a crop of river monsters coming up the sewers!' Mr Harewood finished. He beamed at Ned, who was wedged into the seat beside him. 'My word, but you're a sharp lad! I like the way you think – indeed I do!'

Ned flushed with pleasure.

'Tide tables are easy enough to procure,' the engineer went on. 'As for river monsters, Gilfoyle is the one to ask about *them*. He's made a study of the subject.' Mr Harewood suddenly shifted his gaze to Alfred, who was sitting on Ned's right. 'I should tell you, by the by, that Gilfoyle intends to consult his friend at the Apothecaries' Hall today concerning any toxins that might have been applied to your spear, Mr Bunce. If the news is good, he'll inform us directly.'

'I bin thinking about that,' was Alfred's unexpected response. 'And I've a better idea.'

Ned stared at him in surprise. Even Mr Harewood was taken aback. 'You do?' he asked.

'Aye.' Alfred's voice quavered as their cab bounced over a rut in the road. 'Me old master, Daniel Piggin, were a Derbyshire man. His sister still lives near Derby. She's a "cunning woman", trained in herbs and old lore.' He glanced inquiringly at Mr Harewood, who gave an encouraging nod.

'Folk medicine,' the engineer said. 'I understand.'

'If anyone knows owt about that spear, it's Mother May,' Alfred continued. 'She and her brother was very close, at one time. Afore he moved to London.'

'I see.' Mr Harewood was still nodding. 'Then perhaps you should write to her, Mr Bunce?'

A rare smile cracked across Alfred's dour face. 'I never learned to write, Mr Harewood,' he pointed out, 'and I doubt Mother May ever learned to read. But I thought as how I might take a train to the Peak District, if you've no objection.'

'None at all, Mr Bunce!' Mr Harewood sounded very keen. 'I think it an excellent notion! And I shall ask Mr Wardle to reimburse you for any expenses you might incur, since the committee has a fund to cover such costs. When were you planning to go?'

Alfred shrugged. 'Just as soon as I ain't needed here,' he said.

'Which may be a good while.' The engineer turned his head to peer out the window. 'Personally, I'd encourage you to take your trip before our next meeting, since Mother May's contribution could be vital.' All at once he stiffened. 'Aha!' he exclaimed.

'We've arrived! Good. I told Mr Clegg we'd be here by eleven.'

'Who is Mr Clegg, sir?' Ned asked, as the cab lurched to a standstill.

'He is Chief Clerk to the Secretary of the Postmaster-General.'

Ned didn't find this answer very illuminating. But he climbed out of the cab without saying another word, and was soon standing in the street with Alfred, while Mr Harewood paid their driver.

Ned had never seen the General Post Office up close before. Its immensity awed him, for the building occupied an entire city block. Each column on its facade was at least six feet wide. Each window was nearly as big as Alfred's whole garret room. The entrance was thronged with people, who poured in and out with more parcels and letters and sacks than Ned had ever seen in his life.

There was construction going on across the street, and the noise was deafening.

'Come along!' Mr Harewood said loudly, as their cabman cracked his whip. 'We'll ask for Mr Clegg in the main office.' He began to climb the front steps, with Ned and Alfred close behind him. Though pushing through the crowds wasn't easy, they at last found themselves in a grand public hall full of people. This hall was perhaps fifty feet high, and at least five times as long, but it was so crammed with bodies that Ned had to grab Alfred's sleeve for fear of losing him.

'Stay with me!' Mr Harewood bellowed, over the roar of several hundred voices. Then, instead of joining a line, he went straight to the nearest counter and interrupted a transaction involving a parcel bound for Walthamstow.

'Pardon me,' he said to the bemused mail clerk, 'but I've an appointment with Mr Clegg. Could you direct me to the Secretary's Office, please?'

'You'll have to wait your turn, sir,' the clerk replied, causing Mr Harewood to throw out his chest, square his broad shoulders and scowl impatiently.

'Indeed I shall not!' the engineer snapped. 'I'm here at the request of Mr John Tilly, Secretary to the Postmaster-General! He has engaged my friend, Mr Alfred Bunce, on an urgent matter! Now kindly tell me where I may find Mr Clegg.'

By the merest chance, Ned was glancing around the room when Mr Harewood uttered Alfred's name. So when a nearby newsboy started at the sound of the word 'Bunce', and fixed his penetrating gaze on Alfred, Ned observed that look. For an instant the newsboy stood frozen. Then he bolted towards the front door, before Ned could do more than open his mouth.

'*Thank* you!' Mr Harewood spat. He was still addressing the mail clerk, who must have grudgingly passed him a scrap of information, because he suddenly whirled around and said to Alfred, 'This way! Follow me!'

Ned was given no choice. If he hadn't set off immediately, he would have been left behind. But he kept looking back, trying not to lose sight of the newsboy, until a heavy door suddenly cut off his view of the hall.

After that, there was nothing for him to do but go forward, into the mysterious depths of the post office.

9

THE LOWEST LEVEL

'Mr Harewood. How do you do, sir?'

'Mr Clegg.'

The two men bowed, but didn't shake hands. Mr Clegg was a plump, elegant, grey-haired gentleman wearing a discreet moustache, a gold-rimmed monocle, and a bland expression. His boots shone like polished jet.

'I take it this is Mr Bunce?' he asked, peering at Alfred through his monocle.

'Mr Alfred Bunce. The bogler,' Mr Harewood confirmed.

Mr Clegg nodded. 'Good morning, Mr Bunce,' he said smoothly. Then he gestured at the policeman beside him. 'May I introduce Constable Juddick? We have an Internal Police Office here, and Emmet Juddick is one of our four constables. I have asked him to help you, since I am unfortunately pressed for time.'

Constable Juddick was large and burly, with a broken nose, a freckled face, and bushy red side-whiskers. His voice sounded like gravel crunching underfoot.

'Good morning, Mr Bunce. Mr Harewood, sir,' he growled. When his gaze fell on Ned, he didn't say a word. But his brisk nod was comforting.

Unlike Mr Clegg, the policeman actually seemed aware of Ned's existence.

'Constable Juddick is far better informed than I am on the subject of disappearing boys,' Mr Clegg went on. 'Is that not so, Constable?'

'Yes, sir.'

'I am merely a humble conduit, transmitting his concerns.' The Chief Clerk smirked a little, as if he'd just told a joke. Then he excused himself. 'Do tell me how you fared,' he politely requested, bowing again to Mr Harewood. 'I shall be most interested in your findings. And I'll be expecting a full report from *you*, Constable.'

'Yes, sir.'

'Good day, gentlemen. Please forgive me. I really must go . . .'

Within seconds he'd vanished, leaving his visitors marooned with Constable Juddick in a small, wood-panelled office. Mr Harewood didn't look terribly impressed, Ned thought. And Alfred was becoming impatient.

'Where was them kids last seen?' he asked the policeman.

'Downstairs.' Constable Juddick spoke flatly, in clipped sentences. 'Three of 'em went missing. All telegraph boys. The new Telegraph Office ain't open yet, so the boys still congregate in our basement. They keep their overcoats down there.'

'In that case, you'd best show us the basement,' said Alfred, hoisting his sack up onto his shoulder. With a nod, Constable Juddick turned on his heel. Then he marched into the corridor outside, setting a course for the nearest staircase.

As they made their way down to the lowest level, past a room full of stamping machines, another full of weighing equipment, and a third lined with pigeonholes, Alfred continued to ask questions. How old were the missing boys? Were they small for their age? Had anyone seen or heard anything peculiar before they vanished? To all these inquiries Constable Juddick gave only one answer, in a grinding monotone.

'Corporal Catty will know, for he's the head delivery boy.'

Ned was surprised to hear that telegraph boys had military ranks. Despite their blue serge uniforms, they'd never impressed him as being very disciplined. He was wondering if they saluted each other, like real soldiers, when he found himself in a room full of pipes and valves and pressure gauges – and he immediately lost interest in the telegraph boys.

'This ain't no hydraulic lift!' he exclaimed, before he could stop himself. Ahead of him, Mr Harewood paused and said, 'No. It's warm-air apparatus. For heating the gasometer.' Seeing Ned's awestruck expression, he pointed to one of the smaller devices. 'See that? It regulates the supply of gas to all the burners in this building – including that one over there.'

'I seen dry meters, on occasion, but nothing like this.' Ned spoke absent-mindedly as he gazed at something that looked like a cross between a tank and a steam engine. He knew that he shouldn't linger, because Alfred and the policeman were already out of sight. But he couldn't tear himself away. 'It's a wonder, ain't it?'

Mr Harewood sniffed. 'It does its job, I daresay, but not with any degree of elegance. A *perfect* piece of engineering combines several functions in an aesthetically pleasing manner.' He took Ned's arm and began to lecture him as they slowly made their way out of the room. 'Take Christopher Wren, for instance. Although his Monument was designed to commemorate the Great Fire of London, it is also a giant zenith telescope. By opening a trapdoor in the gilded orb at the top of the tower, you can watch the night sky from a laboratory in the basement.'

Ned had been listening attentively. 'You mean a thing's much better if it does twice the work?' he asked. 'Like the street-lamps on Holborn Viaduct? *They* got vents in 'em as lets out sewer gas . . .'

'Exactly! That is exactly what I mean!' Mr Harewood's grip on Ned's arm tightened. 'Only consider, for example, how ingenious it would be to combine the regulation of the gas supply, in this building, with the regulation of its pneumatic dispatches! For they both rely on a careful manipulation of pressure—'

'Excuse me, sir, but what is a pneumatic dispatch?'

Mr Harewood stopped abruptly. 'Oh, my dear fellow, a pneumatic dispatch is the very *latest* engineering marvel!' He began to describe, in great detail, how mail was now being carried all the way from Euston Station to the General Post Office inside capsules that travelled along an underground tube. Powered by compressed air in one direction, and atmospheric pressure in the other, each capsule acted as a kind of piston, moved by a steam-powered reversible fan that created a vacuum.

Mr Harewood's vivid description filled Ned with excitement.

'Can we see it?' he demanded. 'Is it down here, Mr Harewood?'

'I believe there *is* a terminus,' the engineer replied, then glanced around and winced. 'Oh dear,' he said, dropping Ned's arm. 'We seem to have lost the others.'

It was true. They had taken a wrong turn, and were now standing in a long, empty hallway lined with doors and utility pipes. Two of the doors were sheathed in iron. Another was studded with locks.

'*Hello?*' Ned's raised voice echoed off the vaulted ceiling. '*Mr Bunce?*'

'Oi!' came a sharp rejoinder. 'What're *you* doing down 'ere?'

When Ned and Mr Harewood spun around, they found themselves face to face with two telegraph boys: one sandy-haired and bandy-legged, the other tall, swarthy and chinless. Ned judged them to be between thirteen and sixteen years old.

'We're looking for Corporal Catty,' Mr Harewood informed them.

'Catty? He's in the kitchen.' The taller boy jerked his thumb at an adjoining corridor. 'Did you come with them others? Old Judd and that Go-Devil man?'

'We did,' said Mr Harewood.

'Then I wish you the best o' luck.' The smaller boy, who appeared to be chewing tobacco, spat on the floor. 'I'm right sick o' pairing off. Why, we can't go to the privy alone, now! And must report every other step we take . . .'

He was still grumbling as he and his friend squeezed past Mr Harewood, on their way to something they called the 'dispatch room'. 'Tell Catty we found you,' the taller boy added, 'else he'll send out a search party, the silly old hen.'

'Tell him Joe's too big for a bogle's stomach, and I'm too stringy,' his friend joked, before vanishing around a corner.

Watching them go, Mr Harewood murmured, 'Safety in numbers, eh? I'm not surprised they're pairing off, in the circumstances.'

'Uh – Mr Harewood, sir?' Ned wasn't much interested in the telegraph boys. 'I bin thinking . . .'

'Again?' The engineer flashed Ned an amused look, before starting down the kitchen passage. 'Perhaps we'd better find the others before we distract ourselves with more scientific speculation. We don't want to get lost a second time, do we?'

'No, sir, but – well, there's summat I need to know.' Scampering to catch up, Ned breathlessly inquired, 'If we can't flush them bogles out o' the sewers with water, can we do it with air?'

'Like the pneumatic tube, you mean?' Without waiting for an answer, Mr Harewood continued, 'I doubt it. London's sewer system is so riddled with leaks that the amount of pressure required would be beyond our capacity to generate.'

'Oh.'

'It's a cunning thought, though.' Mr Harewood stopped in front of a closed door at the end of the passage, his hand on the knob and his eyes on Ned's face. 'You're a clever lad. Can you read, by any chance?'

Ned shook his head.

'What a pity,' said Mr Harewood. 'Still, that's not an insurmountable problem. Not at your age.' Then he pushed open the door, revealing a stone-flagged kitchen warmed by a grate full of glowing embers. Alfred and the policeman were standing in front of this grate, together with a skinny youth in a blue serge uniform. Their heads snapped around when they heard hinges creaking.

'Ah!' The skinny youth's worried expression was transformed into one of intense relief. 'Joe found you, then!'

'He did,' Mr Harewood agreed. 'Would you be Corporal Catty?'

'I am, sir.' Without pausing for breath, the youth glanced nervously at Alfred and said, 'I sent all them other lads away. I thought it best.'

'They spend too much time down here in any case, drinking tea and making mischief,' the policeman remarked. He glared at the skinny youth, who stammered, 'I – I do what I can, sir! They're right downy, some of 'em!'

Constable Juddick sniffed as Ned studied the corporal, wondering why he'd been promoted to his present rank. Though very tall, and several years older than the other two boys, Corporal Catty was all skin and bone, with a long neck, stooped shoulders, and anxious, blinking, bloodshot eyes. He had no beard to speak of, and his prominent Adam's apple slid up and down like a piston when he swallowed.

Ned suspected that he'd been chosen because he obeyed the rules – not because he was confident enough to enforce them.

'This is a curious space,' Mr Harewood suddenly observed. He was peering at one of the brick walls, which had three stone pillars embedded in it. Even Ned could see that these massive, rounded pillars were at odds with the rest of the kitchen, which was small and mean. The fireplace was skimpy; the ceiling was low; there was only one gas-jet, and no scullery to speak of. 'I've heard that a crypt was laid open here, when the site was being cleared for construction,' Mr Harewood continued. 'It contained a stone coffin, with a skeleton inside.' As Corporal Catty blanched, the engineer cheerfully concluded, 'Perhaps St Martin's crypt has been incorporated into this basement! It certainly looks older than the building above.'

'If that's true, then mebbe it *weren't* the bogle as took them lads,' said Corporal Catty. 'Mebbe a ghost done it . . .'

'Nonsense.' The policeman snorted. 'Ghosts don't abduct people.'

'What makes you think they was abducted?' Alfred broke in. 'Boys have bin known to run away, on occasion.'

'Not these boys, sir. They never had cause to complain, for all they was the youngest.' Corporal Catty turned to Constable Juddick for support. 'Ain't no bullying here. And the money's good, too. Five shillings a week, they start on.'

Ned blinked. Five shillings a week sounded a little meagre, though he himself had lived on much less. He decided that if Alfred was ever to dismiss him, he'd be glad enough to work as a telegraph boy.

But he didn't like to think about being on his own again . . .

'Was them boys the smallest, as well as the youngest?' Alfred queried. On receiving a nod from the corporal, he went on to ask, 'Where did you last see 'em?'

'The boys, sir? Why – they was last seen here.' As Alfred's gaze flickered towards the fireplace, Corporal Catty added, 'But that don't signify, since we know this ain't where they perished.'

Alfred frowned. His eyes moved back to the corporal's face. 'You do?'

'Of course. Didn't Mr Clegg tell you?'

'Tell me what?'

'We seen the bogle, Mr Bunce. Me and Davy and little Dan. All three of us.'

Ned blinked. Alfred said, 'Where?'

'In there.' Corporal Catty pointed at a door to his left. 'It lives in the lavatory. Didn't you know? Them poor lads never stood a chance, what with their kicksies being down around their ankles . . .'

10

THE PRIVY-BOGLE

Ned was growing hoarse.

He had been standing in the lavatory for a couple of hours, tonelessly chanting nursery rhymes – which were the only songs he really knew. To his left was a row of urinals. To his right, six wooden cubicles each contained a ceramic bowl and suspended cistern. In front of him was an open door leading to a short, narrow passage. Behind him were two basins, complete with cold-water taps, and a covered drain in the floor.

Alfred had identified this drain as the most likely source of bogle activity. So he had traced out his circle of salt just a few feet away from it, then positioned himself in the cubicle closest to the basins.

Half of his shadowy figure was reflected in the mirror that Ned was holding.

Who killed Cock Robin?
I, said the Sparrow,
With me bow and arrow
I killed Cock Robin.

As Ned droned on, he could see Alfred shifting his weight – but he couldn't see Mr Harewood. The engineer was skulking in the cubicle next to Alfred's, having been warned to keep well back, out of sight. No one was visible in the outside passage, either; Corporal Catty and Constable Juddick had been asked to stay in the kitchen.

Yet still the bogle didn't come. Ned wondered if it could somehow sense that there were adults in the room. It seemed unlikely, since Alfred had never encountered any problems before. By keeping still and silent, he had fooled every bogle that he'd ever been hired to kill.

Ned coughed and cleared his throat before launching into the next verse.

Who saw him die?
I, said the Fly

With me little eye
I saw him die.

'Mr Bunce?' It was Constable Juddick's voice, echoing down the passage from the kitchen. Lifting his gaze, Ned saw the policeman's head appear around a distant corner, backlit by a wall-mounted gas-jet. 'We've a lot o' people out here waiting to use the water-closet, sir. Will you be much longer?'

Alfred didn't reply. But his furious scowl was captured in Ned's looking-glass.

'Mebbe there *ain't* no bogle,' the policeman continued. 'If there was, surely it would have showed itself by now?'

Still Alfred didn't answer. Perhaps he was hoping that Constable Juddick would take the hint and withdraw. Ned knew that it sometimes wasn't easy to lure a bogle out of its lair. Birdie had once told him about a three-hour ordeal in an empty tanner's vat.

Ned gnawed at his bottom lip, feeling useless. Could his singing be the problem? Would Birdie have succeeded where he had failed?

He was sure that Alfred must be asking himself the same question . . .

'Mr Bunce?' Suddenly Mr Harewood spoke from

his cubicle, in a rough whisper. 'Should we come back this evening? It will be less busy by then, I daresay.'

Ned winced, expecting Alfred to explode. But instead of snarling at Mr Harewood, the bogler simply remarked, through clenched teeth, 'This place don't close at night.'

'Oh, yes. Of course. How silly of me.' Mr Harewood sounded embarrassed.

'And Catty said them kids disappeared during the day,' Alfred continued, causing a series of gears to turn inside Ned's brain. With a gasp, he swung around to address Alfred.

'Mr Bunce?'

'Shh!'

'I'm sorry, Mr Bunce, but what if it's waiting for a signal?' Before Alfred could do more than glare at him, Ned quickly added, 'Mebbe the bogle comes whenever it hears a cistern flush. Mebbe *that's* what it's bin listening for.'

There was a brief silence. The only sound was a tap dripping. *Plink. Plink. Plink.* Then Mr Harewood murmured, 'I say! What a clever notion!'

'It is.' Alfred stepped into the light, his spear in one hand, his bag of salt in the other. His gaze travelled around the room, darting from the drain to the door to the basins and back to the cubicle. Then he said, 'This here is a trap. You pull the chain, go to wash yer hands—'

'—and the bogle pops up between you and the door!' Ned finished.

'If you're young enough.' Alfred was nodding, his expression grim. 'I mislike this arrangement. It don't give you nowhere to run, Ned.'

He was right. Ned saw that instantly. 'Mebbe if we was to put a ring o' salt in there, I could use it to shield meself,' he suggested, pointing at the booth that Alfred had just left. 'A *closed* ring o' salt. All around the bowl ...'

By this time Mr Harewood had also emerged from his cubicle. 'Are you certain that our bogle is going to come through the grating in the floor?' he asked. 'What if Ned pulls the chain and it comes shooting straight out of the water-closet?'

'T'ain't likely,' said Alfred. 'But if I lay a circle around the bowl, Ned'll be safe enough.' Retreating into the nearest booth, he proceeded to surround the toilet inside it with a ring of salt, as Mr Harewood went to the exit and loudly declared, 'We shan't be much longer, Constable! Have a little more patience, if you please!'

'What about *this* circle, Mr Bunce?' Ned was referring to the ring that already lay near the drain. 'Should it be left?'

'Aye. It won't do no harm.' Emerging from his cubicle, Alfred held the door open as he told Ned to head straight for the nearest basin when he'd flushed the toilet. 'Keep yer eyes on yer looking-glass. I'll be in the farthest booth but one. It's the closest I can get, without alerting the bogle.' His dark, solemn gaze was fixed on Ned. 'I ain't easy in me mind about this, lad. Are you? For if you'd rather not do it, I can allus come back with Jem. He's quicker'n you, though not so canny.'

Ned coloured. He didn't resent the comparison – which was a fair one – but he had no intention of admitting that he wasn't up to the job.

'I can do it,' he croaked, wondering if this were actually true.

'A glass hung up here might have saved three lives,' the bogler went on, his gaze shifting to the blank, tiled wall above the basins. 'Or at least given the poor lads a warning.' Then he sighed and turned to Mr Harewood, who was still hovering on the threshold. 'You'd best get in there,' he instructed, jerking his chin at one of the more distant cubicles.

'But don't so much as blink, if you please, and stay quiet.'

Mr Harewood nodded. He moved into position as Ned asked, in a nervous undertone, 'Am I to sing, Mr Bunce?'

'Aye, lad. Keep at it. You might as well.'

So when Ned finally found himself alone in a cramped little cedar booth, staring down at a white porcelain toilet, he cleared his throat, took a deep, calming breath, and started singing again.

Who caught his blood?
I, said the Fish.
In me little dish
I caught his blood.

He stood with his toes almost touching the ring of salt. There was writing on the toilet, which Ned couldn't read. But that didn't matter. He knew how flush toilets worked, though he'd seen only a handful of them before. Miss Eames owned one, so he'd become thoroughly familiar with its mechanism.

He tried to comfort himself with thoughts of the cistern's ingenious ballcock as he croaked out yet another verse, his pulse racing and his knees trembling.

Who'll make his shroud?
I, said the Beetle.
With a thread and needle
I'll make his shroud.

Ned found it hard to sing, because his mouth was so dry. He couldn't seem to breathe properly, either. And he *certainly* didn't feel ready to confront the bogle. But at last he braced himself, lifted his hand-mirror until his own face was reflected in it, and made a grab for the chain that was dangling above his head.

WHO-O-OSH!

Water was still sloshing down the pipe when he reached the basins. Groping for a tap with one hand, he kept his eyes fixed on the little scene captured in the other. He could see the drain. He could see the exit. He could see Mr Bunce peering out from behind a cedar wall . . .

He could see the bogle, silently appearing.

Who'll dig his grave?
I, said the Owl.
With me pick and shovel
I'll dig his grave.

Ned's voice cracked as he watched a kind of thick, black, bubbling goo dislodge the drain's metal grate and carry it sideways. Then came something long and sticky and featureless, like a giant slug, which reared up and suddenly expanded – *POP!* – the way a bladder inflates. Four long, spiky arms erupted from the bladder, each topped with a bouquet of blood-red talons. A lashing tail was crowned with spikes. There were two clawed feet, and three forked tongues, and a gargoyle's head, and two rows of barbed teeth . . .

But Ned kept singing while Alfred stealthily raised his spear.

Who'll toll the bell?
I, said the Bull.
Because I can pull—

The spearhead flashed. Ned ducked. He leaped sideways into the nearest cubicle, as a deafening screech filled the air. The smell that followed was even worse than the noise. Coughing and gagging, Ned jumped into the ring of salt and scrambled up onto the wooden toilet seat.

He was still perched there when Alfred rasped, 'Ned? Are you all right, lad?'

Ned couldn't speak. He was still retching when Alfred appeared at the cubicle door, holding his nose.

'Are you hurt?' the bogler demanded.

Ned's response was a shake of the head.

'We'd best hook it. This stench may be poisonous.' Alfred ushered Ned out of the cubicle and towards the exit, past the bogle's formless remains. They were so bulky that Ned stopped in his tracks, astonished.

'Why ain't it gone?' he asked hoarsely, aware that most bogles either popped, melted or evaporated when they were killed. They usually left a smear or a scorch-mark, not a heap of singed jelly the size of a small cow. 'I don't understand . . .'

'Neither do I,' Alfred said grimly. He yanked at Ned's arm, pulling him away from the fumes that were making their eyes water. 'I ain't never seen so much gristle left behind, nor heard such a noise, nor smelled such a reek. T'ain't customary. Summat's wrong.'

'Wrong?' Ned echoed in alarm. But Alfred had already turned to Mr Harewood, who was emerging from his hidey-hole, white-faced and gasping.

'Out,' snapped Alfred. 'Now.'

'But I must collect a sample,' Mr Harewood wheezed. 'I promised Gilfoyle—'

'We'll come back when the air's clear.' As Alfred

crossed the threshold, he glanced back over his shoulder. 'And we must clean up that bogle, if it's still there – though I'm puzzled as to how we'd go about it.'

'Wash it down the drain?' Ned suggested.

'Aye, if it don't poison the sewers.' Alfred hawked and spat, then looked up and grimaced as he saw Constable Juddick advancing down the passage towards them. 'Yer friends'll have to wait a little longer, Constable,' he announced. 'The bogle's gone, but I wouldn't go in there just yet. The stench is enough to turn yer stomach . . .'

11

HUNTED

There was a message waiting for them when they emerged from the lavatory. It was a note from Erasmus Gilfoyle, hand-delivered by an errand boy. Mr Gilfoyle was requesting that Alfred come directly to the Apothecaries' Hall, on Water Lane, as soon as he'd finished at the General Post Office.

'Two laboratory boys have vanished in mysterious circumstances,' Mr Harewood explained, as he studied the note. 'Apparently the Superintending Chemical Operator is willing to concede that a "creature of indeterminate origin" may be responsible for their disappearance.' The engineer raised his eyebrows. 'What do you think, Mr Bunce? We could walk to the hall from here. It's straight down Newgate Street, then left at the prison and across Ludgate Hill.'

Ned and Alfred exchanged a wary glance. The bogler looked as tired as Ned felt.

'I daresay we *could* do it,' Alfred rumbled at last, 'if Ned's fit enough.'

'I am,' Ned replied stoutly. Though he was still shaking from his encounter with the bogle, he didn't want to disappoint Alfred – or Mr Harewood. And he fancied that a job at the Apothecaries' Hall might count as official business, for which Alfred was now receiving a handsome wage. 'When I were a mudlark, there was rats as big as bogles on the riverbank, and cutthroats more dangerous still,' he went on, hoping to convince himself, as much as Alfred. 'Ain't no need to fret about me, Mr Bunce. I'm game, sir.'

Alfred eyed Ned sceptically, but refrained from voicing his doubts to Mr Harewood. So when the three of them finally emerged from the post office, they didn't hail a hansom cab. Instead they headed south towards Newgate Street, turning right when they reached the first corner. Mr Harewood took the lead. He marched along energetically, flushed and talkative, carrying a chunk of dead bogle in a china jar obtained from one of the telegraph boys.

'That creature was so *big*!' he gabbled. 'I had no idea! And so difficult to classify. Was it a reptile? A mammal? A curious conflation, like the Australian platypus? Poor Razzy will have a hard time of it!'

Alfred responded with the occasional grunt. He didn't seem to be in a talkative mood. As he shuffled along, bent beneath the weight of his sack, he kept glancing around suspiciously, his dark gaze flitting from face to face. Ned didn't blame him, for they were back in John Gammon's territory. Every step took them closer to Cock Lane, where the butcher's modest little shopfront, festooned with sausages, cleverly concealed the extent of Salty Jack's criminal empire. Walking down Newgate Street, Ned felt as if he were entering a bogle's lair. Despite the rattling carriages and scurrying crowds, there was an ominous quality to the whole scene. Perhaps it had something to do with the wintry light, or the looming bulk of Newgate Prison. Perhaps it was because Alfred had killed a bogle in almost every building that they passed along their way: Christ's Hospital School, the Viaduct Tavern, Newgate Market, St Sepulchre's Church . . .

'. . . I must mark it on our map,' Mr Harewood was saying. 'It's a pity I cannot recall which sewer passes under the post office . . .'

They were approaching Giltspur Street, where Ned had once tackled the fugitive Sarah Pickles and brought her to the ground. She was now in Newgate Prison, awaiting trial. Meanwhile, her accomplice Salty Jack was lurking just around the corner – which was far too close for comfort, in Ned's opinion. As he passed Giltspur Street, Ned caught a fleeting glimpse of Cock Lane, and quickly turned his head to one side.

At the same instant, he spotted a familiar face across the road.

Why, he thought, *it's that newsboy from the post office!*

'. . . and the Chemical Operator might undertake to analyse this sample, if we make it worth his while . . .' Mr Harewood continued, oblivious to Ned's sudden intake of breath. There was no mistaking the newsboy's tartan tweed cap, or bright blue eyes. Though he couldn't have been more than eight or nine years old, he already had the kind of pinched, cagey, watchful expression that marked him as a thief, or a lookout. Jem Barbary had worn the same expression when he was working for Sarah Pickles.

'Mr Bunce?' Ned grabbed Alfred's sleeve. 'We're being followed.'

'What?' Alfred stopped short.

'I didn't tell you earlier ...' As Ned hurriedly explained, Alfred began to frown. But he was smart enough not to glance in the newsboy's direction.

Mr Harewood wasn't quite so quick on the uptake – though he soon turned back when he realised that his friends had fallen behind. He joined them eagerly, his eyes sparkling and his cheeks flushed. On hearing Ned's report, however, his sunny face darkened.

'Why, what a damnable cheek!' he growled. Then, before Ned could stop him, he looked at the newsboy.

'Sst! No!' Ned hissed, but it was too late. The newsboy caught Mr Harewood's eye. There was a heartbeat's pause. Then the boy ducked, swivelled and darted into the nearest cross-street.

'I'll catch the rascal!' Mr Harewood exclaimed. He thrust his china pot into Ned's hands before bolting across the road like a foxhound.

'Wait!' Ned cried. 'Mr Harewood!'

'He'll get hisself killed,' Alfred muttered, setting off in pursuit. With Ned at his heels he dodged a hackney cab, jumped over a puddle, and headed after Mr Harewood, who was struggling to keep up with the newsboy. After dashing past the Newgate pump, Mr Harewood elbowed his way through the crowds that were spilling out of a tavern door, then plunged into a narrow lane opposite the prison.

Alfred swore under his breath. His pace slowed as he eyed the mouth of the lane, which looked dark and seedy. 'I don't like this,' he said. 'This here is a trap, like as not.'

Ned shivered. '*Mr Harewood!*' he yelled. '*Come back!*'

'Mr Harewood! Come back!' echoed a youth who was lounging against the tavern wall. His friends all laughed. Ned blushed.

'You stay close to me, d'you hear?' Alfred told him, ignoring the jeers of their drunken audience. As he slowly advanced, he pulled his sack off his shoulder and tucked it under his arm. Ned couldn't help wondering if he planned to use his spear.

Beyond the tavern, a cobbled passage ran between two rows of sooty, blank-faced shops. The passage was cluttered with carts and barrows. About halfway down its crooked length, another alley opened onto it – and Ned spied Mr Harewood vanishing around a corner into this second alley, pursued by the shrill curses of a woman who'd just been knocked sideways. 'Watch where ye're going!' she squawked, stooping to pick up her basket. One glance told Ned that she probably wasn't a threat, even though she looked a bit like Sarah Pickles. The man near her also seemed harmless; he was small and thin, and wore an ink-spattered apron. But what about the heavily pock-marked porter hovering behind him? Or the man in the blue butcher's smock who was crossing the street up ahead? Were *they* dangerous?

Ned couldn't tell. He'd never laid eyes on John Gammon – or on any of his associates. Except, of course, for Sarah Pickles . . .

All at once a volley of furious shouts was cut short, quite abruptly, as if a door had slammed shut on it. By the time Alfred and Ned rounded the next corner, Mr Harewood was already on his back, in the middle of the alley, with both hands clamped over his nose. There was no sign of the newsboy. But through a screen of startled bystanders – all of whom were converging on Mr Harewood, offering their assistance – Ned saw a man running away.

'There!' Ned shouted, nearly dropping his china pot. '*Stop! Thief!*' As he took a step forward, however, Alfred dragged him back. 'That man!' cried Ned, pointing. 'He'll escape!'

'Leave it.' Alfred wouldn't let go of Ned's arm. 'T'ain't safe here. We shouldn't linger.'

Startled, Ned peered at the people who were clustering around Mr Harewood. Some of them looked quite respectable. There was a stonemason, powdered with white dust; a watchmaker, who wore a bulky eyeglass on a chain; a laundress with a basket of washing; a man dressed in the blue shirt and greasy, fustian trousers of an iron-worker. But there were also several idlers who alarmed Ned. The hatless women were squawking away like hens, while the unshaven men were eyeing Mr Harewood in a speculative manner, as if waiting for a chance to steal his handkerchief.

'John Gammon knows what Jem looks like,' Alfred continued under his breath, 'but that don't mean his cronies do. For all we know, there's folk in this neighbourhood as think *you're* Jem, on account o' you're with me.'

Ned felt a chill run down his spine as Alfred went to assist Mr Harewood, who was already scrambling to his feet. But the engineer pushed away every helping hand extended towards him. He was fumbling in his pockets – for a handkerchief, perhaps. His nose was bleeding, and his voice sounded oddly snubbed when he spoke.

'Thad scoundrel strugg me!' he barked. 'I shall inform the police *ad once.*'

'Mr Harewood? We cannot stay,' Alfred began. Then he frowned on seeing the engineer search through his pockets more and more frantically, without producing anything at all.

'My poggedbook!' Mr Harewood rounded on Alfred, wide-eyed and gasping. 'Id's been stolen!'

There was a murmur of shocked sympathy from his audience. 'Aye, no one's safe in these parts,' said the stonemason. And the watchmaker murmured, 'Are you sure it is nowhere about?'

Ned scanned the surrounding cobbles, but saw no sign of any pocketbook. Alfred, meanwhile, was drawing Mr Harewood aside, away from the curious crowd of onlookers. 'Did you see where the boy went?' Alfred asked in an undertone.

'The boy?' Mr Harewood seemed confused.

'The boy you was chasing,' said Alfred. 'I'm persuaded he had a protector. One o' the butcher's men, I daresay.'

'You thing so?' Mr Harewood accepted the rag that Alfred had produced from his sack, pressing it to his bloody nose before adding, '*I'm* inclined to believe a gang of pigpoggeds lured me here. Thad wretched fellow toog me by surprise.' Before Alfred could object, Mr Harewood turned to Ned and murmured,

'I didden catch more than a glimpse of the boy. Can you describe him to me?'

'Yes, sir,' Ned replied. 'He were eight or nine years old, smaller'n I am, with blue eyes and light hair, wearing brown canvas trousers—'

'Good.' Mr Harewood cut him off. 'And I saw the *other* blaggard well enough – he was a big fellow with no hair and a scar on his lefd eyebrow. So you musd come with me to the nearesd station house, Ned. I believe id's in Smithfield. Or perhaps there's a constable ad the Old Bailey?'

'Ned cannot stay, sir. Not in this quarter.' Seeing the engineer blink, Alfred quickly explained, 'I'm a marked man, hereabouts, and Ned is likely to be mistook for Jem. He ain't safe here.'

'Oh.' Mr Harewood glanced at Ned, then at the small crowd that was dispersing nearby. 'I see . . .'

'And Mr Gilfoyle is expecting me, besides,' Alfred continued. 'I should take Ned straight to Water Lane, while you go to the police.' Eyeing Mr Harewood's stained handkerchief, the bogler finished, 'I'd have that nose seen to, in addition.'

'Very well.' Mr Harewood suddenly capitulated. 'Yes, you should go. Id would be wrong to delay poor Razzy. I shall repord to the police, and perhaps join you in an hour or so.' He nodded at Alfred, but paused for a moment in front of Ned. 'You musd give thad sample to Mr Gilfoyle. He'll know whad to do with id. Can I trusd you with such a commission, my boy?'

'Yes, sir,' Ned answered.

'I hope id's nod been too knogged aboud,' Mr Harewood went on, lifting the lid of the china jar. Then he yelped in dismay and spluttered, 'Why, whad's this? Whad happened? I cannod understand . . .'

For he had uncovered nothing more than a brown smear, where once there had been a great dollop of black jelly.

12

A VERY STRANGE PLACE

The Apothecaries' Hall was a fine old building wrapped around a central courtyard. It was several stories high, constructed of brick and stucco, with a carved coat-of-arms set over its main entrance. To the left of this entrance was a shop that sold drugs, herbs and chemicals. The building also contained a packing room, a warehouse, a mill house, a factory, an accountants' office, a series of examination rooms, and all the various chambers required by any guild or society: a great hall, a courtroom, a library, a kitchen – even a beadle's office.

Not that Ned saw any of these apartments. When he and Alfred arrived at Water Lane, asking to see the Superintending Chemical Operator, they were directed straight to 'the laboratory'. A porter conducted them across the courtyard, past a gas-lamp on a plinth, and through a set of swing-doors into a narrow but well-lit passage. As he walked, the porter listed the building's many features, pointing some of them out along the way.

'The Great Hall is up the stairs to our right ... the library above us contains many rare botanical works ... this colonnade is sometimes used as an extension of the packing room ... there is an old friary well under the gas-lamp—'

'A *well*?' Alfred interrupted sharply, glancing at Ned. But before the porter could reply, they pushed through another set of doors into the laboratory, and Alfred forgot to press for an answer.

Like Ned, he froze in his tracks, drop-jawed and blinking.

'Ah! Mr Bunce!' a familiar voice exclaimed. 'Thank you so *very* much for answering my summons.'

The speaker was Mr Gilfoyle. He was standing with another man in the middle of a sweltering room full of huge copper tanks. Ned instantly realised that these tanks were stills, like the stills he'd sometimes seen in dank cellar kitchens around Wapping, back when he was a scavenger. Such equipment had been used to distil alcohol from old vegetable peelings, though on a very small scale. Ned couldn't understand how these larger versions could possibly work without a fire burning beneath them.

'Mr Warington, let me present Mr Alfred Bunce, our committee's bogler,' Mr Gilfoyle continued. Though rather damp and flushed from the heat, he still looked beautifully groomed in his glossy top hat, gleaming shoes and spotless white linen. 'Mr Bunce, this is Mr Warington, who has kindly offered to assist our committee in its endeavours.'

Mr Warington bowed slightly. He was a short, wiry man with sallow skin, a brisk manner and pale, piercing eyes. Though still quite young, he already had flecks of grey in his dark hair – which was also dusted with some kind of yellowish powder. He wore his shirtsleeves rolled to the elbow, and an apron that reached his knees. Every inch of his clothing was stained, splotched, scorched, smeared or splattered.

'How d'you do?' he said drily. Then his searching gaze settled on Ned.

'This is Ned Roach, Mr Bunce's apprentice,' Mr Gilfoyle explained, before turning back to Alfred. 'According to Mr Warington, it *should* be possible to isolate some of the substances on your spear, Mr Bunce. To do so, however, he would probably have to destroy a good portion of it.'

'To break down the constituents,' Mr Warington added.

'But you can't do that!' Horrified, Ned spoke without thinking – then flushed as everyone stared at him.

'He won't have to,' said Alfred, and went on to describe his planned trip to Derbyshire. Meanwhile, Ned's attention strayed to a nearby set of hanging scales, and to the brick oven that stood beyond it. The scales were big enough to sit in, and the oven was fitted with two iron doors. There were also half-a-dozen boilers, a complex tangle of pipes, a collection of oddly shaped beakers, and two sweating men in dustcoats.

'Well, that does sound like a sensible thing to do,' Mr Gilfoyle observed, when Alfred had finished. 'I've always believed that village healers, with their old tales and traditions, can sometimes be quite helpful.' Hearing Mr Warington snort, he said quickly, 'At the very least, we should leave no stone unturned.'

'Aye. I thought that,' agreed Alfred. Then he changed the subject by addressing Mr Warington.

'I'm told you had two boys go missing. Can you tell me where they was last seen?'

'Downstairs,' Mr Warington replied. 'They were collecting fuel for the steam engine.'

Ned was thrilled. 'You have a *steam engine*?'

'We do. It runs the forcing pump that feeds hot water to the steam boiler heating our distilleries.'

'Ohhh . . .'

'We distil nitric acid, muriatic acid, hartshorn, sulphuric ether – although that, of course, is distilled in an *earthenware* vessel.' Mr Warington cocked his head. 'Are you interested in steam, Master Roach?'

'Yes, sir. Oh, *yes*.'

'Then it may amuse you to know that you are standing on a steam pipe.' As Ned instinctively jumped sideways, the toe of Mr Warington's boot prodded a line of steel plates underfoot. 'The main pipe from the underground boiler branches off into smaller pipes, which run beneath the still-house floor and intersect with each still. The pipes running *out* of each still carry condensed water to a cistern, which in turn supplies the boiler—'

'Ahem.' Alfred cleared his throat suddenly, and Mr Gilfoyle remarked, 'Forgive us, but we're a little pressed for time.'

'I need to know if anything else were seen.' Alfred fixed his sombre gaze on Mr Warington. 'Around the time them lads disappeared. Anything . . . strange.'

'Anything like this,' Ned interjected, taking the lid off his china pot.

Mr Warington and Mr Gilfoyle both peered into the pot. Mr Warington even sniffed at it. Then Mr Gilfoyle asked, 'What on earth is this, Mr Bunce?'

'It's dead bogle,' Alfred said flatly.

'Ah.' Mr Gilfoyle straightened. 'I see.'

'In truth, Mr Bunce, there is such an endless supply of smears and smells in this laboratory that no one working here would be likely to notice anything like this.' Mr Warington tapped on the side of the pot, which he had taken from Ned. 'But if you've no objection, I shall attempt to analyse these remains, it being easier to kill a thing if you know exactly what it is.'

'Why, what an excellent idea!' Mr Gilfoyle began to thank Mr Warington profusely before Alfred could even open his mouth. 'That is *most* kind, sir. Our committee would be *extremely* grateful.'

'As to unusual signs in the basement . . . well, it's a very peculiar place down there.' Tucking the pot under his arm, Mr Warington regarded his visitors with a keen, measuring look. 'I'll show you, shall I? Come. Follow me. And mind what you touch.'

He led them across the still-house, through a pair of large iron doors, and into another, even hotter room full of open fires and furnaces. 'This is our chemical laboratory,' he explained. 'And this is our calcining furnace, and our wind furnace, and our furnace for sulphate of quicksilver . . .'

It wasn't until they entered something he called a 'mortar room' that they finally reached the stairs to the basement, which were tucked away in a corner, near a drying stove. According to Mr Warington, the missing boys had marched down these steps, carrying their empty coal-buckets, and were never seen again – though their discarded buckets were later found.

'Where?' asked Alfred.

'Let me show you.' Mr Warington placed Ned's china pot on top of a steam-press before plunging into the basement ahead of his visitors. When Ned arrived at the bottom of the stairs he found himself in a large, dark, vaulted space, with the biggest chimney he'd ever seen standing squarely in its centre. The chimney was so massive that four other flues fed into it, one on each side.

'Where was them buckets found?' Alfred wanted to know.

'Over here.' Mr Warington moved past the chimney towards a towering heap of coal. He stopped at a point midway between the coal and the chimney. 'Both buckets were discovered in this area,' he said, as Ned scanned the floor.

No drains or steel plates were visible.

'What's that?' Alfred demanded, pointing at a small hatch set into the flue that faced the coal-heap.

'A chimney will not perform its proper function if it can't be cleaned or repaired,' Mr Warington replied, then went on to describe how smoke from every upstairs furnace was directed underground and into the main chimney through a number of flues. Access to the chimney's interior was through the hatch in the flue. 'Now that I think about it,' he murmured, as an afterthought, 'a sweep's boy *was* reported missing, hereabouts. That is to say, some sort of complaint was made to the Warden, though I wasn't informed of the particulars . . .'

'A *sweep's boy*?' Alfred cut in. 'There's *boys* sent up this chimney?'

'Of course,' said Mr Warington. 'But only when the fires are out. And the fires were unquestionably lit when our laboratory boys vanished.'

Alfred looked at Ned. Then they both looked at the

hatch in the flue. It was perfectly placed, Ned realised. You had to turn your back on it if you wanted to shovel coal into a bucket . . .

'I think you got a chimney-bogle,' Alfred announced grimly.

Mr Warington stared at him. 'A what?' he said, as Mr Gilfoyle hurriedly produced a little black book from his pocket.

'It's a bogle as lurks in chimneys,' Alfred rasped. 'I've killed a good few.'

Mr Warington's stare didn't waver, though his mouth twitched. 'Mr Bunce, the temperature in our furnaces can reach six hundred degrees Fahrenheit,' he pointed out. 'No creature could survive such conditions.'

'Can we be sure of that, Mr Warington?' Mr Gilfoyle suddenly came to Alfred's defence, scribbling away in his little black book as he spoke. 'After all, our understanding of bogles is in its infancy.'

'Yes, but—'

'Is that hatch ever left open when there's fires burning?' Alfred interrupted. He was addressing Mr Warington, whose thoughtful gaze moved from Alfred to the hatch and back again before he replied, 'Occasionally. If more air is called for.'

'In that case, we'll open it now,' said Alfred. When he turned to Ned, his expression was grave. 'It'll feel hot on yer back,' he rumbled, 'and there ain't no telling what might come out o' that door. But I'll be close to you, lad. I can hide behind the chimney.'

Ned swallowed. Then he glanced at the huge pile of coal.

'You don't think it's hiding in that coal-heap?' he quavered.

'Mebbe,' Alfred had to admit – at which point Mr Warington said, 'You don't mean to tell me this boy is here as *bait*?'

'He'll be safe enough,' Alfred said. 'I'll make sure of it.' As Mr Warington raised a sceptical eyebrow, the bogler scowled and added, 'You'd best warn all o' them folk up there to stay well away till we're finished.'

'If you'd be so good,' Mr Gilfoyle inserted quickly, with a placating smile.

'Of course.' Mr Warington began to retrace his steps. Upon reaching the bottom of the staircase, however, he paused and studied Ned for a moment. 'It's my belief, Master Roach, that you should consider a different job – especially given your interest in steam,' he remarked. 'Despite the extreme temperature and caustic chemicals involved in laboratory work, you'd probably be safer here than you are in your present position.'

'Except when there's bogles about!' snapped Alfred. And Mr Warington's mouth twitched again.

'True,' he had to concede. 'You have a point.' Then he briskly made his way upstairs.

13

THE SNARE

A drift of smoke curled out of the open hatch. Ned could see it reflected in his mirror. He was standing inside an open ring of salt, with his back to the chimney and his face to the coal-heap. Alfred had given him some extra salt, just in case a bogle happened to emerge from the coal-heap instead of the hatch. 'You'll be safe as long as you close that circle,' Alfred had insisted. 'If anything attacks you from the front, you can allus drop yer salt and stand fast. But I ain't persuaded it'll happen.'

He himself was now skulking by the chimney, ready to leap forward at the first sign of trouble. Mr Gilfoyle was hiding behind the nearest coke-bin. But

Ned couldn't help feeling very lonely as he waited there, his mouth dry and his skin clammy, bleating away like a tethered lamb.

Oranges and lemons,
Say the bells o' St Clement's.
You owe me five farthings
Say the bells o' St Martin's.

Mr Warington was nowhere to be seen. He hadn't returned from his trip upstairs, and Ned wondered what he was doing. Standing guard on the top step? Toiling in the still-house? Either way, he was luckier than Ned – who couldn't help comparing his own job to Mr Warington's.

Given the choice, Ned would have preferred to be doing almost anything else: shovelling coke into a furnace, say, or grinding up toxic powders. Mr Warington had been right. Laboratory work was *much* less dangerous than bogling. If it hadn't been for Alfred, Ned might have considered applying for a position as laboratory boy. (There were at least two vacancies, now.)

But he couldn't desert Alfred. It was Alfred who had rescued him from a life of mud and misery. It was

Alfred who had given him a home. So when Alfred had needed another bogler's boy, Ned had willingly volunteered, even though he couldn't leap like Jem or sing like Birdie.

In fact he was surprised that his cracked voice didn't frighten bogles away . . .

When will you pay me?
Say the bells of Old Bailey.
When I grow rich
Say the bells o' Shoreditch.

Smoke was still curling from the hatch – and it was getting thicker. There was a faint haze in the air now. Ned smelled sulphur and wondered why. Was tainted smoke coming from an upstairs furnace? Or was that sulphurous stench a sign that the bogle was nearby?

Peering into his mirror, Ned could see only smoke emerging from the hatch behind him. But as his eyes began to sting, and his throat became scratchy, something clicked inside his head.

Of course.

There was no *need* for the bogle to emerge. Not if Ned shut the hatch to stop the smoke. For then he'd be within easy reach of any claws or hooks or tentacles.

'Mr Bunce ...' Ned turned and beckoned to Alfred, who was already harder to see through a haze of smoke. When the bogler scowled, Ned motioned to him even more urgently, knowing that it would be dangerous to close the gap between himself and the chimney-hatch by even one step.

At last Alfred moved towards Ned, still scowling. When the bogler finally reached him, Ned put his mouth to Alfred's ear and whispered, 'That creature's not about to show itself. Not till I go over and shut the hatch.'

Alfred hissed. His eyes widened as his bushy brows knotted together. He glanced back at the chimney.

'That there is a smart bogle,' Ned added under his breath. Then he coughed, swallowed and licked his dry lips before quavering, 'If ... if you was to give me yer spear, Mr Bunce—'

'Oh, no. Not that.'

'Ain't nothing else'll work,' Ned pointed out. He actually preferred the idea of confronting the bogle face-to-face, with a spear in his hand. And he felt sure that Alfred's reputation would suffer badly if they just walked away without even *trying* to kill the bogle. 'Please, Mr Bunce. If you go back to where you was, you'll be close enough to grab me. *Or* throw salt. You'll be there if summat goes wrong.'

'Which it's bound to,' Alfred muttered.

'No, sir. It ain't.' Ned spoke staunchly, striving to ignore the sense of black despair that was creeping over him. He recognised it, of course. It was the gloom that every bogle used to protect itself – and Ned knew, by now, that it had no basis in reality. 'I already killed a bogle with yer spear, remember? At Smithfield Market. I can allus do it again.' Seeing that he'd made an impression with this argument, Ned concluded, 'I can't jump like Jem nor sing like Birdie, but I'm stronger'n both of 'em. You know that.'

'Aye . . .' Alfred was gnawing at his bottom lip, his long face growing longer by the second. 'All the same, it don't sit well with me.'

'It sits well with me. For I'd rather – *cough, cough* – walk up to that bogle and look it in the eye than wait for it with me back turned.' By this time the smoke was so thick that Ned could barely see the chimney. Lowering his voice, he concluded, 'We got to do it now, Mr Bunce.'

'Aye,' Alfred said again. Then he surrendered his spear and moved his hand to Ned's shoulder. 'Don't aim twice,' he warned in an undertone, his dark gaze boring into Ned's. 'If you miss yer target, run. You've only one chance, lad. *Drop* that spear if you have to.'

'Yes, sir.'

'It's you I want to keep, not the weapon.' Alfred's hand fell away as he swung around, heading back to his post by the chimney before Ned could say anything else.

By now Ned's eyes were streaming. He was afraid that the smoke must be leaking into the laboratory above him. And when he heard Mr Gilfoyle smother a cough, he realised that he didn't have much time.

So he took a cautious step towards the chimney, raising his voice to drown the choked splutters coming from behind the coke-bin.

When will that – cough! – be?
Say the bells o' Stepney.
I do not know – cough!
Says the great bell o' Bow.

Ned quickly cast aside the salt that he'd been clutching and fastened both hands firmly around the shaft of Alfred's spear. A cloud of black smoke was billowing towards him. He advanced one step. Then another. Then another. The smoke blocked out the light as he carefully adjusted his grip.

Suddenly he couldn't see Alfred. He couldn't see the chimney. But despite the darkness, and the tears in his eyes, he could just make out that there was a dense, black heart to the cloud of smoke – a heart that seemed to be growing bigger.

And though he was gasping for breath, he doggedly kept croaking out another verse of his nursery rhyme.

Here – cough! – comes a candle
To light you to bed – cough, cough!

He raised his spear and aimed it. Then he waited, poised on the balls of his feet, as the black shadow grew ... and grew ...

Here comes a – cough! – chopper
To chop off yer HEAD!

And he rammed the spear home.

There was a jolt – then nothing. Darkness. He couldn't breathe.

Had he failed?

'Ned?' Someone was slapping his cheeks. '*Ned!*'

He opened his eyes. Alfred's face was hanging over him, drawn and anxious. What had happened to the smoke? When Ned's gaze shifted sideways, he saw a whitewashed ceiling behind a ring of heads, and realised that he wasn't in the basement anymore.

'Ned? Can you hear me?' Alfred was speaking again. 'Can you move? Can you talk, lad?'

'Wha – what happened?' Ned croaked. He had spotted Mr Harewood, standing between Mr Gilfoyle and Mr Warington. Mr Harewood's nose was swollen up. One of his eyes was purple and puffy.

'You killed the bogle,' said Alfred. 'Don't you remember?'

'There was an explosion,' Mr Gilfoyle added. He was as white as chalk. 'You were thrown clear across the room.'

'I killed it?'

'You did.' Alfred dangled a dirty rag in front of him. 'We bin cleaning it off you ever since.'

Ned raised his own hand and saw that it was smeared with grey soot. It was also covered in small, reddish spots that stung when he touched them.

'It burned you,' Alfred gruffly explained, on seeing Ned wince. 'Just a little. Nowt to speak of. You was lucky.'

'*Lucky?*' Mr Gilfoyle echoed in disbelief, as Ned struggled up onto his elbows. 'You call that *lucky*? He might have been killed!'

'We're in the mortar room,' Ned suddenly declared. He had recognised the drying oven.

'Aye.' Alfred flashed a quick look at Mr Gilfoyle, whose clenched features relaxed. Even Mr Warington heaved a sigh of relief.

'He must be well enough,' said Mr Harewood, 'if he knows where he is.'

'Of course I do!' Ned sat up. His head was rapidly clearing. 'When did *you* arrive, sir?'

'After you were knogged out,' Mr Harewood replied. His voice still sounded very odd. 'I hear you were as brave as a lion, young Ned.'

'Yes, indeed.' Mr Gilfoyle spoke before Ned could. 'Though I must confess, I'm still unclear as to why he should have been exposed to such danger. I thought the usual technique was to lure the bogle *out* of its lair?'

Alfred gave a grunt. He didn't seem inclined to defend himself. Ned murmured, 'This 'un wouldn't never have showed itself. It stayed in the flue, blowing smoke and waiting for me to come to it.'

'You mean you didn't *see* the bogle? *Any* of you?' Mr Warington's tone was drily incredulous. When

Ned and Alfred and Mr Gilfoyle all shook their heads, he asked, 'Then how can you be sure there was one? That noise sounded just like a gas explosion to me. It's quite possible that you accidentally ignited a combination of volatile chemicals . . .'

'We didn't.' Ned tried not to sound as resentful as he felt. 'It were a bogle. I could feel it.'

'So could I,' said Alfred. He was glaring at Mr Warington. 'This boy killed a bogle. Don't you take that away from him, sir. He's a brave lad.'

Mr Gilfoyle nodded furiously in agreement. Beside him, Mr Warington raised his hands in a half-hearted gesture of submission. Then Mr Harewood remarked, 'I'm persuaded thad there musd be someone with medical training on these premises. Am I ride, Mr Waringdon?'

'Of course.' Mr Warington flashed him a quizzical look. 'This is the Apothecaries' Hall.'

'Then perhaps you could arrange a brief consultation for me? *And* for poor Ned, here, who musd have a lump on his head as big as a crab-apple.' Mr Harewood smiled crookedly as he addressed Alfred. 'Before I hail a cab for us, Mr Bunce, we should probably arm ourselves with a few salves and plasters. Do you nod agree? For I'd argue thad some of us have done enough for one day, and should be off to bed as soon as possible.'

'Aye.' Alfred inclined his head, then muttered something about the importance of getting a good night's sleep. Ned caught the word 'Derbyshire', and suddenly remembered.

He was going to be taking his very first railway journey, the next day.

'Why, yes, of course! Your visid to the Peak District!' Mr Harewood began to rub his hands together. 'I musd say, I'm looking forward to your findings, Mr Bunce. If you can discover the secreds of your spear, we shall all be a *deal* better off . . .'

14

MEETING MOTHER MAY

Ned sat in a second-class carriage on a train heading for Derbyshire. Wedged between Alfred and a fat man with a cold, he didn't have much of a view out the window. He also felt embarrassed every time he caught the eye of the lady sitting opposite, who would sniff and turn away in a very pointed manner. It was obvious that she regarded him as the sort of person who ought to be travelling in third class.

So he'd spent most of the journey staring at his boots, thinking about recent events as the train rocked and swayed and chugged along. St Pancras Station had been so huge – so magnificent – that he'd been dazzled. From a ticket office fitted with cathedral windows and acres of polished wood, he had emerged into a train-shed so large that he could barely see one end from the other. Seven locomotives had been lined up inside it like horses in a stable, with their carriages arranged neatly behind them. Ned had boarded the very longest of these trains, which was more comfortably furnished than he'd ever imagined it would be; the seats were padded, there was glass in all the windows, and the luggage racks were made of solid brass.

Even the train's departure had been exciting. The blast of the whistle and the engine's gathering speed had filled Ned with exhilaration. Plunging into dark tunnels had been quite a thrill, at first. The trip itself, however, had proved to be a bit of a disappointment. The people around him sat quietly, trying not to look at each other. Some of them slept, some of them smoked, and some of them read books or newspapers. The windows quickly steamed up, so that he couldn't see outside. The carriage was cold but stuffy. Passengers would get on or off, but they never did anything of interest. When the shabbily dressed clergyman near the window peeled an egg into a paper bag, his movements were furtive, and he kept his head down.

Alfred slept. With his arms folded and his chin on his chest, he dozed through stop after stop, as

Ned listened to the guards calling out station names. According to Alfred, their destination was a town called Long Eaton. 'We'll change trains at Trent,' he'd explained before nodding off, 'so you must wake me when we reach Leicester.'

In the meantime, Ned had nothing to do but reflect on his situation. He still ached a little from his job at the Apothecaries' Hall, where he'd bruised some ribs, bumped his head, and singed his eyebrows. Luckily, he'd been offered a cab ride home afterwards; *walking* back would have left him feeling much worse. But he'd been forced to spend the whole trip listening to Mr Gilfoyle bicker with Mr Harewood about chimney-bogles. Did the existence of chimney-bogles disprove the theory that bogles used sewers to get around? Mr Gilfoyle had insisted that there were different types of bogles, some of which didn't need underground water. Mr Harewood had argued that the Fleet Sewer ran beneath the very doorstep of the Apothecaries' Hall, so there *had* to be a connection.

Alfred had kept his opinion to himself.

He'd remained very quiet and sombre, even after arriving back at Orange Court – where Jem had been waiting impatiently, anxious to tell them a wonderful piece of news. After spending nearly an hour with

Mr Chatterton that morning, both Jem and Birdie had been hired for the Theatre Royal pantomime. 'We start rehearsing tomorrow,' Jem had grandly announced, 'and they'll pay me two shillings for every performance!' Birdie would be earning more, he'd added, because she had been engaged as a soloist. 'I'm only in the chorus, but if I dance well enough they might give me summat special to do. I might even get to dance with Mr Vokes!'

Remembering the radiant expression on Jem's face, Ned didn't feel the least bit jealous. A stage career wasn't something he'd ever wanted; in fact, the thought of performing in public made his blood run cold. And he was glad that Birdie had achieved her heart's desire, because she deserved to be famous. She was the bravest, prettiest, noblest person he'd ever met, and her voice was good enough to be admired all over the world. As far as Ned was concerned, she *belonged* in the spotlight.

But with Jem employed elsewhere, the burden of the bogling would now fall on Ned. And Ned wasn't sure exactly what that would involve. He didn't even know why he'd been invited to Derbyshire. He had a sneaking suspicion, however, that he wasn't there just to carry the luggage.

Alfred had some sort of plan in mind.

When they finally arrived at Trent Station, some three hours after leaving St Pancras, they found themselves in the middle of nowhere. Though very large and handsome, with lavatories and refreshment rooms and glass canopies over both platforms, the station was surrounded by fields and woods as far as the eye could see. Once the London express had rolled away, and the smoke and steam had cleared, Ned was confronted by a vast expanse of leafless treetops.

'There ain't no town,' he murmured, awestruck. He'd never in his life set foot outside London – and the fresh, scented breeze that blew in his face was a revelation.

'Trent Station's nowt but an interchange,' a passing guard informed him. 'All tha can do here is switch lines.'

''Tis new since I were last in the neighbourhood,' Alfred confessed. 'Where must we go to catch the train to Long Eaton?'

'Ower that way.' The guard directed Alfred to a connecting train, which was almost empty of passengers. As a result, Alfred and Ned had a whole carriage to themselves. And since there was no one else around to overhear them, Ned finally found the courage to ask, 'Is this where you was raised, Mr Bunce?'

Alfred shook his head. 'Nay,' he said, staring out the window as the engine gathered speed. 'I were born in Derby. Daniel Piggin brought me to Long Eaton nobbut two or three times, to visit his sister. She worked on a farm just out o' town.'

Surprised to hear Alfred so chatty, Ned tried another question. 'So where did yer master do his bogling, then?'

'In London, chiefly. I weren't five years old when I moved there. But sometimes we was hired to do jobs up this way, by folk as knew us.' All of a sudden Alfred's pensive gaze shifted back to Ned. 'Daniel Piggin trained me up to take his place. There was other boys as came and went, but I allus stayed close, even when carting loads to make ends meet.' Pausing for a moment, Alfred seemed to expect some kind of comment. But Ned was confused. He didn't know what to say.

So Alfred continued.

'I weren't twenty when Dan passed. A fever took him quick and clean. He left me his pipe and his spear, which I still have.' After briefly surveying Ned from top to toe, the bogler finally said, 'I bin a-thinking I might give 'em to you, in time.'

Ned blinked.

'Jem's found another path for hisself, and I'm glad of it, for he ain't steady,' Alfred went on. 'He's quick and brave, so he made a good 'prentice. But it takes more'n that to be a bogler. A bogler needs to have a clear head and a firm hand.' As Ned shifted uneasily, Alfred finished, 'I ain't never had no other 'prentice kill a bogle – and you done it twice, lad. Seems to me you was born to the job.'

Still Ned didn't know what to say. He should have been honoured; that was clear. Yet his heart sank like a stone at the thought of becoming Alfred's successor.

'Y-you ain't ill, Mr Bunce?' he stammered.

'Nay, lad. I'm tiring, though. And coming back here don't make me feel no younger.' Alfred frowned as his gaze drifted back to the window. 'Wait,' he said, leaning forward. 'What's this? This ain't Long Eaton.'

But it was. To Alfred's dismay, a new railway station had been built since his previous visit. What's more, it was in a completely different part of the town, so when at last he emerged onto the platform, he didn't know where he was. He had to ask one of the guards for directions to Coffee Pot Farm, while Ned stood waiting in a light drizzle, wondering uneasily if they had come all this way for nothing.

If Long Eaton had uprooted its whole railway station, what were the chances that May Piggin still lived at her old address?

'The other station were on Toton Lane, just down the road from Mother May's house,' Alfred observed, when they finally set off. 'Now we must go up Station Street, which used to be Tithe Barn Lane.' They were heading east, across a footbridge suspended over the railway tracks, when he stopped suddenly. 'Look there,' he said, nodding at a cluttered vista of factory chimneys and railway sheds that lay to the west. 'Most o' them mills is new, since I were a lad. It's changed, right enough.'

'It's a big station,' Ned observed.

'It is. And less'n ten years old, that guard said.'

'Will Mother May be living here still, Mr Bunce?'

Alfred shrugged. 'She weren't one for shifting about,' he replied, 'and the farm seems to be where I left it.'

Ned grunted. Though he had begun to doubt that May Piggin was even alive, he obediently followed Alfred up Station Street, which had a strangely patchy appearance at first, as if it couldn't make up its mind whether it belonged to the town or the country. Grand new houses were springing up on brand new streets, but here and there a chunk of old hedgerow or a tumbledown barn remained. The road was macadam for a while, then degenerated into muddy ruts, scattered with puddles.

After about twenty minutes, Ned began to feel as if he was trudging through proper countryside. There were overgrown paddocks and tilled fields, and a horse stood all alone behind a stone fence. Alfred kept muttering under his breath ('Where's Grange Farm? This don't look right. The old tithe barn's gone . . .'), as water slowly dripped from his nose and hat-brim. Ned soon realised that country walking was more difficult than city walking. The road was so dirty and uneven, and the rain was so relentless, that he didn't say another word until they came within sight of their destination.

'There,' said Alfred, pointing at a row of gritstone houses sitting forlornly on an otherwise deserted stretch of road. 'There it is. The one at the end.'

Ned was puzzled. 'That's the farm?' he queried, wondering where the barns were.

'Nay, the farm's up yonder. This here is where the farmhands live. Or *used* to live.' Alfred struck out for the closest cottage, which was a two-storeyed structure attached to another, identical house.

Ned thought it very grim-looking, with its grey walls and tiny windows. The small garden plot in front was full of mud and brown stalks. A leafless vine was growing over the front door, which was set quite low. The smoke oozing from the chimney drifted downwards, as if the damp air weighed on it.

Alfred hesitated for a moment before knocking. Ned thought he was paler than usual, though that might have been because of the cold.

'Hello?' said Alfred. 'Mrs Blewett?'

There was no reply. The only sounds were the trickle of water and the sighing of the wind. Ned couldn't get over the lack of noise; London was never this quiet, not even at two o'clock in the morning.

'Hello?' Alfred repeated. 'Is anyone there?'

Suddenly Ned heard shuffling footsteps, followed by the scrape of a bolt and the creak of hinges. Next thing he knew, he was staring at a little old lady wrapped in a grey shawl. Her hair was grey too, as were her eyes, which were buried deep in two nests of wrinkles. She wore a rather limp white cap on her silvery hair, and carried a wooden cane.

'Who's there?' she cawed, blinking at Ned – who was taller than she was. 'Dost ah know thee?'

'Mrs Blewett?' said Alfred. 'Mrs May Blewett?'

'Aye.' All at once she seemed to get her bearings. Turning to Alfred, she croaked, 'And th'art?'

'Alfred Bunce. I used to work for yer brother Daniel.' As the old woman peered at him, silent and motionless, Alfred cleared his throat and shifted his weight. 'I came here from London, Mother May. There's summat I need to know, and I thought as how you might have the answer.'

'Fred Bunce?' The old woman's face suddenly brightened. 'T' Derby lad?'

'Aye.'

'Well, ah'll be . . .' Smiling a gap-toothed smile, Mother May began to edge backwards into the gloom of her cottage. 'Come in! Come in, tha must be clammed! Ah've some oatcakes for thee, and a drap o' cider . . .'

15

THE BLASTING ROD

Mother May's oatcakes were as dry as dust, but her cider was good. One sip was all it took to warm Ned on the inside. And her fire warmed the rest of him, slowly thawing out his wet feet, his chilled hands and his frozen ears.

The fire was built in a brazier, which occupied one corner of the old woman's huge inglenook fireplace. This fireplace was so big that it seemed to take up half her kitchen. The rest of the low, dark, sooty room was crammed with furniture: a table, a dresser, a chest, a barrel, a sink, a bed, several mismatched chairs, and piles of domestic junk.

Looking at the clothes and pots and tools that

covered every available surface, Ned realised that Mother May was actually *living* in her kitchen. He guessed that the rest of the house was probably unused, except for storing firewood.

As someone who lived in a tiny London garret with two other people, he found such a waste of space hard to comprehend.

'So tha'rt a bogler,' the old woman said to Alfred, in a voice that crackled like the fire. She had lowered herself into a well-worn rocking chair beside the hearth, having placed Ned and Alfred on a rickety settle opposite her. 'And this bonny lad – is he yorn?'

'Nay,' Alfred rumbled. He sounded almost sheepish, Ned thought, and quite unlike himself. 'Ned Roach is me 'prentice.'

Mother May clicked her tongue. 'Ah thought he must be kin, what with t' big, brown eyes that's on 'im. Hast tha no children, Freddie?'

Alfred shook his head.

'Eh, now, that's a shame,' the old women lamented. 'But poor Dan had t' same problem, travelling about as he did. He couldn't settle long enough to find hissen a wife.'

'I don't travel much,' said Alfred. 'I don't need to. There's bogles enough in London to keep me busy.'

'All in t' one place?' Mother May kept dipping her oatcake into her cider, and Ned wondered if she did this because she didn't have many teeth. 'Well, ah never. What a wicked town it must be!'

''Tain't the wickedness as draws the bogles, Mrs Blewett. 'Tis the number o' children living there.' Before Mother May could respond, Alfred leaned forward and said quietly, 'Yer brother gave me all he had when he died. His pipe, his baccy pouch, his boots ... and his spear, ma'am. Do you remember his spear?'

The old woman nodded as she masticated her oatcake. 'That ah do,' she replied, spraying crumbs.

'He told me it were Finn MacCool's spear. Did he ever tell *you* that?'

'*Finn MacCool's* spear?' She began to cough. 'Gerron with thee!'

Alfred frowned.

''Twas nowt but a blasting rod!' Mother May continued, still coughing. She didn't find her voice again until she'd drained her cup of cider. Then she smiled at Alfred. 'Dan was telling thee tales, ah expect, tha being a little laddie. But he cut that spear hissen, and *ah* was t'one that hexed it.'

Alfred stiffened, his eyes widening. Ned asked, 'What's a blasting rod?'

'Why, 'tis a witch's staff, me duck. Made o' black-thorn and used for cursing, though we piggled away at it till we had a bogling spear. Mam taught me how 'twas done, for she was a cunning woman, like her own mam—'

'Blackthorn, you say?' Alfred interrupted. 'That spear is made o' blackthorn?'

'With a head cut by the stonemason down the lane, from a cross blessed by t' owd priest at Duffield,' said Mother May. She looked quite pleased with herself for remembering this. 'Ten shillings, it cost, but Dan knew 'twould pay for issen.'

'So the spear is just a stick o' blackthorn with a consecrated point on it?' Alfred seemed taken aback. 'That's all it is?'

'Nay, lad, 'twould be rammel without herbs!' the old woman exclaimed, balancing her empty cup on an overturned bucket. 'Tha canna cast a bane without herbs, Freddie, else tha'd like to come a cropper.'

'Which herbs did you use?' Ned chimed in. He was genuinely interested – and he sensed that Mother May liked him. But instead of answering his question, she smirked and bridled and said, 'Well now, tha may well ask.'

Ned was surprised. Why was she being so coy,

all of a sudden? He glanced at Alfred, who was studying the old woman gravely, an untouched piece of oatcake in one hand and a full cup of cider in the other.

'You're still in business, Mrs Blewett?' the bogler queried.

'Ah am that,' she replied with a cackle. 'For there'll allus be lassies in love, and lads with grudges. Not to mention owd men with sore teggies.'

Ned still didn't understand. 'What's a teggy?' he asked, bewildered.

Mother May grinned and tapped one of the last teeth in her gums with a crooked finger. 'This is a teggy,' she said, 'and tha may be thankful there's a full set of 'em in that fine head o' yorn.'

'Mrs Blewett, I ain't about to take none o' your potions without paying a fair price,' Alfred cut in – and all at once it dawned on Ned that Mother May's 'business' had to be her magic. She was earning money with charms and cures and curses, and although Mr Harewood had referred to her as a 'folk healer', she was clearly more than that.

Put simply, she was a witch.

Ned stared at her in amazement. So *this* was what a witch looked like! He should have known it; there was something about her dim, damp, untidy kitchen that unnerved him.

'The boy and I – we ain't alone in this,' Alfred was saying. 'We're on a committee, see, as is charged with ridding London of all its bogles—'

'A what?' Mother May cut him off, looking perplexed. 'What's a committee?'

'A kind o' guild,' Alfred explained. 'Like a boglers' guild.'

'Oh, aye.' The old woman nodded.

'And this committee ... well, 'tis a government committee, with government money behind it.' Alfred paused as he allowed this to sink in, then took a deep breath and added, 'If you tell us which herbs is on yer brother's spear, Mrs Blewett, we'll pay you a fair price for the receipt.'

Mother May narrowed her eyes. 'How much?' she croaked.

'Five pounds. In yer hand.' Before the old woman could respond, Alfred continued, ''T'ain't no use asking for ten, on account of our chairman. He's the feller with the final say, and he said five. I cannot bargain with you.'

'Dunna wittle, lad. Ah'll take five pound.' Mother May held out her hand as Alfred produced several gold coins from one of his pockets. But to Ned's surprise, he didn't immediately pass the coins to her.

'Shall I put these in yer chamber pot, Mrs Blewett?'

'Nay!' Mother May spoke sharply. 'Ah dun keep t' money in that no more!'

'Then I'll lay 'em down here.' Alfred placed the coins on a low footstool situated between them. 'And when you've told us what's in yer potion, you may take 'em as you like.'

'Monkshood,' said Mother May. 'That's for deathwork. Also rue and crampweed, which drives away devils. Hag's taper for protection, peppercorn for attack magic, and henbane mixed with black nightshade for poisoning.'

The ingredients came tumbling out as if she couldn't keep them to herself any longer. Ned tried to commit them to memory. *Monks ruing their cramps*, he thought. *Hags and hens, a pinch of peppercorn* . . .

Not for the first time, he wished that he could write.

'Use all of 'em in equal measure,' the old woman went on, 'mixed to a paste with holy water, if you have it. Then add a dob o' goose fat to make it stick.'

'Rue, peppercorn, monkshood, henbane, hag's taper, crampweed, nightshade, holy water and goose fat,' Alfred recited. Then he stood up. 'Thank'ee, ma'am.'

'Tha'll not be staying a little longer?' Mother May protested, as Ned joined Alfred. 'Ah can put the kettle on for tea . . .'

'We've a train to catch.' The bogler reached for his hat, which he'd left hanging from a pot-hook. 'By the by, have you any blackthorn bushes hereabouts?'

'Any blackthorn?' the old woman echoed. 'Why, every blessed hedge in this shire is a blackthorn hedge! There's one down the road.'

'Then I'll take a little, if there ain't no objection.' By this time Alfred had donned his hat, and was edging towards the door. 'Thanks again, Mrs Blewett,' he said gruffly. 'I'll have the committee send you a letter. Mebbe you can find someone as'll read it to you.'

'Thanks for the cake, Mrs Blewett. *And* the cider,' Ned murmured. He felt bad about leaving so abruptly, when she seemed so anxious to have them stay. But with a three-hour train journey ahead of them, they couldn't really linger.

'Art tha bogle-bait, lad?' she suddenly asked him, as she struggled to rise from her chair. On receiving a cautious nod, she turned to Alfred – who was already opening the door. 'There's more'n one way to bait a boggart,' she announced. 'Dost tha know that? They can be raised with herbs, like any spirit.'

Alfred paused to look at her, his dark eyes wary under his hat-brim.

'Elfwort'll do it. Horesheal. Dogsbane,' she continued slyly. 'Tell yer master ah can give thee another recipe for another five pound.'

Shocked by this unexpected news, Ned glanced at Alfred. But the bogler was still regarding Mother May. At last he said, 'Why would yer brother take me on, if all he needed were a potion?'

'A bogle summoned is a bogle primed to fight,' the old woman retorted. 'Lure it with a tender bit o' bait, and it willna be ready for thee.'

She was right. Ned could see that. But Alfred looked unimpressed.

'I'll ask the chairman,' he growled. 'Good day to you, Mrs Blewett.'

Then he opened the door, tipped his hat, and departed – with his hand clenched firmly around Ned's arm. They were well away from the cottage before Ned was finally released, in front of a spiky hedge so overgrown it was more like a copse. 'This here is blackthorn,' said Alfred. 'I'm sure of it.'

'Are we going to make another spear?' asked Ned.

'Aye.' Though it was still drizzling, Alfred took his tobacco knife from his pocket and began to saw at one leafless, thorny branch. Ned stood in the mud, watching, as the silence dragged on.

Finally he said, 'Will you tell Mr Harewood about the summoning herbs?'

'Aye.' It was barely more than a grunt.

'If they work, you'll not need a 'prentice no more.'

'*If* they work,' Alfred replied. There was so much disdain in his voice that Ned was puzzled.

'Don't you think she told the truth, Mr Bunce?'

Alfred shrugged. His face was already damp and red from the effort of hacking away at a thick branch with a small knife. 'She ain't called a cunning woman for nowt,' he spat. 'She wants more chink – that's why she spoke at all.'

'I thought she were trying to make us stay a little longer.' When Alfred didn't comment, Ned observed hesitantly, 'She were happy to see *you*, right enough.'

'All she cares about is money.' Alfred passed his knife to Ned, then began to tug and wrench at the half-cut bough with both hands. 'When I were a lad, I heard her say as how 'twould be cheaper to use stray boys, and let the bogles eat 'em, than to keep feeding a 'prentice.'

Ned's jaw dropped. He had to swallow before stammering, 'Oh, b-but . . . she weren't serious, Mr Bunce? She didn't *mean* it?'

'Who knows what she meant? All I know is, she cares for nowt but that hoard o' coins in her pisspot.' With a mighty yank, Alfred finally managed to detach his chosen bough from the rest of the blackthorn bush. 'She married a man for his house, gave him no children on account o' the expense, and wouldn't stump up for a train ticket to her own brother's funeral,' he finished. 'If she's lonely now, she's got none to blame but herself.'

Having delivered this verdict, he pocketed his knife, adjusted his hat, and headed back towards the railway station, using his new staff as a walking stick.

16

AN EVENING PERFORMANCE

It was early evening before Alfred and Ned finally arrived at Miss Eames's house, on their way home from St Pancras Station. Alfred had told Ned that he wanted to acquaint Miss Eames with his latest discovery, so that she could write to Mr Harewood.

He didn't expect to find Mr Harewood already on the premises.

'Why, what a stroke of luck!' the engineer exclaimed, jumping to his feet as Alfred and Ned crossed the threshold of Miss Eames's front parlour. 'We were just this moment wishing that you were with us, Mr Bunce, and here you are!'

Startled, Alfred gazed around the room – which

Ned had always admired. Like Mother May's kitchen, it was very cluttered, but the clutter was beautiful. There were gilded chairs, framed pictures, glazed bookshelves, embroidered firescreens, and crystal vases stuffed with hothouse flowers. An inlaid work-box sat on a carved writing desk. A glossy piano was draped with a fringed damask cloth. The walls were papered, the floor was carpeted, and a low table was laid for tea.

Surrounding this table were half-a-dozen familiar faces. Miss Eames was wielding the teapot, richly clad in a mauve gown with a low neck. Beside her sat her elderly aunt, Mrs Heppinstall, who owned the house and most of its contents. She wore her usual black silk dress, but to Ned's eyes – fresh from a murky witch's dwelling in Derbyshire – she looked very clean and cheerful with her neat grey ringlets and starched white cap.

Mr Gilfoyle was perched on the couch opposite Mrs Heppinstall. He was all decked out in a white tie and black tailcoat. Mr Harewood, in contrast, was dressed for a day's work, and didn't look entirely respectable – perhaps because of the bruises on his face. Jem and Birdie were sitting on opposite sides of a plum cake, which was already half eaten. Birdie was as pretty as a china doll in an outfit that Ned recognised; it was made of embroidered pearl-grey satin. But Ned *didn't* recognise the sailor-suit that Jem was wearing.

'T'ain't mine,' Jem said sharply, when he saw Ned's raised eyebrows. 'Miss Eames borrowed it from a neighbour.'

'He couldn't have come to the theatre in his own clothes,' Miss Eames quickly explained to Alfred. 'Won't you sit down, Mr Bunce? Ned?'

'We're going to see *Tom Thumb*,' Birdie announced. She had already jumped up, and was guiding Alfred towards a chair. 'Mr Gilfoyle is taking us. Ain't you, Mr Gilfoyle?'

'I thought it only proper,' Mr Gilfoyle agreed, colouring. 'No lady should have to attend the theatre or ballet unaccompanied . . .'

'I want Jem and Birdie to see the show as audience members, before they actually perform,' Miss Eames continued. She sounded embarrassed, and as she went on, Ned realised why. 'Of course you're welcome to accompany us, Mr Bunce, if you could somehow organise a change of clothes . . . and perhaps a wash . . .'

'Nay.' Alfred was wet through, and resisted Birdie's efforts to make him sit in an upholstered armchair. Instead he dropped onto the piano stool, still clutching his blackthorn staff. 'I'll wait till Birdie's up on stage. *That's* when I'll go.'

'And what about you, Ned?' Miss Eames smiled, but Ned wasn't fooled. He could sense from her creased brow and preoccupied gaze that she was wondering where, at this late hour, she could possibly acquire a decent set of clothes for him.

'I'll wait till Birdie's singing,' he mumbled. 'I'll go when Mr Bunce goes.'

'And I'll go with you,' Mr Harewood broke in. He had seated himself again, and was rifling through his coat pockets. 'I'm afraid I'm not dressed for the theatre, at present. In fact I'm not even here at Miss Eames's invitation.' He dragged out a handful of papers and said to Alfred, 'I merely called to show her these. And to find out whether she'd heard from you, of course . . .'

'They're telegrams,' Birdie piped up. 'From all over town.'

Miss Eames shot Birdie a reproving glance, but Mr Harewood proceeded as if he hadn't noticed the interruption. 'I was just telling our friends, Mr Bunce, that the memorandum I circulated among various government departments has had a remarkable response. I've heard from the Customs Commissioners, the London Docks, St Bartholemew's hospital . . . even from some of the railway companies. Word must have got out, I suppose. There seems to be an enormous demand for your services.' Suddenly he leaned forward, his elbows on his knees. 'Which prompts me to ask: did you have any luck in Derbyshire?'

As Alfred began to describe his trip to Long Eaton, Ned reached for a jam tart. He was very hungry, having eaten nothing since Mother May's oatcake. Mrs Heppinstall was the only person who noticed what he was up to.

She poured him a cup of tea while everyone else was listening intently to Alfred.

'. . . henbane, crampweed, and black nightshade,' he was saying. 'She greased the head with it. I brung a piece o' the wood back with me, in case the blackthorn thereabouts is different from London's. I thought as how we could use it to craft a new spear.' And he raised his staff, so that his audience could examine it.

There was a brief silence. At last Mr Gilfoyle observed, 'Mrs Blewett's concoction doesn't sound very difficult to make. I'm sure I could brew it myself, *without* the assistance of a trained apothecary.'

'We'd need help with the spearhead, though,'

Mr Harewood pointed out. He sounded thoughtful. 'I know several good stonemasons, and could apply to one of them for help. But where are we to find consecrated stone?'

'Oh, I'm sure I could do *that* for you,' Mrs Heppinstall unexpectedly offered. Having passed Ned his tea, she set down the teapot and looked around the table with a placid smile.

Miss Eames said quickly, 'My aunt knows a great many clergymen.'

'Why, then we have our plan!' Mr Harewood exclaimed. 'If you can supply the blessing, Mrs Heppinstall, I'll arrange to have the stone shaped to a point, and Razzy can provide the final touches.' He beamed at Alfred. 'You may be testing your new spear by the end of the week, Mr Bunce!'

'Oh dear,' said Miss Eames. 'Won't that be dreadfully dangerous for Ned?'

Everyone stared at Ned, whose cheeks were full of jam tart. He flushed.

'It'll be less dangerous with two spears than one,' Jem remarked, just as Alfred cleared his throat.

'There's summat else I should tell you,' the bogler said. Then he went on to describe Mother May's offer of a summoning recipe. 'She'll need to be paid, and I ain't sure we'll be getting our money's worth. But I thought as how, if the new spear works, we should mebbe go back and buy the other charm. The one as lures bogles.'

'My word, yes!' said Mr Harewood. Meanwhile Jem and Birdie were exchanging wide-eyed looks. When they turned to Ned he shrugged, embarrassed by all the attention.

'A summoned bogle is more dangerous, on account of it's primed to fight,' he muttered. 'That's what the old witch told us. Bait is better, she said.'

'But not if the bait is a child!' cried Miss Eames. 'I've always maintained that there must be an alternative to using children, and here it is! Though of course we must be sure that the herbs actually work.' Suddenly she swung around and appealed to the engineer. 'Would it not be a marvellous thing, Mr Harewood, if Ned could be replaced by a potion?'

'Er . . . well . . . yes . . .'

'Mr Harewood and I were just discussing Ned,' Miss Eames continued, addressing Alfred. 'We agreed that he's a very clever boy, and wasted as a bogler's apprentice.' She then turned to Ned. 'I'm sure you'd prefer to be doing something else with your life. Wouldn't you, dear?'

Ned swallowed. It was true; he *didn't* like bogling. But he had a duty to Alfred.

'I'm a bogler's boy,' he answered at last. 'Mr Bunce needs me.'

'Not for much longer,' Miss Eames reminded him. Her tone was brisk. 'Not if he can replace you with a herbal solution.'

'Ain't no herb can replace a good 'prentice!' Alfred snapped. And seeing the bogler leap to his defence, Ned felt even more indebted to him.

'Mr Bunce needs me,' Ned repeated. 'No bogler can do his job without a 'prentice.'

He wanted to say more, but didn't get the chance. Suddenly there was a knock on the parlour door and, as everyone glanced around, a maid appeared on the threshold. She had frizzy red hair, and wore a white apron over her black dress.

'Begging yer pardon, Miss, but yer carriage is here,' she announced.

'Oh, dear. Is it that late? Thank you, Mary.' Miss Eames stood up, prompting everyone else to do the same. 'We must go now, Mr Bunce, but we'll certainly discuss this at a later date,' she went on. Before Alfred could reply, she said to Birdie, 'Find your mantle, there's a good girl. Have you seen my gloves, Aunt?'

'On the piano, dear . . .'

During the bustle that ensued, Ned and Jem managed to polish off five more jam tarts between them. Mr Gilfoyle offered Alfred a ride to Drury Lane. Mrs Heppinstall wished the theatre party a very pleasant evening, and Alfred said to Mr Harewood, 'Will you be coming with us?'

'I doubt I'd fit. It will be rather cramped in that vehicle with six passengers, let alone seven.' When a confused chorus of voices assured Mr Harewood that room could certainly be found – that children could sit on knees – that a spacious hackney coach had been ordered, rather than a hansom cab – he hastily added, 'I'm heading east, in any case. Please don't concern yourselves.'

'If you ain't coming with us, sir, may I ask how you fared with the police?' Alfred inquired. 'Only I bin a-thinking on it, and wondering what they might have done about finding the feller as struck you.'

'Oh.' As every eye turned towards him, Mr Harewood smiled crookedly. 'To tell the truth, I've not had much satisfaction on that front,' he admitted. 'There must be so many footpads around Newgate that my black eye simply doesn't measure up to all the cracked skulls and cut throats that infest the neighbourhood. I certainly haven't heard from the police. They seemed quite unimpressed when I spoke to them, as I believe I may have mentioned yesterday . . .'

Alfred frowned. 'You went to Smithfield station house, did you not?'

'I did indeed. On your recommendation, Mr Bunce.'

'You should have talked to Constable Pike,' said Birdie.

'Oh, yes.' As Jem and Ned began to nod in agreement, Mr Gilfoyle declared, 'Constable Pike is the man you want. *He* would have helped.'

'Who is Constable Pike?' asked Mr Harewood.

Alfred explained that Constable Pike was a market constable at Smithfield, who had helped to arrest Sarah Pickles. 'He knows all about Salty Jack Gammon,' Alfred explained. '*And* he's seen me bogling.'

'Then the next time I'm assaulted, I shall certainly appeal to Constable Pike,' Mr Harewood remarked in a bantering tone. 'Meanwhile I must take my leave, or you'll be late for the theatre. Good evening, Miss Eames. Mrs Heppinstall. Many thanks for the tea. Have fun, old boy.' He flipped Mr Gilfoyle a mocking salute, bowed to the ladies, and said to Alfred, 'Let me take your blackthorn staff, Mr Bunce. I want to see what I can do with it. And I'll look you up tomorrow, shall I? For I've a pocketful of bogles here, and you must decide which of them you should tackle first. Personally, I'd begin with Tothill Fields prison, since no one there can actually *run away* from an attacking bogle . . .'

Even as he spoke, he was donning his hat. Then he turned on his heel and plunged through the front door, which was standing open. By the time the others had emerged onto the street – fully equipped with hats, gloves and umbrellas – he had disappeared into a thick fog.

'I just hope he don't get run down,' Alfred muttered. 'He's a fearless sort o' cove, ain't he?'

'Which is why he ends up with so many black eyes,' said Mr Gilfoyle, before rushing forward to help Miss Eames into the waiting carriage.

17

BEHIND BARS

The entrance to Tothill Fields prison was a large granite gateway in a massive wall of beige brick. Its double doors were made of iron, set under a raised portcullis. Its door-knockers were as big as dinner plates.

As Alfred lifted one of them, and let it drop again, Mr Harewood remarked, 'Did you see the streets we passed on our way here? Pool Place. Pond Court. I've heard that this prison was built on a swamp, and those names seem to confirm it.'

Alfred didn't comment. He was too busy watching a little hatch in the right-hand door, which suddenly snapped open.

'State yer business,' a deep voice growled.

'My name is Mark Harewood.' Consulting the telegram that he was clutching, the engineer added, 'This is Alfred Bunce and Ned Roach. We are here at the request of Mrs Spraggs, the Principal Matron.'

'One moment, please, sir.'

The hatch closed again. Ned heard a murmur of voices, and the squeal of bolts being drawn. Suddenly the door opened, revealing a uniformed warder with brass on his collar and keys at his belt. His waxed moustache was so large that it stuck out on either side of his head, eclipsing his ears.

'Kindly step inside,' he barked. 'Mrs Spraggs has bin sent for.' He then ushered his guests into a little office just inside the gateway, which contained a clutch of chairs, a desk, a small fireplace, and a row of cutlasses strung together on a chain. With four people squeezed into it, the room felt very cramped.

'May I inquire as to what yer business is with Mrs Spraggs, sir?' the warder asked Mr Harewood, who promptly gave him the matron's telegram. As soon as he'd read it, a great change came over the warder. He lost his stiff, military air and addressed Mr Harewood in the mildest of tones.

'Are you the bogler?' he asked.

Mr Harewood shook his head. 'Mr Bunce is.'

'Then I'm right glad to meet you, Mr Bunce. *Right* glad,' the warder said, vigorously shaking hands with Alfred. 'It's time we did summat about this here bogle, for we've lost too many girls already.'

Ned blinked. 'You have *girls* in this prison?' he exclaimed. The telegram had mentioned three missing children – but not that they were girls.

'We take women, girls, and boys under seventeen,' the warder replied. 'It's the females as work in the laundry, and that's where the bogle is.'

Alfred frowned. 'Are you sure there's a bogle?' he said.

'That's what I bin told, Mr Bunce.' The warder went on to explain that the missing girls had all been laundry workers, and had disappeared in the vicinity of a hot closet. 'The first time it happened, 'twas called an escape. The second time, we thought the first lass had set a bad example. But the third time . . .' He shook his head sadly. 'The third time, someone heard a scream.'

Ned shuddered. Though it wasn't an unusual story, it somehow seemed much worse in these grim surroundings – which filled Ned with a deep sense of unease. He hadn't wanted to come to the prison. But after carefully considering Mr Harewood's pile of telegrams, Alfred had ruled against the job at St Bartholomew's hospital because it was too close to Newgate. Crossness Pumping Station, on the other hand, would be too far out of London. And the job at the docks would be so close to the job at the Custom House that Alfred had felt they ought to be tackled together. As for Blackfriars Station, or the Thames Tunnel ... well, they both belonged to private companies, and Mr Harewood wanted the government jobs tackled first.

So Alfred had decided to start at Tothill Fields prison – despite Ned's misgivings. Because his own father had died in gaol, Ned had always feared imprisonment more than anything else. And he wasn't the only one. That very morning, Jem had quietly confessed to an abiding dread of the 'stone jug', before wishing Ned good luck with heartfelt sympathy – even though *Jem* was the one about to face his first matinee performance. ('I'll stay at the back o' the line till I've got me steps right,' he'd declared, when asked if he was ready.) Birdie wouldn't be on stage for a few nights yet, because she was still working on her new part. But she was far too busy to help Alfred.

So it was Ned, and Ned alone, who found himself standing next to Alfred inside Tothill Fields House of

Correction, hoping desperately that he wouldn't catch sight of someone he knew among the inmates.

'Ah! Here's Mrs Spraggs,' the warder suddenly observed. He stepped out of his office to greet a tall woman in a grey gown, whose brown hair was parted in the middle and drawn back severely under a starched white cap. She had a long face, a square jaw, and small, dark, chilly eyes that seemed to weigh up everything they focused on. A set of keys jingled at her waist.

As the warder introduced her to Alfred and Mr Harewood, Ned's gaze drifted towards the huge courtyard framed in the doorway behind her. This green space was divided by straight gravel paths and dotted with drooping ash trees, so that it looked more like a public garden than a prison exercise yard.

'And who's this?' Mrs Scraggs inquired, peering at Ned – who stiffened.

'That's Ned Roach,' Alfred told her. 'He works with me.'

Mrs Spraggs nodded slowly. 'You must mind what I tell you, Ned Roach,' she warned. 'Don't stray from the path I set, nor speak to none o' the prisoners. We follow the silent system, here, and if they talk, they'll be punished.'

Ned swallowed, speechless. Alfred growled, 'He's a good lad, ma'am, and may be trusted anywhere.'

'I'm sure that Ned may be trusted, Mr Bunce. But our prisoners, on the whole, cannot,' Mrs Spraggs replied. Her voice was as cold as her eyes. 'Happily, we'll be passing through no busy places to reach the laundry, which is well away from our dormitories and workrooms. If you'll follow me, gentlemen, I'll take you there.' Without further ado, she swung around and set off, heading in an easterly direction down the path that ringed the octagonal courtyard.

Alfred and Mr Harewood exchanged a doubtful glance, as the warder said to them, in a very low voice, 'She's a trifle abrupt in her manner, but she knows what she's about. By gad, she does! You're in safe hands, gentlemen.'

'I can see *that*,' Mr Harewood muttered, with a crooked smile. Alfred simply gave a grunt. Then they both followed the matron past a series of doors and windows, with Ned trailing along behind them.

He was acutely conscious of being watched. Nearly a dozen buildings ringed the courtyard, many of them multi-storeyed, and he sensed that the worst of the prison was concealed behind their bland, symmetrical facades. He felt as if hundreds of eyes were fixed on his scurrying figure – and was greatly relieved when they finally plunged into one of the more modest, single-storeyed structures.

'Can you tell me about the missing girls, Mrs Spraggs?' Alfred suddenly asked, his voice echoing off the stuccoed walls of a long passage lined with doors. Some of these doors stood open, revealing rooms stacked from floor to ceiling with box-shaped pigeonholes – each of which contained a bundle of clothes, a pair of shoes, and a bonnet. If the clothes had been identical, Ned would have assumed that they were uniforms. But since they were all very different, he realised that they must be the inmates' own garments, stored until their owners were released.

He shivered as Mrs Spraggs answered Alfred's question.

'Clara Birks was eight years old. She was serving a three-month sentence for stealing a pair of shoes. Mercy Radbourne was a year older, sentenced to twelve months for picking pockets. Georgina Dugby was twelve, but stunted. She was in for six months – theft of four silk handkerchiefs.' Mrs Spraggs came to an iron gate and unlocked it, talking all the while. 'Laundry work is popular, so it's mostly women and older girls in the laundry. But they need young 'uns to fetch and fold – and to crawl into the hot closet.' After locking the gate behind Ned, she turned to Alfred and said, 'The boggart's in the closet flue, Mr Bunce. There's no doubt o' that. Each girl went in there to pick up fallen garments, and not one of 'em was ever seen again.'

Ned didn't ask what a 'hot closet' was – he didn't want to sound stupid. He just followed the others silently into a large, triangular yard bounded by the prison wall on two sides. Tucked into a corner of this yard was a squat building with two wings. One contained the washroom, Mrs Spraggs said; the other contained the laundry.

This hardly needed explaining, since the yard was full of sheets flapping on laundry lines. A girl in a blue-and-white spotted dress was hanging out rows of flannel drawers.

'Maud!' Mrs Spraggs addressed the woman sharply. 'Come here!'

Maud spun around and curtseyed. She was about sixteen years old, with a pink nose, flaxen hair and almost invisible eyelashes. As she scuttled over to Mrs Spraggs, the matron said, 'Maud is a witness. She saw Clara go into the hot closet, and heard her scream. Is there anything you wish to ask her, Mr Bunce?'

'Nay,' mumbled Alfred, who couldn't even meet the girl's eye. Mr Harewood looked just as uncomfortable; his face was red, and he kept adjusting his collar.

'Very well.' Mrs Spraggs dismissed Maud, then ushered her guests into the laundry. It was large and steam-filled, with wooden troughs ranged around the walls. A giant mangle in the centre of the room was being turned by a woman in a spotted uniform and white calico cap. Other women, identically dressed, were standing on wooden grates, sloshing clothes about in troughs or scrubbing flannels against ridged boards. Scattered around their feet were baskets full of wet towels and dry blankets.

Ned noticed a large boiler, a stove for sad-irons, and a curious cupboard made up of eight long, thin doors, each bearing a steel handle.

'That is our hot closet,' Mrs Spraggs announced, striding towards the cupboard without acknowledging the other women in the room. Ned tried to do the same, but it was hard. The women kept stealing glances at him – and at Alfred – and especially at Mr Harewood, who looked very large and handsome in that dingy, bedraggled place, despite his black eye.

Ned thought he heard a smothered giggle.

'*Who was that?*' Mrs Spraggs whirled around, enveloping the room in a ferocious stare. '*I did not give anyone permission to speak!*'

A deathly silence fell. The washerwomen scrubbed away furiously, their eyes on their suds. *Creak-creak-creak* went the mangle.

After a brief, tense pause, Mrs Spraggs turned back to Alfred. 'This is the hot closet,' she said with eerie calm, before seizing a handle and dragging one of the skinny doors out of the wall. As she did so, a cloud of steam engulfed her. But when the steam cleared, Ned saw that the door was connected to a kind of upright frame, or ladder, of which there were eight all told, lined up in a small room like books on a shelf. Each could be pulled out separately, and each was laden with damp petticoats.

'You see how the closet is heated,' Miss Spraggs continued, pointing to a hot-water pipe that coiled around the walls of the little room. 'The steam escapes through a flue in the ceiling.' Her gaze fell on Ned, who was peering into the closet. 'I wouldn't get any closer, if I were you,' she added drily.

At the same instant, Alfred pulled Ned back out of harm's way – though not before Ned had caught a glimpse of the gaping void above the row of drying frames.

'If a garment falls to the floor, someone must be sent in to retrieve it,' said Mrs Spraggs. 'We thought Georgina must have climbed the horse and escaped up the flue, under cover of all that steam—'

'But she didn't,' Alfred finished. He was squinting into the closet. 'Aye,' he muttered, 'this feels like a bogle's lair to me.'

It didn't feel like one to Ned. He hadn't been overwhelmed by any creeping sense of dread and despair. Then it occurred to him that he'd been so full of dread and despair since arriving at the prison that he wasn't well placed to judge.

'This ain't going to be easy, Mr Bunce,' he murmured.

'I know it,' Alfred replied, his gaze drifting down to the sopping wet floor.

Then, without warning, a pair of newcomers appeared on the laundry threshold. One of them was a warder, jingling a set of keys.

The other was Erasmus Gilfoyle.

18

TESTING

'Pardon me, Mrs Spraggs, but this gentleman was inquiring after the other gentlemen. So Mr Crimp told me to bring him in here,' the warder announced.

Beside him, Mr Gilfoyle looked like a startled rabbit. Sweaty and breathless, the naturalist kept darting nervous glances at all the silent women labouring away at their troughs. 'I'm – I'm so sorry to intrude,' he stammered, 'but I thought you might need this, Mr Bunce . . .' And he held up a canvas-wrapped, stick-shaped bundle.

Before Alfred could answer, Mr Harewood exclaimed, 'Is that the new spear, Razzy?'

'It is. Yes.'

'Bravo!' Catching the matron's eye, Mr Harewood added, 'Oh – er, this is Mrs Spraggs, the Principal Matron. Mrs Spraggs, this is Mr Gilfoyle.'

Ned heard a muffled snigger as the matron nodded briskly at Mr Gilfoyle, who bowed back. But if Mrs Spraggs was aware of the snigger, she didn't show it. Instead she turned to Alfred and said, 'Do you want this room cleared, Mr Bunce?'

Alfred nodded.

'I thought so.' Suddenly the matron raised her formidable voice. 'All inmates form a line! On the double! Leave everything where it is!'

Though none of them uttered a word of protest, the prisoners resented having to leave. This much was obvious from their disgruntled expressions. As Ned watched them line up, their arms still red and soapy, he could almost hear what they were thinking. *Bloomin' old haybag. Hatchet-faced cow.*

Even after they'd marched out, escorted by Mrs Spraggs, the steamy air felt thick with suppressed anger.

'Thank heavens,' Mr Harewood remarked, once the last, shuffling figure had gone. 'Now we may speak freely.'

'What a dreadful place!' Mr Gilfoyle was pale with distress. 'Such very young women! I had no idea—'

'Is that spear blessed and greased, Mr Gilfoyle?' Alfred interrupted curtly. 'Can we use it now?'

'I believe so,' the naturalist replied. He went on to explain that, at Mr Harewood's request, he had collected the finished spear from a Board of Works stonemason that very morning. He had then delivered the spear to Miss Eames's house, where Mrs Heppinstall had been entertaining a helpful clergyman. Finally, once the spearhead had been consecrated, Mr Gilfoyle had carried it to his own residence. 'I mixed a herbal paste last night, after the show,' he revealed, 'so it took me no time at all to add the finishing touches.'

'Well done, old boy.' Mr Harewood was rubbing his hands together. 'We'll be able to test it here – eh, Mr Bunce?'

'Aye,' Alfred rumbled. He took the spear and examined it, while the others clustered around him. Unwrapped, it looked rather disappointing. Its shaft was roughly sanded, its head crudely chiselled. But it was sharp and well-balanced, and covered in a smelly coat of brown grease that had a very toxic appearance.

'Where's the bogle?' Mr Gilfoyle murmured. 'Does anyone know?'

'In there.' Mr Harewood jerked his chin at the hot closet.

'Dear me,' said Mr Gilfoyle. 'How are you going to work inside that?'

'We ain't.' Alfred spoke flatly. 'We cannot use salt in here – it's too wet. And I'll not put Ned in that closet. 'Twould be like throwing him into the bogle's mouth.'

Everyone considered the cluttered space beneath the flue. Mr Harewood began to nod thoughtfully.

'If we was to take one o' them blankets,' Ned finally suggested, thinking aloud, 'and lay it flat on the floor out here, and trace a circle on it—'

'The damp's in the air, lad. That salt won't stay dry for more'n a minute.' Alfred raised his eyes to the beams overhead. 'I bin thinking about the roof.'

'The *roof*?' Mr Gilfoyle echoed, aghast.

'The pitch is low enough. And there's chimneys to hide behind.' Turning to Ned, Alfred said gravely, ''Tis a dry day, with no wind to speak of. If there's steam, it won't linger. I'm persuaded it'll be safer on the roof than it is in here.'

Ned swallowed. He glanced at the ceiling.

'If you baulk, lad, I'll not hold it against you,' Alfred went on. 'But I'll tie us to the roof with ropes. And if the bogle takes its time, we shan't wait about. Not this late in the day—'

'All right.' Ned cut him off. 'I'll do it.'

'Are you sure?' asked Mr Harewood, frowning. 'It seems rather unwise ...'

'I'll do it,' Ned repeated stubbornly. He had a duty to Alfred, who deserved – and required – a brave apprentice. Besides, he trusted Alfred. If Alfred said that the roof was safe, then it probably was.

Only after he'd scrambled up onto its slippery slates, and felt an arctic chill on his cheek, did Ned begin to wonder.

'You don't think it'll snow, Mr Bunce?' he quavered, squinting up at the sky.

'If it does, we'll stop,' the bogler answered grimly. 'Hush, now, and stand still. For I must tie this rope around yer middle ...'

The roof had a very low pitch, as Alfred had promised. It was also quite close to the ground, and easily reached by the ladder that Mrs Spraggs had provided. The chimneystack was large enough for Alfred to crouch behind, and sturdy enough to tie a rope to. Thanks to the encroaching walls of the prison, there was only one stretch of gutter to fall from. And, as a final touch, Alfred had placed a row of laundry baskets beneath this gutter, to ensure a soft landing if something went wrong.

But with the grey walls looming over him, and the dark sky pressing down on him, Ned felt a bit queasy. *Mebbe it's the bogle*, he thought, as he edged his way along the roof towards Alfred's ring of salt. The ring had been laid near the washroom chimneystack, instead of the one built above the laundry – and Alfred had also tied Ned's rope to a washroom chimneypot.

Not that Ned was expected to jump off the roof. If something went wrong, Alfred wanted Ned to stand and fight.

'I'll be testing this 'un,' Alfred had explained, holding up the new spear. 'If it don't work, you've nowt to fear, lad – for you'll have Mother May's blasting rod. You must hold fast and defend yerself, as you did in Water Lane. I know you can do it. I *seen* you do it. But I'm hoping you'll not have to.'

Ned wasn't so sure. He didn't entirely trust the new spear. And he didn't know how well he would use the old one, either, with his chilled fingers and unsteady foothold. As he positioned himself inside the magic circle (which was keeping its shape quite nicely, despite the slant of the roof), he couldn't help wishing that he was Jem. For someone as spry as Jem, the roof would have presented no problems.

All Ned could do was take off his shoes and hope.

Turning his back on Alfred, he clasped Mother May's spear to his chest and braced himself. Reflected in his mirror was a bank of chimneys. Smoke and steam mingled above the chimneypots, behind which Alfred was hunkered down, spear in hand. Beyond the chimneypots lay the prison wall, which drew Ned's eye northwards, towards a distant wedge of exercise yard. Trapped by a high wire fence, dozens of hunched figures were circling the flagstones, round and round, with their heads down and their feet dragging. They looked bone-tired, freezing cold, and utterly miserable. Yet Ned would gladly have changed places with any one of them as he cleared his throat, took a deep breath, and launched into a nursery rhyme.

Simple Simon met a pieman
Going to the fair.
Says Simple Simon to the pieman,
'Let me taste yer ware.'

His voice didn't seem very loud; it was whisked away by a fitful breeze. Somewhere beneath him, inside the laundry, Mr Harewood and Mr Gilfoyle were anxiously waiting. Mrs Spraggs had retreated back into the depths of the prison. The warder had returned to his post. Apart from the prisoners trudging around the exercise yard, there wasn't another soul to be seen.

Ned felt very lonely – and very exposed. His coat wasn't thick enough to keep him warm. As he chanted away, his breath emerged in filmy white clouds.

Says the pieman to Simple Simon,
'Show me first yer penny.'
Says Simple Simon to the pieman,
'Indeed I have not any.'

All at once Ned spotted a gush of steam issuing from a flue behind him – and knew instantly that the bogle was on its way. Sure enough, instead of dissipating, the steam grew thicker. It seemed to bubble out of the flue and roll across the slates like foam. And it was followed by something that briefly plugged the mouth of the flue; something big but not black.

To Ned's amazement, *this* bogle was the colour of salt, bleached and stringy and hairless. Though it seemed to have no eyes at all, its mouth was as big as a manhole cover – and its long snout twitched like a pig's as it tested the air. When Ned saw this, he felt grateful that the wind was blowing from the east instead of the west. Otherwise the bogle might have smelled Alfred.

Simple Simon went a-fishing
For to catch a whale.
All the water he had got
Were in his mother's pail.

Ned watched the bogle haul itself out of the flue behind a veil of steam. One arm popped out, then another, then another. They lashed about, as boneless as whips, before attaching themselves to the roof with suckers. Then the bogle slithered down the chimney and began to slide across the slates towards Ned – who suddenly spied Alfred in his mirror. The bogler was edging into view, a dark shape at the very edge of the frame. He braced himself, aimed his spear, and flashed a warning glance at Ned.

Simple Simon went to look
If plums grew on a thistle—

'NOW!' yelled Alfred.

Ned hurled himself towards the washroom chimney. There was a sharp hiss, like steam from a kettle, but no 'pop'. No 'bang'. Ned almost lost his footing, but managed to grab a chimneypot just as Alfred cried, 'Ned!'

Looking around, Ned saw that the bogle was still alive. It had rounded on Alfred, its writhing arms raised. Alfred's spear sprouted grotesquely from its head, which was collapsing like a blister. Grey steam spurted from its wound.

Ned didn't stop to think. He moved instead, lunging forward. But the rope tied around his waist wasn't long enough; it brought him up short. He lost his balance, threw his own spear, and flailed about frantically as he stumbled towards the edge of the roof. Luckily, his spear found its mark.

The bogle imploded.

Then Ned tripped and fell. He didn't hit the ground, though; his rope wasn't long enough. He ended up swinging off the gutter like a fish on a hook, his bare toes brushing the fluffy pile of sheets packed into the basket below him. Alerted by his cries, Mr Harewood and Mr Gilfoyle burst out of the laundry. Within seconds the engineer was supporting Ned, as the naturalist frantically picked at a knot in the rope.

'Mr Bunce!' Ned croaked. 'Is Mr Bunce all right?'

'*Mr Bunce!*' shouted Mr Harewood. '*Are you hurt?*'

'Nay.' Alfred's head suddenly appeared above them. 'How's the lad?'

'He's fine,' said Mr Harewood. 'And the bogle?'

'Dead. No thanks to this 'un.' Alfred waved the new spear at Mr Gilfoyle, before adding crossly, 'Summat went wrong. There's a fault here somewhere. The first wound weren't mortal.'

'Oh, dear,' said Mr Gilfoyle.

'I ain't testing no more spears on live bogles,' Alfred growled. 'Either we find another way to test 'em, or we don't test 'em at all. For this here job is too perilous to take chances with. And Ned's future ain't going to lie in a bogle's belly.'

Then he disappeared again, muttering to himself. Moments later, Ned heard him stamping across the roof, his anger clearly expressed in every footfall.

19

'MURDER!'

'Mebbe the fault were in the blessing,' Ned mused. 'Mebbe the stone should have bin cut *after* it were blessed, instead o' the other way round.'

Alfred grunted, then spat on the floor.

'Either that, or we shouldn't have used plain stone,' Ned went on. 'Mother May hewed her spearhead from a church cross. Mebbe we should have done the same.'

'Who knows?' Alfred sounded impatient. He had dragged on his nightshirt and wrapped himself in his old green coat. Now he sat on his rickety bed, puffing away at his last pipe of the day, while Ned threw more coals onto the fire. 'T'ain't our job to worry about potions and blessings,' the bogler added gruffly. 'Our

job is killing bogles. You leave the science of it to
Mr Gilfoyle.'

'If it *is* science,' Ned muttered. He was beginning
to think about bogles in a whole new way. What
were they? Where did they come from? Were they
animals? Demons? Something in between? He knew
that Alfred, who was only interested in killing them,
didn't much care. Alfred's customers were even less
concerned. To them, a bogle was something to be
exterminated, as quickly as possible.

It was Miss Eames who'd first taken a scientific
interest in bogles – and Ned was starting to see why.
He was starting to realise that people like Miss Eames,
and Mr Gilfoyle, and even Mr Harewood, were always
asking questions about things that didn't directly
relate to them. Was it because they were educated? Or
was it because they didn't have to worry about where
their next meal might be coming from?

Whatever the reason, they seemed fascinated by the
world – and by the way it worked. Ned had always
been fascinated by machines, and how *they* worked.
It hadn't occurred to him before that the world itself
might be a giant machine, with parts that all fitted
together like gears in a watch . . .

'He-e-elp! Murder!'

Ned straightened. As he looked around, he saw Alfred jump up.

'That's Jem,' the bogler rasped.

'*Murder! Help me!*'

The noise was coming from somewhere outside. Ned and Alfred both lunged for the window, which Ned shoved open with a *bang*.

'*He-e-e-elp!*'

Shutters were slamming. People were yelling. As he leaned out over the windowsill, Ned caught sight of candles flickering in at least a dozen windows overlooking the alley – which wasn't well lit. No gas-lamps had been erected in Orange Court. No lanterns were hung above doorways. But thanks to a full moon, a clear sky, and the golden glow of the candles, Ned was able to spot Jem.

'There!' Ned cried, pointing at a dark shape hanging off a downpipe. Jem had climbed the wall of a neighbouring house. He was two floors above ground, and still moving.

Below him a door swung open, casting a square of light onto the cobbles.

''Ere!' A girl appeared on the threshold. 'What's all the bloody fuss about?'

'He tried to kill me!' Jem wailed. 'He's got a knife!'

'Who does?' It was Alfred, speaking loudly and roughly. He jostled Ned aside, craning his neck to catch a glimpse of Jem. 'Who tried to kill you?'

'I – I dunno.' Jem turned his head gingerly to peer at the dark alley beneath him. 'He ain't there no more . . .'

'I'm coming down,' Alfred declared.

'No! Don't you come down! I'll come up!'

'But—'

'He may be hiding! He may come back!' Before Alfred could even begin to argue, Jem swarmed up the pipe until he reached what seemed to be a washing line. By following this line from shutter-hook to shutter-hook – hand over hand, feet swinging – he made it to the window just two floors beneath Alfred's garret. By this time Ned was almost falling out of the garret window in his struggle to see what was going on. As far as he could tell, Jem was quite right; Orange Court looked deserted. No one was skulking among the coster's carts, or sidling back into Drury Lane.

Two floors below, however, a pair of thin, white arms reached for Jem as a sickly neighbour begged him to crawl into her room. 'You'll fall to yer death!' she screeched, over the fretful whimpering of her youngest. 'You'll dash yer brains out!'

But for some reason Jem kept climbing. Perhaps he didn't trust the neighbour. Perhaps he didn't have any faith in the strength of her arms.

It was Alfred who finally pulled Jem inside, with a heave that sent them both sprawling. For a moment they lay on the floor, stunned. Then Ned sprang forward to help Alfred, while Jem staggered to his feet.

'What happened to yer coat?' was the first thing Alfred said, once he'd recovered.

Jem glanced down at himself. Even in the leaping yellow firelight he looked pale. His hair was ruffled, his knuckles were grazed, and there was a rip in the knee of his trousers.

'I – I lost it,' he admitted.

'You *lost* it?'

'T'weren't down to me, Mr Bunce.' Jem's voice cracked. But he cleared his throat, took a deep breath, and continued. 'That cove out there – he tried to nobble me. I only got away by slipping out o' me coat.' He glanced at the window. 'It might still be in the street,' he faltered. 'He might've left it where it fell . . .'

'Did you see him?' asked Ned. 'D'you know who done it?'

Jem wiped his eyes, which were bloodshot. His

grubby hands were shaking. 'It's dark as a chimney out there,' he said. 'But he were big. I could see *that*. And he didn't have no hair.'

Ned blinked as Alfred sucked air through his teeth.

'No hair?' the bogler repeated sharply.

'I seen his bonce gleaming like glass,' Jem insisted.

'Did he have a scar on his brow?' Ned demanded. He clearly recalled Mr Harewood's description of the footpad who had attacked him in the court off Newgate Street.

'I told you, I couldn't see much.' Jem turned to address Alfred. 'He followed me, Mr Bunce. I'm sure of it. I were coming home from the theatre, and when I turned into Orange Court, he grabbed me from behind.'

'Aye,' said Alfred, retrieving his pipe from the bed. 'I'm a-thinking he were one o' John Gammon's cronies. Same cove as struck Mr Harewood, I'll wager.'

'But how did they find us?' Ned couldn't understand it. 'We bin so careful! How did they track us here?'

'I'll tell you how,' said Jem. His tone was flat, his expression grim. 'They bin reading playbills. Like half o' London.'

'Playbills?' Alfred echoed.

'They was posted yesterday. New 'uns. With Birdie's name on 'em.' Glancing from face to face, Jem added hoarsely, 'That there bald cove must have bin watching the Theatre Royal. I expect he wanted to follow Birdie, in case she met up with me—'

'But he didn't have to,' Ned interrupted.

Jem gave a curt nod. He was still very pale. In the pause that followed, Alfred squatted down and reached under his bed.

'Playbills,' Ned muttered at last. 'I never thought o' that...'

Jem shrugged. 'Why should you? None of us can read. *I* only found out about them bills from Birdie.'

'Birdie?' Ned was struck by a sudden, horrible thought. 'Don't tell me you saw *Birdie* there tonight?'

Jem quickly assured Ned that Birdie had left the theatre much earlier that day, after rehearsing with some of the cast. She wouldn't be making her debut until Saturday, he said, because Saturday night pulled the biggest crowds. 'Mr Chatterton decided to wait a few days, so as word would get about,' Jem went on. 'He's bin posting bills and advertising in newspapers. '*Birdie the Bogler's Girl ... Child Prodigy Astounds Theatrical Profession ... London's Latest Marvel.* That kind o' thing. He thinks she'll boost the takings.'

'So no one followed Birdie home?' asked Ned.

'I doubt it.' Jem's attention suddenly shifted to Alfred, who was unwrapping Mother May's blasting rod. 'W-what are you doing, Mr Bunce?' he stammered. 'You don't think that feller'll be coming up *here*?'

'I ain't taking no chances,' Alfred replied coolly.

Ned and Jem exchanged a frightened look. Then Jem croaked, 'Mebbe we should leave.'

'And go where? To Miss Eames's house?' Ned frowned at him. 'We can't have no lurking nobbler follow us to Bloomsbury. Mrs Heppinstall would die o' fright!'

'We ain't going nowhere. Not while it's dark.' Alfred was heading for the door, his stool in one hand, his spear in the other. 'Shut that window, Ned, and bolt it. I don't expect no one'll come over the roof, but it's best to be careful.'

As Ned rushed to the window, Alfred stationed himself by the door. It was somehow obvious, from the way he settled down with his back to the wall and his spear across his knees, that the bogler intended to stay there all night.

'Are you taking the first shift, Mr Bunce?' asked Jem.

'Nay, lad, I'll be here 'til morning.' Before anyone could protest, Alfred continued, 'Did you leave tonight's pay in yer coat pocket, by the by?'

'No, sir.' Jem plunged a hand into his trousers and pulled out a modest collection of coins. 'I didn't lose me wages.'

'Good.' With his teeth clenched around the stem of his pipe, Alfred remarked, 'You can keep half o' that, if you think you earned it.'

'I earned it, right enough. I didn't put a foot wrong tonight, though I did mistime one exit.' Jem hesitated, then asked, 'How did you fare at the gaol?'

Ned shrugged, but didn't comment. It was Alfred who said, through a puff of smoke, 'Ned killed another bogle.'

'*Ned* did?'

'The new spear didn't work. Not like the old one,' Ned hurried to explain. He didn't want Jem thinking that he had somehow taken over Alfred's job. 'The bogle seemed uncommon, too. White as snow. Slightly stunted. And so much of it left behind, the warders talked o' shovelling it into a boiler.'

Jem's eyes widened as he turned from Ned to Alfred, who growled, 'Aye. Summat's wrong. There's strange things afoot. But we'll not fret on it tonight

– we've enough to worry us. You boys go to bed, now. I've bolted the door. If anyone tries to break it down, I'll gut him like a fish.'

There was an edge to Alfred's tone that made the boys flinch. Finally Jem asked, 'But what'll we do tomorrow, Mr Bunce? If that feller's still sneaking about . . .'

'Tomorrow we'll speak to Constable Pike,' said Alfred. 'He knows all the streets around Newgate, *and* those as live in 'em. I'm persuaded he'll have a notion of who that bald villain might be, and how we might lay our hands on him.' As the two boys absorbed this plan, Alfred concluded, 'Constable Pike will listen. He'll not turn us away with an empty promise.'

'But I'm due at the theatre for a matinee tomorrow,' Jem pointed out.

'Aye. And I'll take you there meself, once we've talked to Constable Pike.'

Jem seemed satisfied with this assurance, though Ned wasn't. To Ned, it seemed that Alfred had left a lot of questions unanswered. Constable Pike was stationed at Smithfield, just a stone's throw from John Gammon's shop. How were they going to smuggle Jem into the neighbourhood without putting him in danger? Would they hire a cab? And what if the bald man was waiting for them as they left their room the next morning? What if he was *just outside the door?*

Ned decided that he would have to be ready for anything: a midnight raid, a morning ambush – even a fire, if someone decided to burn the house down. So before going to bed, he quietly moved the water-bucket, tucked a kitchen knife under his palliasse, and made sure his boots were standing, loosely tied, where he could easily find them.

Despite these precautions, however, he took a long, long time to fall asleep.

20

POLICE BUSINESS

'You're in luck, Mr Bunce,' Constable Pike announced.

He was standing with his hands behind his back, straight and stocky and trimly dressed in a dark blue uniform. Behind him, flames danced in a modest fireplace under a portrait of the Queen.

'It so happens we've a gentleman in our custody who matches the description you've just given me,' he continued. 'Tobias Fitch is his name, and he was arrested early this morning on a charge of unlawfully uttering counterfeit coin.' The policeman's keen gaze shifted from Alfred to Ned to Jem, taking in every detail: the bags under Alfred's eyes, the knife-handle protruding from Ned's pocket, the torn flannel shirt that Jem wore instead of a coat. Constable Pike's own eyes were large and grey, and ringed by thick black lashes. With his curly hair, full cheeks and red lips he looked almost cherubic – though his rigid posture and toneless drawl undermined this impression. 'Fitch is an associate o' John Oswald Gammon, butcher, and is well known to us here at Smithfield station house,' he continued. 'We were about to send him off to the police court, with our regular delivery o' felons. But you caught him just in time, Mr Bunce. He's still here for your lad to identify.'

Ned grimaced. He didn't envy Jem. Looking Tobias Fitch in the eye wouldn't be easy.

'Mebbe we should fetch Mr Harewood,' Alfred murmured. '*He* saw the feller in broad daylight.'

'The more the merrier,' said Constable Pike. 'Our only witness to the counterfeit charge lives in White Hart Street, which is a deal too close to Gammon's shop for my liking.' Spotting another policeman across the room, he suddenly stiffened. 'I must have a word with my sergeant. If you'll wait here, Mr Bunce, I'll be back directly. It won't take long.'

He strode off briskly, leaving the others marooned like driftwood on a mudflat. The station house was an unfriendly place, lined with hard benches and studded with barred windows. The policeman who stood behind a high desk at one end of the room never raised his eyes from the ledger that occupied him. Distant wails and moans issued from one dark doorway; another was protected by a locked gate. Everywhere he looked, Ned saw chains and keys and bolts and batons.

'We needn't have hired a cab to get us here after all,' Jem muttered at last. 'Not with Fitch banged up in a police cell.'

'You still don't know if Fitch is the one,' Ned pointed out.

But Jem snorted. 'He must be. How many big, bald men could be working for John Gammon?'

'Shh! Hold yer tongues!' Alfred snapped. By this time Constable Pike was on his way back, jingling a set of keys. But instead of stopping, he walked straight past Alfred.

'We'll go downstairs now,' the policeman said, 'and if Fitch don't prove to be your man, I'll send him off to Clerkenwell with the rest of 'em.' He led Alfred's party along a short passage lined with metal doors, as the sound of moaning grew louder. 'It's a stroke o' luck you're here, Mr Bunce,' he went on, 'for I've bin hard at work trying to break Fitch. Now that he's lagged, I thought he might open up a little on the subject o' Salty Jack. I promised him no end o' trouble, if he didn't. But he refused to cooperate.' Constable Pike paused at the end of the passage, where a stone staircase plunged into the bowels of the station house. 'Seems to me he's less scared o' the *gallows* than he is o' John Gammon – but then most people are, hereabouts. That's why I can't find one solid witness against the worst villain this side o' the Thames. But your boy's appearance might shake Fitch, especially if I threaten the fellow with two counts o' felonious assault. That's a hanging crime. He'll not be doing six months' hard labour for *that*.'

'T'aint Fitch as wants Jem dead,' growled Alfred.

'Exactly. It's Gammon. And I'll remind Fitch it's Gammon who should swing for it, not him.' Having made this promise, Constable Pike continued on his way, down two flights of narrow stairs and into a cellar almost as foul as the slaughterhouse beneath Newgate Market. After years spent scavenging along the banks of the Thames, Ned was familiar with foul stenches. But the air in the lock-up nearly choked him, smelling as it did of sweat and vomit and even worse things.

Jem began to cough as Alfred covered his nose.

'We've had ten drunkards come in overnight,' Constable Pike said cheerfully, without flinching, 'and won't be able to clean up till they leave. But Fitch is in his own cell.' Suddenly he raised his voice, pitching it high above the sound of moaning. *'Be quiet now, Mr Bates! You'll be out o' here in a minute!'*

The moaning stopped. It had been coming from behind one of the numbered doors that lined the dim, dank passage in front of them. Bustling down this passage, Constable Pike finally stopped at another door – iron-studded, double-bolted, and fitted with a small metal grate. He then turned to Jem, indicating the grate with a jerk of his chin.

For a few seconds Jem hesitated. But after Alfred had given him a prod, he shuffled forward and stood on tiptoe to peer into the cell behind the door.

Almost immediately, he ducked down again.

'Well?' said Constable Pike.

Jem hesitated. Ned could tell that he was loath to pass judgement. But Constable Pike wasn't about to let Jem express any doubts – not within earshot of Tobias Fitch.

'He's the one, is he? I thought as much.' The policeman raised his voice. 'You're in trouble, Fitch. D'you hear me? I've a boy here who was attacked on his way home last night, and he's identified you as the culprit.' There was no reply. Ned couldn't even hear the prisoner breathing.

So Constable Pike continued, 'You also punched a gentleman in Angel Court, on Tuesday – a respectable gentleman who'll have no qualms about testifying against you, and who'll cut a fine figure in the witness box.' The policeman turned to Alfred. 'What was the gentleman's name, Mr Bunce?'

Alfred gave a start. 'Er . . . ah . . . Mark Harewood,' he mumbled.

'D'you hear that, Fitch? You're facing two counts of felonious assault. Even one conviction'll send you to the gallows.'

Still Tobias Fitch didn't speak. It was another prisoner who suddenly erupted into a stream of abuse, somewhere down the passage.

'*Shut your mouth, O'Flaherty, or I'll shut it for you!*' barked Constable Pike, before once again directing his comments through the grate in front of him. 'We know you were hired, Fitch, and we know why. John Gammon don't like witnesses. Not living ones, at any rate. But Jack's a fool. If he'd let the boy alone, we wouldn't be here now. There'd be no cause for the lad to peach – he'd have too much to lose. What's he got to lose now, though? He's dead if he talks and he's dead if he don't. So he might as well talk.'

Ned saw the colour drain from Jem's face.

'I want you to think about it,' the policeman continued. 'I want you to think about what you owe John Gammon, who's happy to let you swing for his own misdeeds. It was Gammon who sent you after Jem Barbary. It was Gammon who set you to watch over that newsboy, with orders to nobble anyone who might pursue him. Why – for all *I* know it was Gammon who paid you with counterfeit coin!' Again Constable Pike paused, peering into Fitch's cell. But as the seconds ticked by, and no one answered, he caught Alfred's eye and gave a rueful shrug. 'You've ten minutes before I send you off to King's Cross Road, Fitch, with two more names on your charge sheet,' he finished. 'And if I do that, you're done for. You'll be hoisted in Newgate yard before the month's out. Think on that, for it's worth pondering.'

The policeman then sniffed, sighed, and motioned to the others. As he was walking away, a voice like a creaking millstone suddenly said, "Ere! You! Peeler!'

Constable Pike halted and glanced back at the cell. 'What?' he asked.

'I got summat for you.'

From where he was standing, Ned could see that Tobias Fitch was now right behind his cell door. A wedge of cheek was visible through the bars of the grate. The cheek was heavily scarred, and bristling with a two-day growth.

Constable Pike hesitated for a moment. He seemed to be weighing his options. At last he approached Fitch's door again.

'What is it?' he asked, upon reaching the grate.

A gob of spit landed on his collar.

Ned gasped. Even Alfred winced. But the policeman simply turned on his heel and marched off.

He was dabbing at his collar with a starched white handkerchief by the time he reached the bottom of the staircase.

'I've had worse,' he told Alfred, who was just behind him. 'Policing can be a dirty business.'

'Shall we send for Mr Harewood?' Alfred said gruffly. He seemed rattled, Ned thought.

'By all means.' The policeman began to head upstairs. 'I'm not convinced we'll get any more out o' Fitch, though. It's my belief he's more scared o' Gammon than he is of anything else. And I daresay he thinks Gammon'll spring him from gaol by getting rid o' witnesses. It's happened before.'

Ned swallowed. As he trudged after Constable Pike, he couldn't help glancing back at Jem, who was bringing up the rear.

Poor Jem looked as scared as Ned felt.

'I'll be the talk o' the division, now that you've paid me a visit,' Constable Pike was saying. 'By the by, have you bin hunting down bogles in any station houses lately? The newspaper said you've bin hired to exterminate all the bogles on government premises – and there's a good many police stations with drains under 'em.'

Alfred stopped in his tracks, halfway up the stairs. He looked shocked. 'What newspaper are you talking about?' he demanded.

'Why, today's *London Times*,' the policeman said. 'Haven't you read it?'

Alfred opened his mouth, then shut it again. Ned wondered if the bogler was too embarrassed to admit that he couldn't read. Breaking into the sudden silence, Jem piped up, 'Mr Bunce?'

'Wait.' Alfred set off again, with Ned close at his heels. Upon reaching the top of the stairs, Alfred asked Constable Pike, 'What did that newspaper say about me?'

'It said you were employed by the Sewers Office,'

the constable replied. Fixing Alfred with a quizzical look, he added, 'The tone of it wasn't too friendly, sir, if you get my meaning. Questions were asked about wasting public funds on fairytales. But you'll be accustomed to that, I expect – folk who don't believe in bogles.'

'Aye,' Alfred growled. 'There's plenty as don't . . .'

'Mr Bunce?' By this time Jem, too, had reached the top of the stairs, and had jostled Ned aside in his eagerness to communicate.

'What is it?' Alfred glared at Jem, but didn't manage to quell him. Instead Jem grabbed Alfred's sleeve, dragged him aside, and hissed, 'There's one thing as might scare Tobias Fitch more'n the butcher – and that's a *bogle*, Mr Bunce.' Seeing Alfred's blank expression, Jem continued in a low voice, 'What if we threaten Fitch with a bogle?'

Ned's jaw dropped. He couldn't believe his ears. As Constable Pike gave a snort of laughter, Alfred said, 'Don't be a fool, boy. We can't do that!'

'Believe me, lad – if there was a bogle in this here station house, I'd know about it,' the policeman drawled.

Jem, however, ignored him. 'It wouldn't be a *real* bogle, Mr Bunce! We'd just pretend it was.' As Jem glanced uneasily towards the staircase, Ned wondered if he was serious. He certainly *looked* serious, with his white face and furrowed brow. 'We'd have to find a good cellar, with a sufficiency o' places to hide,' Jem continued. 'There's a man at the Theatre Royal can make a puff of smoke appear wherever you want it. And if Constable Pike could hold onto Fitch just a *little* longer, I know someone we could ask to play a bogle.' Seeing Alfred narrow his eyes, Jem's tone became more urgent. 'He's at the penny gaff on Whitechapel Road, Mr Bunce. *You* know where I mean. The cove I'm a-thinking of – why, he plays bogles for a living! And all we'd need to do is make it worth his while . . .'

21

A BOGLE FOR HIRE

Josiah Lubbock was the manager of a penny gaff on Whitechapel Road, where he mounted shows featuring dwarves, snakes, clockwork heads, stuffed freaks of nature, and anything else that people might pay to see. Ned had met Mr Lubbock several times: once at Alfred's place, once in Giltspur Street, and once outside the derelict house where Salty Jack had tried to feed Jem to a bogle. But never had Ned visited Mr Lubbock's establishment in the East End.

He'd heard a lot about it, though. It was a small, two-storeyed building tucked between a pastry shop and a public house. Standing in a bitter wind, with snowflakes drifting and whirling around him like ash, Ned studied the shopfront with keen interest.

There were playbills all over its windows, and its front door was firmly shut.

'Too early in the day for a show,' Alfred speculated.

'Does anyone *live* there?' asked Ned.

Alfred shrugged. His hands were buried deep in his pockets. His voice was muffled by the thick scarf wound around the bottom half of his face. 'I wish there were some way o' doing this without alerting Lubbock,' he said morosely, 'but I don't expect there is. Whatever money's on offer, he'll get his cut of it, I've no doubt.'

'He might not reckanise me,' Ned observed. 'Mebbe *I* should knock on the door. What's the name o' the feller we want?'

'Eduardo.' Alfred heaved a sigh that turned to steam when it hit the air. 'Nay,' he said, 'I ain't no sneaking speeler as juggles with the truth. Not like Josiah Lubbock. I'll walk up and speak out, like an honest man.'

Alfred then boldly stepped off the pavement into the dirty, slushy street. Ned followed him. Whitechapel Road wasn't as busy as usual – perhaps because the weather was so bad. It was the kind of weather that made Ned offer up a silent prayer of gratitude. As a mudlark, on a day like this, he would have had to choose between starving or freezing. But thanks to Alfred, he now had to endure nothing more taxing than a walk from the nearest omnibus stop.

They had taken an omnibus from Smithfield, instead of a cab. It was Jem who had been sent to Spring Gardens in his very own hired vehicle, with orders to inform Mr Harewood that he was needed at Smithfield station house. 'See if Mr Harewood will give you a ride to Drury Lane for yer matinee,' Alfred had urged Jem. 'And be sure he sets you down on the theatre's very doorstep, lad. Tell him you ain't safe on yer own. Tell him Tobias Fitch may not be Salty Jack's only nobbler.'

As Alfred banged on the door of the penny gaff, Ned wondered uneasily if Salty Jack *would* send someone else to kill Jem – and what could possibly be done to prevent it. Even if he moved lodgings, Jem would still be working at the Theatre Royal. Unless he gave up his job there, he would be easy enough to find again.

The only real solution was to get rid of John Gammon. And the only way to do *that* was to get him locked up in gaol . . .

'Who's there?' a shrill voice demanded. It was coming from behind the door.

Alfred cleared his throat and spat on the ground. 'It's Alfred Bunce,' he rasped. 'I'm looking for Eduardo.'

'For whom?'

'*Eduardo.*' After a moment's hesitation, Alfred admitted, 'I don't know his other name.'

There was a pause, then a scraping of bolts. At last the door swung open to reveal a short, plump girl with dirty blond hair and a pasty face. There were dark circles under her eyes, and traces of make-up above them. She wore an untidy collection of garments, topped off by a mangy fur stole.

Ned judged her to be about sixteen.

'I remember you,' she said accusingly. 'You're the Go-Devil man.' Before Alfred could confirm this, she suddenly cried, 'I ain't played Birdie McAdam in weeks! Birdie's name is off our boards, now! I'm Delia the Dragon-slayer – can't you read? We don't *have* a Birdie in the show! Not since you was here last.'

'I don't—'

'If you've come to complain, you needn't talk to me. It's Mr Lubbock you want, and he's out.' The girl was closing the door when Alfred wedged his foot in it.

'Wait,' he said. 'I ain't here to fret you, Miss. I know you don't use Birdie's name no more.'

'We want to talk to Eduardo,' Ned interrupted. 'We want to hire him.'

The girl blinked. '*Hire* him?' she echoed.

'To play a bogle.'

For a moment the girl stood motionless, wide-eyed and open-mouthed. Then her expression brightened. 'A job, is it?' she asked Alfred, who nodded.

'Aye.'

'Well, come in, then!' She pulled open the door. 'I'll fetch Eduardo – he's backstage, at present. *I'm* Bedelia Moss. I don't recollect if we was formally introduced, last time we met.' Bedelia peered at Ned as she bolted the door behind Alfred. 'What happened to the other lad? The one with black hair? Did he get ate by a bogle?'

'No!' snapped Alfred.

'Jem's a dancer now,' Ned mumbled. 'I'm Ned Roach.'

'A dancer, is he? So am I. I can dance *and* sing. But I ain't engaged at the Theatre Royal.' There was a waspish edge to Bedelia's tone – and Ned suddenly realised that she must have seen one of Mr Chatterton's playbills. Upon following her into a dim, dusty vestibule, which contained an empty ticket booth and three large display cabinets full of stuffed and pickled creatures, Ned could see why Bedelia might be jealous of Birdie. Mr Lubbock's penny gaff was a far cry from the Theatre Royal on Drury Lane.

'*Eddie! You got visitors!*' the girl bellowed, pushing aside a plush curtain to reveal a very large room with a raised platform at one end. From the rows of wooden benches facing this platform, Ned deduced that he had entered the actual theatre – which smelled of stale sweat and sawdust. A door to the left of the platform was standing open. Beyond it stood a rack of clothes and a chest piled high with props.

'Whatta you want?' a deep voice roared. 'I'm-a very busy!'

'Job for you, Eddie!' Bedelia turned to Alfred. 'Is it regular work?'

'No,' Alfred had to confess. 'We'll not be needing him more'n once.'

'When?' asked Bedelia.

'Tomorrow morning. Early.'

'Well, *that's* all right. We don't do morning shows.' Bedelia suddenly turned to address a hulking figure framed in the open doorway. 'D'you remember Mr Bunce, Ed? He came here last month, with Birdie McAdam.'

Ned stared in astonishment at Eduardo, who was immensely tall, with a massive, square-jawed head, the shoulders of an ox, and legs like tree-trunks. His black hair was shaved very short all over his skull, but was thick and luxuriant on his arms and hands and chest – all of which were clearly visible because he wore only an open shirt with rolled-up sleeves, over a loose pair of canvas trousers.

'What job?' he said, his eyes flicking from Bedelia to Alfred and back again.

Alfred cleared his throat. 'Last time we came here, Mr . . . er . . .'

'Miniotto,' Bedelia supplied.

'Last time we came here, Mr Miniotto, you was playing a bogle on stage.'

'He still is,' Bedelia interjected.

Alfred stared at her for a moment from beneath his bushy eyebrows. Then he turned back to Eduardo and said, 'We need a bogle. For an hour or two tomorrow morning, around six o'clock, at the Clerkenwell station house on King's Cross Road.'

Eduardo frowned. He looked puzzled.

'They don't want a *real* bogle, Eddie, they want you,' Bedelia explained. 'Ain't that right, Mr Bunce?'

'Aye.'

'And we want his costume too,' Ned added quickly. 'He'll need to wear that.'

'Of course!' Bedelia exclaimed. 'He can't be a bogle without a pelt!' Smirking, she put her hands on her hips and announced, 'It'll cost you ten shillings.'

'Ten shillings!' squeaked Ned. It was a monstrous sum.

'Five,' said Alfred.

'Come now, Mr Bunce, you can do better than that,' Bedelia protested. 'I read about you in the newspaper this morning. You've a fancy new position with the Sewers Office.' Seeing Alfred scowl, she reduced the fee. 'Eight shillings.'

'Five,' Alfred repeated. 'That's me final offer.'

'His position ain't *that* fancy,' Ned murmured, just as Eduardo stepped forward with his hand extended.

'Five-a shilling issa good,' he announced.

Bedelia squealed, 'But *Eddie—*'

Eduardo cut her off. 'I put on a suit, stamp and roar, make-a good money. For a fee, I do this.' He shook hands with Alfred, then asked for an advance.

Alfred gave him half a crown. 'Clerkenwell station

house, six o'clock in the morning,' he repeated.

'Why do you need a bogle in a police station?' Bedelia seemed genuinely curious. But instead of answering her, Alfred changed the subject.

'If you'd keep this to yerselves, I'd be grateful. Once Josiah Lubbock finds out, he'll want a cut o' the fee. And he'll make a nuisance of hisself, besides.'

Bedelia and Eduardo exchanged a quick glance. At last Bedelia replied airily, 'Don't you worry about Josiah. We know how to get around *him*.'

Alfred gave a satisfied nod. Then he tipped his hat and turned to go. Before heading back into the vestibule, however, he paused and addressed Eduardo.

'Bogles seldom roar,' he growled. 'They hiss. You'd best remember that.'

With a final nod, he took his leave – and was out in the snow again a minute later. Ned followed him. As they trudged down Whitechapel Road, weaving their way between scurrying pedestrians and rattling carts, Ned's gaze drifted longingly back towards the pastry shop.

He could smell hot pies.

'Where shall we go now, Mr Bunce?' he asked, hoping that Alfred, too, might be feeling hungry. But before the bogler could respond, someone else answered Ned's question – in a roundabout kind of way.

'*Mr Bunce! Ahoy!*'

Startled, Ned spun around. He was astonished to see Mark Harewood leaning out of a hackney carriage, just across the road.

Alfred had stopped in his tracks. 'Mr Harewood?'

'Come quickly!' The engineer beckoned to him. 'You're wanted!'

The bogler obediently struck out for Mr Harewood's vehicle, with Ned at his heels. They dodged a coster's cart, splashed through a puddle of slush, and finally ended up at the door of the carriage – which Mr Harewood was holding open for them.

'Mr Daw has called an emergency committee meeting,' he said, reaching down to grab Ned's arm.

'Mr Daw?' For a moment Ned was stumped. Then he remembered that Mr Daw was the Principal Clerk at the City of London Sewers Office. 'Oh! Mr *Daw* . . .'

'I've been sending messages all over London,' Mr Harewood continued. He moved aside for Ned, then shut the door behind Alfred. 'I thought I'd *never* find you. But when Jem arrived, he told me where you'd gone.'

'We ain't neither of us bin back to Smithfield yet,' remarked Jem, who was sitting in one corner of the carriage. Ned offered him a weak smile.

Alfred didn't seem to notice Jem at all.

'What's this about?' he demanded, peering at Mr Harewood.

The engineer shrugged. 'I'm not sure, but I've a notion it may have something to do with today's newspaper article.' Dropping into the seat opposite Ned, he thumped on the roof with his stick and cried, 'Guildhall, please! Quick as you can!' As the carriage gave a lurch, he added, 'This is my fault. Someone must have passed my memorandum to the press. But what else could I have done? After all, we can't investigate bogles unless we know where to find them. And how can we possibly find them without the public's help . . .?'

22

MR DAW'S DISPLEASURE

Mr Joseph Daw's office at the Guildhall was handsome enough to be a chapel. It had stained-glass windows, a coffered ceiling, velvet curtains and dark, heavy furniture. Mr Daw himself was dressed in priestly black. His waistcoat was made of silk, and his spectacles were gold-rimmed. Despite his slight build and sickly complexion, he somehow managed to fill the room with an atmosphere of chilly disapproval, as though he were a schoolmaster confronted by eight disobedient children.

'I assume that you have all read this piece,' he said, pushing a newspaper clipping across the desk in front of him.

Mr Harewood nodded. So did Mr Wardle. Mr Gilfoyle murmured, 'I'm afraid so . . .', as Miss Eames leaned forward to get a better look.

'Oh, dear,' she remarked. 'Yes. I did see that.'

Ned and Jem glanced at each other, but didn't comment. From the moment of their arrival, Mr Daw had treated them as if they didn't exist. Perhaps it had something to do with Jem's missing coat, or Ned's muddy shoes. Whatever the reason, Ned knew that anything they said would be roundly ignored. So, like Jem, he remained silent.

It was Birdie who spoke up. Because she was so nicely dressed, in chestnut cashmere trimmed with silk braid, she had received a guarded nod from Mr Daw upon entering his office. Now she sat up straight and defiantly announced, 'Not everyone here can read, Mr Daw.'

'Aye, but I know what's in the newspaper,' Alfred hastened to assure her. 'Mr Harewood told me the gist of it.'

'I see.' Mr Daw's stern gaze travelled from Alfred to Birdie, then from Birdie to Miss Eames. After skipping over Jem, Ned and Mr Wardle, it finally came to rest on Mr Gilfoyle, who was standing shoulder to shoulder with Mr Harewood, because there weren't enough chairs. 'Did I, or did I not, convey to you from the very start that this committee was convened *unofficially*?' said Mr Daw. 'Did I not make it clear that the Chief Engineer was anxious not to arouse too much interest among the public?' Without waiting for an answer, he ploughed on. 'Perhaps the wisdom of this request has become apparent to you, now that the Sewers Office is a laughing stock. May I ask, Mr Harewood, how this came about? As Chairman of the committee, you must have *some* notion.'

Mr Harewood shifted uncomfortably. He was looking a little ink-stained, and his black eye was turning mauve and green and yellow. 'I'm not sure how the news got out,' he confessed, 'but it might have had something to do with my memorandum.'

He then explained what he had done, as Mr Daw's expression became more and more sour. When the engineer proposed that some government clerk must have leaked the memorandum to a journalist, Mr Daw produced from one of his desk drawers a wad of crumpled paper. Some of the sheets were telegrams; some were letters; some appeared to be jottings on ledger-leaves.

'Since the article was published, I have received more than two dozen requests for help,' he said tightly. 'Some of these messages concern missing children. Others relate to sightings in sewers. One is about a blocked drain.' He shot a withering look at the engineer. 'This is not what I had in mind when the committee was formed, Mr Harewood.'

'No, sir. I quite see that.' The engineer fished a handful of papers from his own pocket. 'As a matter of fact, I've also received further communications this morning. From a military barracks, and the Treasury Department—'

Mr Daw cut him off – quite rudely, Ned thought. 'Clearly the problem is widespread. Are you confident of solving it, at this point?'

There was a pause, as everyone else looked at each other. It was Miss Eames who finally answered Mr Daw's question.

'I believe we *have* made strides. At present we have high hopes of reproducing Mr Bunce's spear. And with more spears we can train up more boglers—'

'Ahem.' Mr Daw raised his hand suddenly. 'The Sewers Office does not work with boglers. The Town Clerk has already made a statement to this effect.'

Ned caught his breath as his eyes swivelled towards Alfred. Even Mr Gilfoyle looked startled.

'The Committee for the Regulation of Subterranean

Anomalies has undertaken to hire Mr Bunce,' Mr Daw continued, 'but this committee was never convened by the Sewers Office.'

'Not officially, perhaps—' Mr Harewood began, as he stuffed his telegrams back into his pocket. But he was quickly corrected by Mr Daw.

'Neither officially *nor* unofficially. Your committee was formed on a whim by various interested parties, including Mr Eugene Wardle, who happens to work for the Sewers Office but who has been participating in a *private capacity*, and whose presence in no way implicates this department.'

Mr Wardle's jaw dropped. Aghast, he stammered, 'B-but Mr Daw ... you've already covered a good portion of our expenses—'

'Because of a payroll accounting error. The money you received was in advance of your wages, Mr Wardle, and must be repaid.'

'But—'

'Luckily, Mr Edward Rider Cook, a member of the Metropolitan Board of Works, has undertaken to fund the committee as a private patron. So the Sewers Office will apply to him for recompense. I would advise that you communicate with Mr Cook as soon as possible, at his address in Woodford Green.' Mr Daw pushed another slip of paper across his desk, ignoring the gasps and stares that greeted this announcement. 'Naturally, the Sewers Office will be interested in any discoveries you might henceforth make,' he went on. 'And we'll do our best to provide assistance where it's needed. But the Sewers Office will have no *direct* involvement in the funding of boglers or bogle-related research.' Leaning back in his chair, he steepled his fingers and let his chilly gaze sweep over the people arrayed before him. 'Do you understand me, gentlemen? Ladies? I hope I have made myself clear?'

'*Quite* clear, thank you,' Miss Eames replied crisply. Ned caught Birdie's eye and grimaced. He knew exactly what was going on. Mr Daw didn't want any more newspapers accusing his department of wasting rate money. So he had devised a clever, roundabout way of ensuring that the committee continued to exist without his direct involvement.

Not that it mattered much. As long as Alfred was being paid, Ned didn't care where the money came from.

'You must address your reports to Mr Cook, in the future,' Mr Daw advised the engineer. 'He is a soap manufacturer with a high regard for all forms of scientific research, though he has a special interest in chemistry. No doubt he will keep me apprised of your progress.' Rising, he executed a stiff little bow and said to the group as a whole, 'May I wish you the very best of luck in your endeavours? If you have any further questions, you should direct them to Mr Cook.'

The others exchanged stunned glances. Birdie was scowling. Mr Wardle had turned pale. Alfred didn't look at all impressed.

Mr Harewood asked, with an edge to his voice, 'May we hold our next meeting at Spring Gardens, Mr Daw? Or is it closed to us, now?'

'As I said, Mr Harewood, you should apply to Mr Cook for an answer. He is, after all, on the Board of Works.' As Mr Wardle opened his mouth, Mr Daw added, 'If you'll excuse me, I'm very busy. I had to postpone several meetings to make time for this one. You know your way out, I think? It's left, then left again . . .'

Two minutes later, the entire committee was standing in a Guildhall corridor, cut adrift like castaways.

'Well,' Mr Harewood said at last, 'I suppose I should have foreseen *that*. Clerkish fellows always scuttle for cover when a storm threatens.'

'But what is expected of us, Harewood?' Mr Wardle spoke plaintively, his plump face creased into anxious lines. 'Is it our duty to attend these meetings? Will we benefit from doing so? Is the committee part of my job anymore, or not?'

Mr Harewood shrugged.

'I'm persuaded that Mr Daw wants you to continue as before, but doesn't want to know anything about it.' Miss Eames turned to the naturalist. 'Did you receive that impression, Mr Gilfoyle?'

'Perhaps. It's hard to say. Mr Daw was curiously *oblique* in his manner.'

'You must go and speak to Mr Cook,' Birdie suddenly declared. She was addressing Mr Harewood, her tone sharp, her cheeks flushed. 'You must go now, and tell him that Mr Bunce needs his wages. *Every week.*'

Miss Eames winced and clicked her tongue. Alfred quickly said, 'He cannot go now, lass. He's wanted in Smithfield. Urgently.'

Alfred then went on to explain that the man suspected of assaulting Mr Harewood was being held at Smithfield station house. But he didn't mention Jem's violent encounter with Fitch the previous night.

Ned wondered if he was afraid that Miss Eames would kick up a fuss.

'I'll go in search of Mr Cook as soon as I've formally identified this Fitch blackguard,' Mr Harewood promised Birdie. 'Once I've discovered Mr Cook's plans for us, I'll make sure you're all acquainted with the particulars.' He shuffled aside to let a black-suited clerk hurry past. 'Meanwhile, we must carry on as before. Our best hope still lies in replicating Mr Bunce's spear. I believe Gilfoyle is on the trail of a cross that we can use for a spearhead. Isn't that right, old boy?'

'It is,' Mr Gilfoyle conceded. 'Though I cannot imagine what difference it will make. Whether you consecrate the stone before or after it's carved, you end up with the same material, scientifically speaking.'

'Except that bogles ain't scientific,' Birdie pointed out. 'They're magic.'

Mr Gilfoyle sniffed, but said nothing. It was Ned who quietly remarked, 'I used to think the same, Birdie. Now I ain't so sure. There's things in this world we don't understand – mebbe bogles is one of 'em.'

There was a brief silence. Mr Gilfoyle studied Ned with a gratified look on his face. Finally Mr Harewood cleared his throat and said, 'Once the cross is in our hands, I'll arrange to have a new spearhead made. And while that's being done, Gilfoyle will be testing his herbal mixture on some of the samples he's collected. As for you, Mr Bunce . . .' The engineer once again produced a handful of rustling telegrams from his coat pocket. 'I assume you'll keep responding to every legitimate appeal for help?'

'Aye. I'll do that,' Alfred mumbled.

'As I said earlier, I've received several more – from St George's Barracks, and the Treasury, and the Monument—'

'I'll get to 'em.' Catching Ned's eye, Alfred added, 'First I've some business to attend to, back in Drury Lane.'

Ned knew what *that* must be. Having secured Eduardo's services, Alfred now wanted to hire one of the gas-men at the Theatre Royal. According to Jem, this was the stagehand who could produce a cloud of smoke at the drop of a hat.

'You won't forget about tomorrow night, Mr Bunce?' Birdie piped up. 'You'll come and hear me sing? You and Ned?'

'We'd not miss it for nowt,' Alfred replied solemnly. 'Would we, lad?'

'No.' Ned racked his brain for a pretty way of

assuring Birdie that he would sooner miss tea with the Queen. Before he could think of the right words, however, Mr Harewood forestalled him.

'I believe we'll *all* be there. Isn't that so, Wardle?'

'Oh . . . er . . .'

'The research subcommittee will certainly be attending,' Miss Eames interjected. 'Mr Gilfoyle has kindly offered to escort me to the theatre.'

Ned saw Mr Harewood shoot a sideways look at the naturalist, who coughed and rubbed his nose. Then Alfred rasped, 'Mebbe you can tell us about Mr Cook tomorrow night, Mr Harewood.'

'Yes, indeed,' the engineer drawled. 'We can have a committee meeting in the theatre's crush bar, like civilised people.' He spoke in a sardonic tone that Ned found puzzling. It wasn't until later, when Mr Harewood and Mr Gilfoyle were being terribly polite to each other about sharing a cab, that Ned suddenly understood.

Mr Harewood was jealous.

23

AN UNEXPECTED GUEST

Clerkenwell Police Court stood next to Clerkenwell station house. They were separated by a large iron gate, which opened onto a cobbled yard behind the two buildings. Peering through this gate, Ned could just make out that the yard was enclosed by a string of smaller structures: a stable block, a carriage house, and a row of prison cells, small and mean and dismal in the murky dawn light.

'Gives you the jitters, don't it?' said Humphrey Cundle, the gas-man from the Theatre Royal. He was wizened and middle-aged, with a mouth so full of big, yellow teeth that he couldn't seem to shut it properly. His scalp gleamed through his close-cropped grey hair, and his sallow skin was spotted with burns, scars and splotches.

On his back he carried an enormous basket, tied across his shoulders with a pair of leather straps.

Ned could only assume that the basket contained Humphrey's apparatus – a smoke-pot, perhaps, or a flash-box. The previous afternoon, Humphrey had shown Alfred and Ned a huge collection of stage equipment, starting with a tiny jar of magnesium and ending with a large pair of bellows mounted on a brazier. The tour had been accompanied by a running commentary, as the gas-man tried to explain the function of every pipe, flap, wire and screen. 'A flash-box is full o' lycopodium powder. If you blow the powder through a flame, you get a nice, bright flare . . . Or I can make you a smoke-pot out o' sugar and saltpetre. You'll get more smoke from a smoke-pot, though it ain't so easy to manage . . . A bit o' salt will turn a flame yellow . . . Coloured smoke's best done with lights and gauze . . .'

In the end, Alfred had told Humphrey to bring along whatever he thought suitable – and had grudgingly agreed to pay an extra twopence for sulphur. 'It'll give you a lovely brimstone stench, as if yer bogle's come straight from the fires of hell,' Humphrey had promised, on pocketing Alfred's twopenny bit.

Now, as they stood outside the station house waiting for Eduardo to arrive, the gas-man was talking again. Excited, perhaps, to have a captive audience after so many years spent working in the wings, he entertained Alfred and Ned with grisly tales of all the backstage accidents he'd witnessed until a policeman suddenly hailed them from the door of the station house.

'Hi! You, there! Would you be the bogling party, by any chance?'

The policeman was young and slim, with shiny black hair and thick black eyebrows. There was a five o'clock shadow on his chin, despite the early hour.

He looked just like a gypsy, Ned thought.

'Aye,' said Alfred. 'I'm Bunce the bogler.'

'And I'm Constable Evans.' The policeman darted forward to shake Alfred's hand. 'Pleased to make your acquaintance, Mr Bunce – I read about you in the newspaper. Seems you've made quite a name for yourself.'

'Oh, aye?' Alfred didn't look very pleased.

'Len Pike told me what you wanted, and I think I've found it. But you'd best hurry in, for your felon will arrive with the next delivery, and I'm expecting *that* within the hour.'

'We're a-waiting for one more—' Alfred began, but Ned interrupted him.

'There he is.' Ned pointed. 'There's Mr Miniotto.'

An enormous figure was lumbering towards them down King's Cross Road, which was practically deserted and swathed in a damp, grey mist. Ned had recognised Eduardo because of his size. The showman looked even bigger than usual because of his tall hat, his bulky dreadnought coat, and the over-stuffed burlap bag on his shoulder.

Constable Evans blinked at the sight of him.

'Well, now,' said the policeman, 'I hope *that* one'll fit in the basement.'

'You're taking us down to the basement?' Alfred asked, frowning. 'But I saw a dozen cells off the yard, back there . . .'

'You'll not find what you want in those court cells. They're whitewashed boxes, and noisy besides. But this station house is brand new, built straight over the old cellars, and down below there's a lot still left unfinished. It's where you'll find any number of boltholes, ideal for your purposes.' The policeman's blue eyes glinted as a smile tugged at the corner of his mouth. 'I'll tell your friend Fitch that we've run out of room in the cells, and must confine him downstairs, instead.'

By this time Eduardo had joined them. He was quickly introduced to Humphrey and Constable Evans, both of whom regarded him warily, as if he were an exotic animal. 'He ain't no Englishman, that's clear enough,' mumbled the gas-man. And the constable declared, in a dry voice, 'Len Pike has vouched for you, Mr Bunce, and I know you're well respected in your profession. But I tell you now, if this gentleman here makes one misstep, or smuggles anything untoward into the lock-up – such as might be used as a weapon – he'll end up in the same cell as Toby Fitch. For I know foreigners are partial to stiletto knives, and the like.'

Ned wasn't sure if Eduardo fully understood what was being said; there was a puzzled expression on the performer's big, square, unshaven face. It was Alfred who scowled at Constable Evans and rasped, 'You've no call to insult Mr Miniotto. He's a working man like me. And there's nowt in that bag but his bogle-pelt.'

'If you say so, Mr Bunce.' The policeman shrugged, then turned on his heel and plunged back into the station house – which was a looming box four storeys high, made of brick and stone and dull grey slate. After a moment's pause, everyone else followed him. They passed through the front entrance into a lofty hallway that was lined with closed doors. The air smelled of soap, sweat and fresh paint. The scarred walls were hung with signs that Ned couldn't read.

It was still so early that the gas-lamps were lit.

Constable Evans turned right when he reached a stairwell near the end of the hallway. He led his visitors down two flights of stairs and across a small room cluttered with stacks of loose timber and old paint pots. Dust was lying everywhere – mostly brick and plaster dust. But the air felt damp, all the same.

'I'll have to fetch a lamp,' the policeman remarked, as he pushed open a door made of raw, unpainted wood. 'There's no gas laid on down here. No steam pipes, either. And no facilities, of course . . .'

There wasn't, in fact, much of anything. Ned saw this at once when he peered through the open doorway into the dim space beyond it, which looked half-finished. Old stone walls jostled with new brick ones oozing clots of dried mortar. Rusty, iron-barred grates alternated with neat sets of shelves made from fresh-cut wood. A brand new boiler stood beside a blocked-up fireplace.

'See that gate?' Constable Evans pointed. 'There's a key in the lock. Beyond it lies a disused storeroom.' He stepped aside, allowing the others to shuffle past him. 'You'll find it well supplied with nooks and crannies,' he continued, 'though they'll be hard to see in this light. I'll fetch a lamp, so you may judge what suits you best. Watch where you put your feet, in the meantime.'

He disappeared suddenly, leaving his guests huddled together near the door to the stairwell. It was Alfred who finally made a move. He let his bag slide off his shoulder before crouching down to rake through its contents.

Ned could only assume that he was searching for his dark lantern.

'This place smells bad,' Ned muttered, unnerved by the darkness and the mouldy, swampy odour.

'It does,' Alfred grimly agreed. For an instant the match in his hand fizzed and flared. Then he lit his lantern, straightened up, and tossed away the spent match. Ned followed him as he picked his way carefully through the shadows towards the gate, which swung open on creaky hinges when the bogler touched it.

In the soft gleam of Alfred's lantern, Ned could just make out a series of cupboard doors set into the wall opposite. Some stood open, revealing black holes framed by fluttering cobwebs. Some were bolted shut.

'What do you think, Mr Bunce?' Humphrey asked from the stairwell. 'Is there space enough for the big lad?'

'Hush! Stay back. You too, Ned. Don't take another step.'

Ned stared at Alfred in surprise. 'Why? What's wrong?'

'*Quiet!* Keep yer mouth shut, d'you hear?' As Ned subsided, his heart pounding and his stomach clenching, Alfred turned to the others. 'I mislike this. T'ain't what it should be. I'm a-thinking there might be bogles about.'

'*Bogles?*' Humphrey echoed, as Ned's jaw dropped. 'You mean *real* bogles?'

'Aye.'

Ned didn't understand. He hadn't felt the presence of a bogle – not the way he usually did. There was no telltale sense of despair.

But he kept silent, because Alfred had told him to.

'Stay back,' the bogler repeated. 'None o' you come no closer. Not till I give you leave.' To Ned he muttered, 'Fetch the spear, there's a good lad.'

Ned promptly obeyed. Then he retreated to the doorway at the foot of the stairs, where he stood while Alfred checked the cupboards one by one.

How can he say I'm a born bogler, Ned thought morosely, *when I didn't feel a thing?* It was more than embarrassing; it frightened him. He couldn't stay safe if he wasn't skilled enough. And what if he let Alfred down? What if he put them *both* in danger?

Beside him, Humphrey Cundle stood hunched beneath the weight of his basket, riveted by the movement of Alfred's lantern. Eduardo, on the other hand, looked frankly puzzled. Ned would have liked to explain things to him, but couldn't speak. Not until Alfred gave permission.

All at once a muffled voice was raised above them, in surprise or anger. Ned heard footsteps over-head, followed by a loud bang. More footsteps followed. They began to move closer until they were clumping down the stairs.

Ned turned to intercept Constable Evans, who clattered into view carrying an oil lamp.

'Mr Bunce?' the policeman exclaimed. 'Your man's arrived. He came with the rest. Are you ready for him?'

'Not yet,' Ned replied, from the foot of the staircase. 'Mr Bunce is still checking cupboards . . .'

'Well, he'd better hurry. We cannot hold Fitch for more'n a few minutes, up there. We need him put under lock and key.'

'Mr Bunce thinks there's a *real* bogle,' Humphrey unexpectedly remarked. He had sidled up to Ned, his expression wry, his basket still on his back. 'I don't know what *that* means for me and the big foreigner. Do you, lad?'

Ned didn't. He opened his mouth to say so, but was prevented from answering by Constable Evans.

'A *real* bogle?' the policeman spluttered. 'What nonsense is this?'

'T'ain't nonsense.' Alfred spoke up suddenly, startling them all. He stood framed in the doorway, his lantern held high, his face drawn and sombre. 'There's a bogle in that fumigation cupboard,' he announced. 'See for yerselves.'

He swung his lantern towards the storeroom. As Ned gaped at him, aghast, Humphrey said, 'You can *see* it?'

'Aye.'

'But . . .' Ned was confused. Bogles only showed themselves when they were lured out of their lairs. Stealth was their greatest weapon. They didn't lie around in basements, waiting to be discovered. They *crept up* on people.

'If I didn't know better, I'd say it were poorly,' Alfred went on. 'At first I thought it were a bag o' coal stuffed in the back o' the oven, down there. But then it moved.' In a tone of wonder he added, 'The light seemed to be fretting it.'

There was a short, stunned silence. At last Constable Evans said, 'Are you sure? No one has ever reported anything strange in this basement.'

Alfred shrugged. 'Mebbe the bogle ain't bin here long.'

'But what does it *mean*?' Humphrey demanded. 'Am I needed or not? Will I be paid, Mr Bunce?'

'You'll be paid,' Alfred said shortly. 'As to whether you're needed . . . well, I'm inclined to think we must change our plans to fit the circumstances.'

'Mr Bunce.' Though he was almost too scared to talk, Ned couldn't remain silent. 'Please sir,' he croaked, 'ain't . . . ain't we going to kill it?'

'Not yet.' Alfred's gaze shifted back towards the wall of cupboards. 'I want to see what it does.'

'But we've no time for that!' Constable Evans protested. 'What about Fitch?'

'I want to see what it does to Fitch,' said Alfred. Then he glanced at the policeman, smiling a cold little smile. 'Why don't you go and fetch him?'

24

BOGLE BAITING

'What's all this, then? This ain't right! I don't belong in no basement...'

Standing in a circle of salt, Ned heard Tobias Fitch long before the man himself actually appeared. He heard Fitch's heavy tread and deep, hoarse, rumbling voice, which he recognised from Smithfield police station. He heard grunts and curses. Then he heard Constable Evans say, 'The basement is *just* where you belong, Fitch, make no mistake.' And all at once three figures staggered over the threshold.

One of them was Constable Evans. With him was another policeman, small and stocky and silver-haired. Caught between them was a big, bald man dressed in

corduroy trousers, a red neckerchief, and a frock coat
that looked much too tight for his bulging muscles.
Though the scar on his eyebrow wasn't visible in the
poor light, there was no mistaking Tobias Fitch.

Ned felt sick at the sight of him.

'There weren't but six other coves in that van!'
Fitch growled, as the two policemen shoved him
across the room. 'How can the cells be full? You've a
round dozen of 'em at least, and I *know* how tight you
pack 'em . . .'

'You weren't our first delivery, Fitch. Besides, we
had Clerkenwell lags here already.' Though Constable
Evans wasn't half Fitch's weight, he somehow
wrestled his prisoner through the open gate of the old
storeroom – which he managed to shut and lock before
Fitch had even turned around. It was only at this point
that the prisoner finally noticed Ned and Alfred, both
of whom were lurking in the shadows nearby.

Humphrey and Eduardo had already been dismissed. They had left reluctantly, with many a curious
backwards glance, taking with them six shillings
of Alfred's hard-earned money. But the bogler had
assured Ned that Jem was worth the price.

'What the devil . . .?' Fitch spluttered. His
face looked like a gargoyle's, all glaring eyes and

gap-toothed snarl. 'Who's that? What's yer caper? I ain't no mad cove in Bedlam, to be gawked at like a monkey in a cage!'

'This here is Mr Alfred Bunce,' Constable Evans replied flatly. 'We hired him on account of our bogle problem. Which is *your* problem too, Fitch. We have a bogle, see. And it's in that cell with you.'

The prisoner snorted. 'I dunno what you're prating about,' he said, without so much as a glance over his shoulder. Ned wondered, with a sudden chill, if Tobias Fitch might be immune to the threat of bogles. It occurred to Ned that Sarah Pickles had spent months feeding babies to a bogle that lived in her chimney, and had never once come to any harm. Maybe Fitch knew that. Maybe he understood that bogles didn't normally attack adults, unless the creatures felt threatened.

'D'you hear me, Fitch?' Constable Evans continued, following a script that he and Alfred had already prepared together. 'There's a bogle in that cell with you, and unless you tell us the truth about Salty Jack, we'll not let you out.'

'I ain't never heard o' no Salty Jack,' Fitch retorted. It was such an outrageous claim that both Constable Evans and his colleague had to smile.

'We know you work for Gammon, Fitch,' Constable Evans said patiently. 'I don't believe there's a soul living between St Paul's and Chancery Lane who *doesn't* know it. But we want to hear it from your own lips, in front of witnesses. We want to hear how John Gammon told you to kill Mr Bunce's apprentice.'

Fitch's blank stare swung towards Ned, who flinched.

'I don't know Mr Bunce,' the prisoner growled. '*Nor* his 'prentice.'

'Well, that's hard to believe, since Mr Bunce is by way of being a famous man.' Constable Evans spoke in a light drawl, his head cocked and his arms folded. He didn't hold himself stiffly, like many other policemen of Ned's acquaintance, and his voice was as flexible as his carriage. 'Come now, Fitch. This is your last chance. Tell us why Salty Jack wants this boy dead – or I swear, Mr Bunce'll bring down the wrath of hell upon you.'

'T'ain't *me* was attacked!' Ned blurted out. But Alfred hushed him, and Tobias Fitch spat on the floor.

'You must think I'm glocky,' the prisoner scoffed. 'This here is a racket, and you're all flamming. There ain't no bogle. And I ain't no fool.'

Constable Evans glanced at Alfred, who jerked

his chin at Ned. It was the signal that Ned had been waiting for. He cleared his throat, took a deep breath, and began to chant the first song that sprang to mind.

This is the house that Jack built.
This is the malt as lay in the house that Jack built.
This is the rat as ate the malt
As lay in the house that Jack built.

'You calling me a rat?' Fitch cut in, hoarse with fury. 'Is that yer game? Well, I ain't bringing down Jack's house no matter *what* yer malt is, for I don't know nothing and I'll not say nothing!'

Ned wondered if the prisoner's loud, angry voice would frighten off the bogle. It seemed likely. Yet Alfred had been willing to take that chance, rather than kill the creature and replace it with a man in a furry suit. According to Alfred, there was no substitute for the real thing. 'Besides, I don't fancy putting Mr Miniotto in a cage with Toby Fitch,' he'd said, 'for all that they're a good match when it comes to size.'

Ned could see why Alfred had chosen the riskier course. And it wasn't *too* risky, if the bogle itself was old and sick. Not that they were taking any chances;

Ned was standing in a closed circle of salt, and the locked gate would provide added protection, should the creature decide to emerge from its lair. But as he listened to Tobias Fitch ranting away, Ned began to doubt that the bogle *would* emerge. Healthy bogles favoured unaccompanied children. Why should a sick bogle be any different?

If Birdie was here, he thought glumly, *she'd lure that bogle out no matter what.* And as he launched into the second verse, he tried to make himself sound irresistible.

This is the cat as killed the rat
As ate the malt as lay in the house that Jack built.
This is the dog as worried the cat as killed the rat
As ate the malt as lay in the house that Jack built.

Suddenly Fitch stopped cursing to peer at the wall of cupboards behind him. Then, as Ned paused to take another breath, he heard a faint scraping sound, followed by a dull knock. It was the sound of something rearranging itself inside a small space.

There was a moment's silence, which the prisoner finally broke. 'Hah!' he exclaimed. 'So you've put a dog in here to scare me, have you? Well, I'm more'n a match for the best ratter in London, and will tear the throat out of any dog as tries to sink its teeth into *this* carcass!' He probably would have said more, if a creak of hinges hadn't interrupted him.

Squinting into the gloom, Ned saw that a little hatch in the fumigation cupboard had swung open. The doors above it were already hanging ajar, exposing the slatted shelves where lice-ridden clothes had once been stacked before they were engulfed in clouds of sulphur-laden smoke. These shelves were now empty – but the oven below them was not. Ned could just make out a dark, shiny, squirming shape in its depths, despite his obstructed view.

He immediately tried to coax the mysterious shape out of its bolthole.

This is the cow with the crumpled horn
As tossed the dog as worried the cat
As killed the rat as ate the malt
As lay in the house that Jack built.

As he sang, a long, grey, triple-jointed arm slowly unfurled, flopping out of the oven onto the floor. The end of this arm was forked, crowned by two curved talons that buried themselves between the flagstones.

Each talon was iron-grey, six inches long, and barbed like a fish-hook.

Fitch took one look and froze. Ned heard someone gasp. He felt a sudden pang of hopeless dismay that announced, as clearly as any fanfare, that he was in the presence of a genuine bogle.

Tobias Fitch must have felt something similar, because he clamped his hands around the bars of the gate and squawked, 'Lemme out! You can't keep me in here! *Lemme out!*'

'Not until you tell the truth,' Constable Evans replied. He sounded shaken, but was obviously trying to remain calm. 'Who told you to nobble Jem Barbary?'

Even as he spoke, another long grey arm joined the first, followed by another, and another. Reaching across the flagstones, they groped about in a slow, sinister way, fanning out like antennae.

The gate began to rattle furiously. 'Lemme go! Now!' Fitch screamed.

Ned's voice failed him for an instant. He shot an anxious look at Alfred, who caught his eye and gave a nod.

So Ned kept singing.

This is the maiden all forlorn
As milked the cow with the crumpled horn
As tossed the dog as worried the cat
As killed the rat as ate the malt—

'Please! Lemme go! I'm begging you!' Fitch's voice was a high-pitched squeal. He was reaching through the bars, his eyes bulging with fear. Behind him, the bogle was halfway out of the oven, drawn to Ned's voice like a fish on a line. Ned caught glimpses of a flabby grey mass puddling on the floor. He couldn't see much, because of the walls, the bars, and Fitch's large frame – but it did look as if the bogle wasn't very well. It moved sluggishly, its eyes dull.

'John Gammon did it!' the prisoner wailed. 'He hired me! He said to kill the kid before he – gawd help us! Lemme go, *please*!'

'Before he what?' Constable Evans took a step forward, his face as white as salt. 'Before he *what*, Fitch?'

'Before the kid peached on him, and got him nibbed!'

'Will you swear to that in court?' the constable asked roughly.

'Yes! *Yes!*'

'Mr Bunce.' Ned couldn't stand it any more – the fear, the screeching, the darkness, the groping claws and growing stench. He gazed beseechingly at Alfred, just as Constable Evans threw a harassed look in the same direction.

'Time we killed that bogle,' said Alfred. Then he and Constable Evans both converged on the gate, one carrying a spear, the other carrying a bunch of keys. Tobias Fitch, meanwhile, was throwing himself against the iron bars in a frenzy. *Bang! Bang! Bang!* And the bogle was slowly spreading across the floor, like a grey tide with teeth . . .

CRASH! Fitch fell through the gate as it slammed open, colliding with Constable Evans, who lost his balance. But the other policeman quickly jumped on Fitch, and in the ensuing scuffle, Fitch ended up flat on the floor with both constables piled on top of him.

'Don't you . . . try anything . . . you'll regret . . .' Constable Evans breathlessly warned the prisoner, who was bleating, 'Shut the gate! Shut the gate, you halfwits!'

'There ain't no need,' said Alfred. He had stepped into the storeroom, where he stood prodding the motionless bogle with the tip of his spear. 'It's dead.'

Ned gasped. 'But – but it can't be!' he stammered. 'You ain't barely touched it!'

'I don't claim I'm the one as caused it to die.' Without warning, Alfred lifted his spear and drove it into the bogle – which didn't so much as twitch in response. 'Best to be on the safe side, though,' he remarked. Then he yanked the spear free and wiped it with the handkerchief that he'd removed from his pocket.

Ned stared at the bogle in amazement. It hadn't shrunk. It hadn't exploded. It hadn't evaporated. It had died like a sick rat, leaving a sizeable corpse.

'What's happening, Mr Bunce?' he croaked.

'That I can't tell you,' said Alfred. 'This ain't summat I ever seen nor heard of.' He glanced at the two policemen, who were hauling their captive to his feet. 'I don't know if it starved, or were poisoned, or died of old age,' he went on thoughtfully. 'But whatever killed it, we got to find out what happened. For if we can, our troubles will be over.'

25

MR CLUNY'S MONSTER

Clerkenwell was a long way from Billingsgate. So Alfred decided to catch a green omnibus from Gray's Inn Road, then walk to the Custom House from Fleet Street. 'Once we've done our work at the Custom House, we may have time for the Monument, which is close by,' he said. 'But I'll not attempt no job at the London Docks. Not today. For we must return to Drury Lane in good time for Birdie's show this evening.'

Ned gave a start. The show! Of course! He had forgotten all about it. *I should be ashamed o' meself,* he thought, though he understood why Birdie's debut performance had briefly slipped his mind. He'd been distracted by the sick bogle, by Fitch's confession, and by the fearsome prospect of tackling all the other bogles on Alfred's list – which the bogler must have memorised, since he wasn't able to read the pile of telegrams that Mr Harewood had given him the previous afternoon.

Now, as Ned trudged past the great wholesale warehouses on Cannon Street, he wondered how he could broach the subject of his own incompetence. Alfred was relying on him. Ned knew that. But was he really all that reliable . . .?

'Did you hear what Constable Evans said, when you was packing away the salt and the spear?' Alfred suddenly asked. 'He said he'd be sending word straight to Constable Pike, so as John Gammon may be nibbed.'

Ned grunted.

'We'll neither of us have to fret about Salty Jack, no more,' Alfred continued. 'Nor Tobias Fitch neither, now he's bin fingered by Mr Harewood. Mr Harewood must have gone to Smithfield station house last night, for he were due in court this morning, to testify against Fitch. Constable Evans told me so. He told me they'd be laying charges of assault and attempted murder on Fitch, in addition to the counterfeit coin charge.' Alfred frowned, his expression preoccupied. Against the majestic backdrop of the City Terminus Hotel, he looked soiled and shabby as he shuffled along in a light drizzle. 'I'm glad Mr Harewood will be there in court,' he muttered, 'for Jem'll need a deal of encouragement. He's bin called to give evidence – did I mention that? Mr Harewood promised to collect him from Drury Lane, though I ain't no longer greatly troubled as to his safety on the streets. Not now Fitch is banged up, and his master about to be.'

'Mr Bunce?' Ned finally found the courage to speak. A wagon was rattling past, however, and Alfred didn't hear him.

'Constable Evans promised to have a word with the inspector on duty at Clerkenwell Police Court, who will tell Mr Harewood about recent events,' the bogler went on. 'I must confess I ain't so sanguine on that score, for police courts is all noise and confusion. But at the very least, Jem is bound to spot Mr Harewood. And with Mr Harewood backing him up, Jem'll make a better witness than he would have once, when it were his word against Gammon's . . .'

'Mr Bunce?' Ned tried again – and this time he was heard. Alfred glanced at him from beneath the sodden, sagging brim of his hat.

'Aye?'

'How did you know a bogle were in that basement?' Before Alfred could reply, Ned glumly admitted, 'For I could not feel it. Not till it showed itself.'

'Well . . . that ain't so strange,' said Alfred. 'It had no strength left with which to poison the air.'

'But *you* felt it. You knew it were there before I did.'

Alfred shrugged. 'When you bin around bogles long enough, lad, you get a nose for 'em.'

'I don't think I have a nose for 'em, Mr Bunce.' Ned came out with it at last – the bald truth – his feet dragging and his gaze on the ground. 'You said I were born to the job, but that ain't so. I didn't feel the bogle at Clerkenwell. I fainted when I speared the bogle on Water Lane—'

Alfred cut him off. 'That weren't no faint. You was knocked out.'

'Which *you* never was, while killing a bogle.'

'Lad, I'm nearly twice yer size, at present. Though I don't expect I shall be for much longer, the way you're growing.' In the pause that followed, Ned shot a quick glance at Alfred – who was studying him intently, with narrowed eyes. 'You expect too much o' yerself,' Alfred said at last. 'You'll make a fine bogler. I'd swear to it, if that's what's troubling you.'

Ned didn't answer. He didn't know what to say. How could he tell Alfred that he didn't *want* to make a fine bogler?

'What you need is a bite to eat,' Alfred unexpectedly announced. 'No man feels equal to nowt if his belly ain't full.' And he stopped by a cart selling roasted chestnuts, buying a pennyworth for each of them. After that, the rain set in with a vengeance; Ned soon found himself too preoccupied with the challenge of eating hot chestnuts in wild weather to chat with Alfred about anything.

At last they reached the Custom House, which stood on the river next to Billingsgate fish market. It was a lofty building that seemed to stretch for miles along the quayside, though Alfred and Ned didn't enter it from the river. Instead they used the northern entrance on Lower Thames Street, which was thronged with clerks carrying umbrellas, and seafaring men in oilskin coats.

'Mr Harewood told me to ask for Mr Spiddle at the Queen's Warehouse,' said Alfred, casting a practised eye around the building's noisy, crowded vestibule. Spotting a man with a porter's knot on his shoulder, he lunged forward and caught the man's sleeve. 'Can you direct me to the warehouse?' he asked, raising his voice above the din.

With a jerk of his head, the porter indicated a door at the rear of the vestibule. Then he spat on the floor and disengaged himself.

'Thank'ee,' said Alfred. He hustled Ned past a knot of customs-house officers in brass-buttoned jackets, through a pair of heavy oak doors, and into a big, square, unadorned room full of shelves and counters that overflowed with goods. Scattered among the boxes and barrels and crates were loose rolls of cloth, stacked jars of chutney, several acres of East India matting, great sheaves of slate pencils, and a piano wrapped in woollen pads.

'May I help you?' A man addressed Alfred from behind one of the counters. He was pale and pinched, with a bushy grey moustache that looked as if it had been pasted on. There were heavy pouches under his oyster-coloured eyes, one of which was magnified by a monocle on a black ribbon. He wore a dark serge waistcoat over a crumpled white shirt.

'I'm looking for Mr Spiddle.' When Alfred plucked a thin sheet of greenish paper from his pocket, Ned recognised one of Mr Harewood's telegrams. 'Concerning this here message he sent to the Board o' Works.'

'I'm Spiddle.' The man set down his pen and

emerged from behind the counter, adjusting his monocle as he did so. His voice was unexpectedly rich and sonorous, as if produced by a pipe organ. 'Would you be Mr Mark Harewood?'

'No, sir, I ain't. The name's Bunce. Alfred Bunce. I'm a Go-Devil man.'

'Ah!' One of Mr Spiddle's sparse eyebrows climbed halfway up his balding head. The other stayed clamped to his monocle. 'I read about you in the newspaper, Mr Bunce. You're the man who kills bogles, are you not?'

'I am.'

'Well, I'm afraid you're a little too late. I was about to send word, in fact.'

Alfred frowned. 'Beg pardon, sir?'

'It's been days since we communicated with Mr Harewood. So rather than wait any longer, Mr Cluny solved the problem himself.' Before Alfred could respond, Mr Spiddle shouted across the room. '*Alan! Would you come here, please?*'

Alfred and Ned exchanged a startled look as a short but very burly young man suddenly popped up from behind a heap of hatboxes.

'Mr Cluny is our locker,' Mr Spiddle told Alfred, 'and first apprised me of the problem after our last

Customs sale. We regularly sell off the goods that we've confiscated, as you probably know, and at such times our warehouse is open to the public. In the circumstances, it's rather difficult to keep out some of the riffraff, and of course the first thing an accomplished thief will try to do is get down into the cellars, where we keep our wine and spirits.' He suddenly turned to address Mr Cluny, who had joined them at the counter. 'Alan, this is Mr Bunce, the Go-Devil man. He has come about our bogle.'

'Ah!' Alan Cluny had thin, sandy hair and grey eyes. He was red-faced and sweaty, and the sleeves of his grubby flannel shirt were rolled up, exposing his thick, sinewy forearms. 'Ye'll be wanting to see it, I expect?'

'*See* it?' Alfred repeated in amazement.

'Aye. We killed it this morning, and havenae disposed of it yet.'

Ned couldn't believe his ears. Nor could he keep silent any longer. '*You* killed it?' he exclaimed.

'I did,' said Mr Cluny. 'With a cutlass and a poker.'

It must have bin sick, thought Ned. *It must have bin!* He opened his mouth to say as much, but Mr Spiddle was already speaking.

'During our last sale, we had a clutch of young thieves make their way down to the cellars. They came screaming straight up again, claiming that one of their party had been eaten by a subterranean beast.' Mr Spiddle pulled a wry face as his restless gaze moved past Alfred, towards a porter with a grandfather clock. 'I wasn't inclined to believe a word of it, until Cluny spotted something unwelcome among the hogsheads.'

'A peat-black boggle,' the locker interjected. 'With blood-red eyes.'

'He reported it to me,' Mr Spiddle continued, 'and I was put in mind of it again when Mr Harewood's memorandum arrived. But then nothing came of my telegram, and the creature was making *such* a nuisance of itself—'

'There are men amongst us who wouldnae go near it,' Mr Cluny cut in, 'though 'twas making its home among the wine-cases and the brandy-pipes.'

'Indeed it was,' Mr Spiddle agreed. 'And being the warehouse keeper, I could not have the efficiency of this place imperilled by vermin. So I allowed Alan to do as he thought fit, and he cornered the wretched thing in the vaults.'

'Which once I would have baulked at, when I thought boggles were something mair than flesh and blood,' the locker confessed, sounding sheepish. But he brightened as he added, 'Now I ken well enough that the Board of Works wouldnae be charged with exterminating demons, or suchlike, but would be concerned only with common beasties. So I set to work with good courage.'

Ned was dumbfounded. Alfred asked suspiciously, 'You're *sure* it were a bogle?'

'Come see for yeerself.' Mr Cluny flung out his arm. 'I'll show ye.'

Within a few minutes, he had guided Ned and Alfred down a flight of stone stairs and into the gloomy basement, which was divided into a series of groin-vaulted bays. Each bay contained wine casks of every size – barrels, hogsheads and butts – all stacked on top of each other. The air was saturated with the smell of spirits, yet beneath it Ned could detect a faint whiff of the river, which lay just beyond the granite wall to the south.

'A sair job I had of it, shifting the thing,' Mr Cluny declared, as he stopped to turn up the gas-lamps. 'Like half a ton of gelatine, it was. But I packed it into a sturdy butt, and was about to dispatch it to the docks with the other condemned goods, to be burnt in the kiln there.' Picking up a long steel prybar, he asked, 'Did I do right, Mr Bunce?'

'Aye. Like enough,' said Alfred in a dazed voice. He then followed Mr Cluny over to a large, upright cask, which the locker proceeded to prise open. Hovering beside Alfred, Ned marvelled at the size of the cask. Surely the bogle hadn't left *that* much of itself behind?

'What do ye think?' Mr Cluny demanded, wrenching off the cask's wooden lid and tossing it aside. 'Is that no a boggle, Mr Bunce?'

Ned craned his neck to peer into the cask, which was full of something that looked like treacle jelly. When Alfred hesitated, Mr Cluny suddenly plunged the hooked end of his prybar into the mess and hauled out a floppy, drooling, distorted body part. Ned spied a gaping hollow lined with teeth . . . a blank, bleary, reddish orb . . . a flap like a giant pig's ear . . .

'That's a bogle,' Alfred confirmed, retreating several steps. And Mr Cluny let the grisly thing drop back into its final resting place.

26

MUDLARKS

'Mr Bunce! Are you still about?' Mr Spiddle's voice came echoing down the stairs. 'I've a bit of news you may want to hear!'

Ned shot a puzzled look at Alfred, who cleared his throat and loudly answered, 'I'll be there directly, Mr Spiddle!'

'Shall I nail this cask shut again, for dispatch to yon kiln?' Mr Cluny wanted to know. 'Or is it best dumped in the river?'

'Burn it, Mr Cluny, if it don't disappear in the meantime.' Alfred tipped his hat and retraced his steps, with Ned drifting along behind him. When they reached the top of the stairs, they found Mr Spiddle waiting impatiently, a sheaf of paper in his hand and a pen tucked behind one ear.

'There's a dead bogle at Fresh Wharf,' he announced.

Alfred blinked. Ned croaked, 'What?'

'I just had it from one of our rummage crew. When I mentioned you were here, he said that a waterman had pointed it out to him.' Mr Spiddle paused, but Alfred was speechless. So the warehouse keeper continued. 'If you want to see it, you'd best hurry. For it's under the pier, and will vanish at the next high tide.'

Alfred took a deep breath. 'Will you – can you . . .?' Though he trailed off, Mr Spiddle seemed to understand that he wanted help.

'Go down to the quay and ask for Donny Donkin. He's the waterman you want to speak to. If he's not about, ask someone else. All those fellows know each other.' As Alfred and Ned glanced at the door through which they had entered the warehouse, Mr Spiddle flapped his hand towards another door, on the south side of the room. 'That's the way to the quay. Try the west stairs. You'll need ferrying, mind – you'll not be able to see a thing on foot.'

Ned frowned. Even a short trip on a wherry-boat would cost them money. But Alfred simply nodded and mumbled his thanks, which Mr Spiddle received with a brisk farewell. Two minutes later, Alfred and Ned were bustling across the wide, stony surface of Custom House Quay, heading towards the west stairs and the forest of masts beyond them.

Though it had stopped raining, dark clouds hung low over the river, mingling with yellowish smoke from hundreds of chimneys. Everything looked grey: the water, the mud, the boats, the buildings – even the fish being unloaded at Billingsgate Market. The only touch of colour that Ned could see was a clutch of red flannel shirts on the crew of a Dutch eel-boat. Among all the vessels packed together so tightly around the docks and wharves, there wasn't a touch of gilding that hadn't tarnished, or a lick of paint that hadn't weathered. Even polished brass looked dull in the drab, wintry light.

Most of the watermen who were waiting for business around the quay wore slate-coloured oilskin coats and sou'westers. As he neared the water, Ned spied a knot of these men at the foot of the west stairs. Some were smoking. Some were chatting to a uniformed customs-house officer. One or two of them glanced up when Alfred appeared at the top of the stairs.

'I'm in search o' Donny Donkin,' said Alfred, raising his voice over the clamour from the nearby market. Below him, every eye swung towards a man sitting in a shallow wherry-boat that had beached itself on the mud.

'I'm Donkin,' the man rasped. He had huge shoulders, grizzled hair, and hands that looked as if they'd been hacked from chunks of walnut. His face was as brown and seamed as a peach pit, but his eyes were a bright, clear blue.

'The name's Bunce,' said Alfred. 'I were given yer name by Mr Spiddle, at the Queen's Warehouse.' When Donkin didn't so much as grunt in response, the bogler added, 'He told me you saw a dead bogle by Fresh Wharf.'

The customs-house officer snorted. 'Dead bogle!' he scoffed. 'Aye, and that tangle o' fishing nets out by the bridge is a sea monster, I daresay.'

But Donkin ignored him. 'You want to see it?' the waterman asked Alfred, who gave a nod. 'It'll cost you sixpence. And a penny more for the lad.'

Sixpence was an extortionate fee for two dozen strokes of the oar. Seeing the smirks of the other watermen, Ned opened his mouth to protest.

Alfred, however, cut him off. 'Tuppence,' said Alfred. '*With* the lad. Or I'll find someone else as can do it for less.'

'Paid in advance,' Donkin countered. Then he rose from his seat as Alfred began to descend the stairs.

Ned followed, taking care where he put his feet. The stairs were damp and slimy, and strewn with people who hardly bothered to step aside as he passed. Some of them snickered when Alfred nearly fell while stepping into Donkin's boat; his sack would have dropped into the mud if Ned hadn't caught it in time. Luckily, the bogler managed to right himself without losing more than his balance.

'Boy in the bow; you in the stern,' growled Donkin. But even after Alfred and Ned had settled themselves, the waterman wouldn't cast off until he had received his twopenny bit – which he inspected carefully, then tucked into his waistcoat pocket. 'If you want a piece o' that there crayture at Fresh Wharf, you'll have a fight on yer hands,' he said, as he grabbed his oars. 'For there's a crowd gathering already, and them mudlarks'd sell a dead man's skull if it washed up on the tide.'

Ned flushed, but didn't say anything. He knew that Thames watermen viewed mudlarks as dirty, greedy, thieving pests. He'd suffered enough abuse himself in the past, though he'd done nothing to deserve it. The smell of the river stirred up bitter memories for Ned;

he found himself wondering if he was about to see anyone he knew at Fresh Wharf, and what he would say if he did.

'Ned!' Alfred hailed him from the back of the boat. 'Watch the water.'

'The water . . .?' Ned echoed in confusion.

'Lest there's bogles about.'

'Oh.' Ned's heart skipped a beat. He peered overboard, but realised at once that, even if the river *was* full of bogles – dead or alive – he didn't have a hope of seeing them. For one thing, the water was filthy, full of floating debris and as cloudy as pease porridge. For another, very little of the river was visible between the keels of all the boats clustered about the wharves. Ned could almost have *walked* to Billingsgate Market, using boats as stepping stones – except, of course, that some of the vessels were quite large, with towering masts and high bulwarks. It was amazing to see how Donny Donkin threaded his way between them, darting around like a fish in his little wherry.

'Tide's on the rise,' he remarked. He had pulled away from the market towards Fresh Wharf, which reared up out of the water on rickety wooden stilts. But soon, through a thicket of masts and pilings, Ned was able to make out dark figures on a mud slope beneath the wharf.

'Be quick, for I'll not stay long,' Donkin warned. His vessel glided between two brigantine hulls, then gradually slowed until it passed under the wharf and bumped gently against solid ground. By this time he had already raised his oars. 'Why, there's Mizzle Meg!' he exclaimed, upon craning around to check the scene behind him. '*Meg! What's yer game? That ain't no eel, you nickey old dollymop!*'

Ned assumed that he was addressing the only woman in sight, who stood hunched over something that looked, from a distance, like a bloated pony's corpse. She was ragged and middle-aged, with a face that could have been made out of melted yellow candle wax, and a straw pad tied on top of her crushed calico bonnet.

Around her were half-a-dozen grimy boys, ranging in age from about eight to fourteen. Ned didn't recognise any of them.

'Where's yer basket, Meg?' Donkin continued. 'Ain't you going to load it up? That thing'll taste no worse'n the eels you normally sell, I'll be bound.'

The woman didn't answer. Instead she glared at Donkin and waddled away.

'Mute,' the waterman said to Alfred, by way of an explanation. 'No one knows why. Someone cut out her tongue, I expect, on account o' she were a scold.'

Alfred, however, wasn't listening. Having climbed out of the boat, he'd begun to stagger through a dense, oily mud that sucked at his boots like glue. Ned would have liked to remove his own boots, but realised that it would be too risky because of all the jagged spars and mussel shells that were probably buried just below the surface. So he vaulted over the side of the boat, only to end up ankle-deep in sludge.

'It's a boggart, sir!' one of the younger boys informed Alfred. 'And *I* found it!'

'You don't know it's a boggart,' the eldest boy cut in. He was rake-thin and pallid, with lots of shaggy red hair. 'You ain't never seen no boggart before.'

'But what else could it be?' a third boy interposed. 'T'ain't no pig. T'ain't no horse, neither.'

'Could be summat as dropped off one o' them foreign ships,' the redhead speculated. 'A seal or a hippomouse, or some such thing . . .'

'It's a bogle,' said Alfred. He had already reached the mysterious shape, and was bending over it. When Ned finally joined him, the bogler straightened up and murmured, 'I ain't seen nowt like this. Not in all me years on the job.'

Ned studied the bogle. It was covered in a sodden mat of jet-black bristles or thorns, which had bits of thread and peel caught in them. Two barbed grey horns sprouted from its head. Its snout gaped open, displaying a limp forked tongue and three rows of razor-sharp fangs. One fixed yellow eye sent a shiver down Ned's spine.

'It's a bogle,' he confirmed hoarsely.

'How do *you* know?' the redhead demanded. His tone was abrupt – almost rude – but Ned didn't take offence. The boy was so thin and dirty and ragged that Ned could hardly bear to look at him.

It was like looking at what might have been . . .

'I'm a bogler's boy,' Ned declared, more boldly and gratefully than he ever had before. 'And Mr Bunce is a bogler.'

To Ned's surprise, the reaction was one of muted disappointment. 'You mean you're going to take this here thing away?' the youngest boy asked Alfred, who shook his head.

'Nay,' replied the bogler, frowning. Then he turned to his apprentice. 'I seen enough,' he rasped. 'Let's go.'

Ned was startled. 'What about Mr Gilfoyle? Won't *he* want a piece?'

'Ain't no time for that. The tide's coming in.' Alfred began to retrace his steps, lurching and stumbling towards Donny Donkin's boat through water that had already risen a good six inches. Ned set off after him, moving more nimbly, thanks to years of practice.

'Real bogle teeth!' a voice piped up behind them. It was the youngest boy speaking; Ned recognised his high-pitched squeak. 'I'll wager they'd fetch a pretty penny – eh, Barnabas?'

'Don't you touch them teeth!' Alfred stopped abruptly, his hand on the wherry's bowsprit, his head snapping around. 'There's poison on a bogle's teeth, and worse besides! You leave that creature alone and get along now, afore you all perish.'

'Won't be no great loss if they do,' Donkin rumbled. He spat into the river, then steadied his boat as Alfred clumsily boarded it. He didn't, however, extend the same courtesy to Ned, who only reached the vessel when it was already afloat, and had to throw himself into it before it glided away from the shore.

Once Ned had finished flopping around like a landed fish, and was sitting upright in the bow again, he craned his neck to see if the mudlarks had scrambled out from beneath Fresh Wharf. But it was too late. His view was already obscured by distance, by shadow, and by the waterman's bulky silhouette.

'What's happening, Mr Bunce?' Ned couldn't keep silent any longer. Bogles were dying like flies. They were being killed by untrained men with household tools. It made no sense. There *had* to be an explanation. 'Is some sort o' poison weakening them creatures?' he asked Alfred, who was staring off into the distance.

'I don't know, lad,' Alfred replied. 'Mebbe it's poison. Mebbe it ain't.'

'If bogles keep dying like this – if people keep killing 'em with pokers—'

'Then there won't be no need for a committee,' Alfred finished. 'Nor for a bogler like me.'

He then lapsed into a thoughtful silence, and stayed silent until long after their boat had arrived back at the Custom House Quay.

27

THE HIDDEN LABORATORY

'There's plenty o' poisons dumped in the sewers by tanners and fullers and the like,' Ned observed. 'And new poisons must be devised every day, what with all the factories opening up across London.'

'Aye,' said Alfred. 'That's true.'

'But I don't know how one load o' poison could sicken the bogles in Billingsgate *and* Clerkenwell.' Ned was thinking hard as he trudged along Lower Thames Street. 'It can't be the same sewer as passes under both. Unless the poison is in the river, and the bogles come from there?'

Alfred didn't answer. He was too busy navigating his way towards the Monument, which lay quite close to Billingsgate Market. From Lower Thames Street he turned right into Pudding Lane, through a district of rotting warehouses, dilapidated churches, and sooty, dismal little churchyards. Ned spotted a few handsome structures here and there – including two that might have been guild or company halls, judging from the coats-of-arms set over their front doors – but for the most part the streets were lined with ugly office buildings or dank, ancient, half-timbered inns converted into shops or cheap lodging houses.

'If it ain't poison, it might be magic,' Ned suddenly remarked, wondering if Birdie had been right after all. 'Mebbe it's a curse, or a spell.' He shot a doubtful glance at Alfred. 'That Morton feller's still in gaol, ain't he?'

It had occurred to Ned that someone, somewhere, might be using magic against London's bogle population. And there could be no likelier candidate than the wicked Doctor Roswell Morton, who fancied himself as a necromancer, and who had once fed several young boys to a bogle in order to gain power over it. But why would he want to destroy the city's bogles?

'Aye, Morton's still in gaol,' said Alfred. 'He ain't going nowhere.'

'So he couldn't be laying spells, then.' Ned frowned. 'You don't suppose it might be Mother May?'

'I don't suppose nowt,' Alfred replied shortly, 'and neither should you. We ain't sure if every bogle is affected, and won't for a good while yet. Not until we visit all the people as wants to see us.'

'But what if they *don't* want to see us no more? What if they don't need to?'

'Stop fretting on it, lad, for you'll get nowhere.' Alfred refused to discuss the subject any further. It was impossible to tell how he felt about this unexpected threat to his livelihood. Ned didn't know how he felt about it himself; on the one hand, it was frightening news, because it meant that Alfred might be reduced to killing rats, or making flypaper. It also meant that Ned would have to find work as a mudlark or a coster's boy again. And none of those jobs would pay well – certainly not as well as bogling did.

But mixed with Ned's fear and anxiety was a growing sense of relief. If all the bogles died, he would never have to face another one. He would no longer have to be a bogler's boy. And it wouldn't be because he had quit his job; it would be for a perfectly justifiable reason. How could Alfred be disappointed in him for abandoning work that didn't exist anymore?

'If all the bogles die, no more kids will be eaten,' Ned blurted out. 'That'll be a wonderful thing. Won't it, Mr Bunce?'

'Aye,' said Alfred. 'A thing I never expected to see.'

All at once he turned left, into a narrow alley that widened into a spacious square. The square was ringed by fine, big, ornate buildings, and at its centre was the Monument, like a giant grey candle with a gold flame on top. The towering stone column stood at least two hundred feet high, on a square plinth as big as a watch-house. Ned was aware that it had been built by someone called Christopher Wren, to commemorate something called the Great Fire of London, because Mr Harewood had told him so. But he knew nothing else about it, and had never actually been close to it before – though he *had* caught glimpses of its fiery crest, rearing above the rooftops.

'Mr Harewood told me to speak to the guard,' said Alfred, peering across the cobbled expanse that surrounded the Monument. Sure enough, a door had been punched through the base of the column's pedestal, and a man sat by this door, smoking a pipe. As Ned drew closer, he saw that this man wore brass buttons on his fraying blue coat, and a stiff cap rather like a telegraph boy's – beneath which his warty, weathered face was set in lines of blank boredom and resentment.

'It's threepence a body to get in,' the man drawled, before Alfred had even opened his mouth.

'Not for me, it ain't,' Alfred replied. 'I'm here on a job. Bunce is the name. Alfred Bunce. You sent for me.'

'*I* did?'

'You got a bogle,' said Alfred, causing the guard to straighten so abruptly that he nearly fell off his chair.

'Oh – ah – yes!' Recovering himself, the guard jumped to his feet, his face reddening. He looked quite shocked, Ned thought, and not at all pleased to see Alfred. 'So you're the bogler, then?'

'I am.' Alfred produced a crumpled sheet of paper from his pocket. 'You sent this telegram to the Sewers Office, asking for help. Well, I'm yer help.'

Watching the guard take the telegram and stare at it dumbly, Ned began to doubt that it *had* been sent by such a seedy-looking fellow. And his suspicions were confirmed when the guard said, 'This telegram weren't down to me, though it were me as told Clarkson about the bogle. I expect he sent you this.'

'Clarkson?' Alfred echoed, frowning.

'At the Guildhall. He's the one as banks the fees.'

Squinting up at the mighty edifice that loomed over them, the guard added, 'I can't let you in just yet. There's a lady and a gentleman still up at the top, and we cannot have *them* eaten by a bogle.'

'Bogles don't eat ladies and gentlemen,' Alfred pointed out, eyeing the guard in a speculative manner. Ned wondered fleetingly if it were still true that bogles didn't eat adults. The city's bogles had been behaving so oddly over recent weeks, he wouldn't have been surprised to learn that the bogle in the Monument had started attacking every human being in sight.

'How do you know it's there?' Alfred inquired of the guard. 'This bogle. Did you have a child go in and never come out?'

'I seen it,' the guard replied. 'It's in the cellar.'

Suddenly Ned remembered something else that Mr Harewood had told him. There was a basement laboratory under the Monument – and this, Ned assumed, must be where the bogle was hiding.

'I don't normally go down the cellar, save to fetch a mop or a bucket,' the guard continued, his gaze skipping around the square as if in search of potential sightseers. 'But the other day I heard a strange growling noise, and when I lifted the grate, I spotted the bogle.'

Alfred regarded him intently for a moment, then said, 'You're sure it were a bogle?'

'Ain't no mistaking a bogle, Mr Bunce.' The guard began to wave his pipe around, his voice rising dramatically. 'It had huge great claws, and great big teeth, and it roared like a lion!'

Ned caught Alfred's eye. It was unlikely that the bogle had roared, since the creatures tended to be rather quiet until you stuck a spear into them. But Ned had already decided that the guard was either imagining things or embroidering the facts. And Alfred must have thought the same thing, because he remarked drily, ''Tis strange behaviour for a bogle, Mr . . . uh . . .'

'Copperthwaite,' the guard supplied. Then the click of a latch made him turn his head. 'Ah! Here's the other visitors come down again.'

At that very instant the Monument door swung open, and two people emerged. One was a man with luxuriant dark whiskers, who wore a tall hat and carried a cane. The other was a lady dressed in the very latest fashion, with a huge bustle and lots of feathers in her bonnet.

Both were damp and red and puffing like bellows.

'I must sit down!' the lady whined, leaning on her companion's arm.

'I'll take you to a tea-shop,' the gentleman promised, before fixing his angry gaze on Copperthwaite. 'Those stairs are a deal too much for a well-bred young woman!'

'Three hundred and forty-five of 'em, sir,' was the guard's jovial response. 'I told you they'd be a challenge.' As the couple moved away, he said to Alfred in a sly undertone, 'It's worth twice the money to stop down here, but folk will never be warned. Oh no!'

'You'd best show us the basement,' said Alfred, 'afore someone else comes along.'

'You can't miss it. It's under a grate in the middle of the floor.' Without warning, Copperthwaite abruptly sat down again. 'I'll stay and guard the entrance. You'll not need *me* in there.'

Ned decided that Copperthwaite must be telling the truth after all; why else would he be scared to step inside? Alfred sniffed, but didn't comment. Instead he jerked his chin at Ned and advanced towards the Monument's shadowy little door, which looked so much like the door to a tomb that Ned found it quite unnerving.

But he summoned up the courage to follow Alfred into the darkness, only to discover that the

Monument's interior wasn't so dark after all. The endless shaft above them was lit by a series of windows set into deep alcoves, which were placed at regular intervals up the circular staircase. This staircase was made of black limestone, and was coiled around a gap that reached all the way from the ground floor to the column's highest point – which Ned couldn't even see, from where he was standing.

He remembered Mr Harewood's words: '*By opening a trapdoor in the gilded orb at the top of the tower, you can watch the night sky from a laboratory in the basement.*' This gap, then, was obviously part of the 'giant zenith telescope' that Mr Harewood had mentioned. And if the trapdoor in the orb was directly above Ned, then the entrance to the basement had to be . . .

'Down there,' said Alfred. 'Under yer feet.' As Ned quickly stepped aside, Alfred let his sack drop to the stone floor. Only after he had retrieved his spear did the bogler stoop to shift the circular manhole cover in front of him. 'Stand back, now,' he warned his apprentice. 'We don't know what's down there.'

Ned swallowed. Though he couldn't actually *feel* the presence of a bogle, he knew quite well that this meant nothing – not anymore. Edging towards the doorway, he kept his eyes fixed on Alfred, who was dragging aside the heavy iron cover.

Clan-ng-g! The cover hit the floor, exposing a round, black hole just big enough for a man to squeeze through. Ned was craning his neck to peer into it when the Monument door swung shut behind him.

'Tell Copperthwaite to open that up again, will you?' Alfred was squatting by the hole, studying it intently. 'Tell him we need an escape route.'

The words were hardly out of his mouth when Ned heard the clink of a key turning in a lock. '*Mr Copperthwaite?*' he cried. '*We need that door open, sir!*'

But no one answered. And as Ned spun around to hammer on the iron-studded door panels, he was nearly deafened by a huge explosion.

BO-O-OM!

Someone had fired a shot inside the Monument.

28

THE VIEW FROM THE TOP

'*Ned! Run!*' yelled Alfred.

He had fallen back onto the floor, and was groping for the spear he'd just dropped. In front of him, someone large and dirty had reared up through the open hole – someone with a shining bald head, bushy black side-whiskers, and a huge moustache.

When Ned saw the smoking pepperbox revolver clasped in this stranger's hand, he screamed, '*Open the door! Please! Mr Copperthwaite!*'

The door didn't open. But Ned's raised voice distracted the hulking intruder, whose pale eyes swung towards him. At the same instant, Alfred's fingers closed around the shaft of his spear. And as the intruder aimed his revolver at Ned – who stood frozen with shock – Alfred suddenly lunged forward, thrusting his spear into the gunman's arm.

The gunman roared. He fired wide and his pistol-ball ricocheted off one wall, spraying tiny chips of stone. Ned ducked and ran. There was nowhere to go but up, so he made for the circular staircase, screaming for help. Then another shot rang out.

BOOM!

'Mr Bunce!' Ned cried, glancing over his shoulder. But Alfred, he saw, was already behind him, still clutching the bloody spear.

'*Run! RUN!*' Alfred shouted.

Ned obeyed. He pounded up the stairs, frantic with terror, expecting a ball in his back at any instant. He could hear Alfred gasping for breath.

'*Ain't no way out!*' a cracked voice called after them. '*And I got one more shot in this here pepperbox!*'

'Keep going,' Alfred wheezed to Ned. 'Don't stop.'

Ned had no intention of stopping. As he passed one of the alcoves, he briefly wondered if it would provide any cover, then decided it wouldn't.

'*I'll shoot you first, Bunce!*' the man continued roughly. '*And then I'll throw that boy off the top o' the tower!*'

Ned couldn't suppress a frightened moan. He heard Alfred pause just a few steps behind him.

'You can't do that, Gammon!' the bogler rejoined, panting heavily. 'Ain't *no one* can jump off the gallery no more – not since they shut it up in a cage!' To Ned he whispered, 'Go! *Go!*', because Ned had stopped and turned at the sound of the word 'Gammon'.

'Then I'll just have to chop him into pieces, and throw the pieces through the bars!' John Gammon bawled. He was mounting the stairs at a clumsy canter, stumbling occasionally, his feet dragging. Ned wondered how badly hurt the man was. Would he bleed to death before he could reach the top? Suddenly Ned caught a glimpse of Gammon's dark head, bobbing into view against the curving wall opposite, and saw that the butcher would soon have a clear shot at Alfred – since there was no stone core in the middle of the winding staircase.

'Go, boy – *run!*' Alfred bellowed. And Ned ran as Gammon laughed.

'You can't escape! Ain't nowhere to go!' the butcher taunted. *'You're trapped in here like rats in a barrel!'*

'You got the . . . wrong boy . . . Gammon.' Alfred's lungs were labouring so hard that he could barely speak as he staggered after Ned. 'This here . . . ain't

Jem Barbary. You'll do . . . yerself no good . . . killing *him*.'

'T'ain't the boy I want, it's *you*. You've crossed me once too often.' Before Alfred could reply, Gammon continued doggedly, in a harsh tone, 'Oh, I devised all this to catch the boy. *That* I'll own to. I put a nobbler o' my acquaintance down here to cut yer throats, and sent the telegram meself to summon you. For Copperthwaite is an old mate – the Monument being so close to the Butcher's Hall – and he's bin useful when I've had things worth concealing. No one ever thinks to look under the Monument.'

The Butcher's Hall, Ned thought in despair, as he heaved himself up the staircase. He remembered several nearby buildings with coats-of-arms above their doors, and for the hundredth time cursed the fact that he couldn't read. For if he'd passed the words 'Butcher's Hall' on his way to the Monument, it would have put him on his guard, at the very least.

' . . . but I had to change me plans,' John Gammon was saying. Though breathless, he didn't sound weak. And his footsteps didn't seem to be slowing down. 'I heard what you done to Fitch, this morning.' As Alfred choked on an indrawn breath, the butcher snarled, 'Oh, yes. You think I ain't got spies at Smithfield station house? I skipped out o' Cock Lane just ahead o' them coppers as came to nib me, and took my nobbler friend's place.'

By this time Alfred was lagging so far behind that Ned had to run back and tug at the bogler's sleeve. 'Come *on*, Mr Bunce!' he whispered. 'I got an idea, but you have to hurry!'

'Ain't no one else knows I'm here, save Copperthwaite, and he ain't going to blab. So I can't be letting *you* out to peach on me, can I?' The butcher seemed almost to be thinking aloud as he stamped up the stairs. 'I'll hide you both in the basement, then go out tonight and arrange a berth on one o' them eel-boats. Eelers is no strangers to smuggling – I know *that* well enough. And they'll not baulk at dropping remains overboard, providing the remains is a manageable size . . .'

'Ssst! Mr Bunce!' hissed Ned, who had finally reached the open door that led to the caged viewing gallery. It was a solid door with a hefty lock, but Ned didn't have a key. And there was no way of bolting it from the outside.

If we lean against it to keep it closed, he'll just shoot straight through it, Ned decided. Then he glanced down at Alfred, who was still catching up. The bogler was bent double, pouring sweat and coughing like a consumptive.

Catching his eye, Ned pointed at the ladder set into the wall some distance above them both. This ladder started where the stairs stopped, and Ned knew exactly where it led: straight to the trapdoor in the golden orb.

Alfred nodded as Ned closed the gallery door with a *bang*.

'*Ain't no good shutting that door, Bunce! It won't keep me out!*' John Gammon yelled. '*I got a filleting knife in me pocket and one shot left in this here revolver! If you had any sense, you'd let me put a ball through yer head, nice and clean – for if I wing you, you'll not like what follows!*'

By this time Alfred had heaved his apprentice up onto the ladder. Ned immediately began to climb through the narrow shaft that led to the very top of the Monument, pursued by the sound of Alfred coughing and John Gammon shouting, '*Think you hurt me, Bunce? Think again! I've had worse wounds cutting sides o' pork in the shop!*'

Suddenly Ned's hand struck something metallic. It was the lid of the flaming orb, and it wasn't locked or bolted down. He gave it a mighty shove, then pulled himself through the hole he'd exposed.

Almost immediately, he was hit by a blast of wind that almost took his breath away. For an instant he froze, feeling dizzy and terrified; beyond the golden spikes that ringed him like a crown of thorns he could see nothing but grey clouds and wheeling pigeons. But then he felt something nudging his feet, and quickly swung them up until he was crouched amid the gilded flames – which were twisted strips of metal, too thick to be razor-sharp.

Grabbing the spear that Alfred was passing up through the trapdoor, he set it aside carefully, placing it so that it wouldn't fall. Then he reached down and grabbed Alfred's arm, helping the bogler to scramble up into the whistling wind.

One glimpse of the cloud-capped steeples surrounding them made Alfred's face turn white as he edged away from the hole, allowing Ned to seal it again. The gilded flames gave them both something to cling to – and also provided excellent footholds – but Ned's natural instinct was to freeze like a cat stuck in a tree. He had to fight that instinct when he craned his neck for a better look at the structure below him.

He saw at once that the cage around the viewing platform was a long, long way away. Even further away was the ground beyond it. The people down there looked like ants, and the buildings like toys. Ned's original plan had been to climb down from the orb and spear John Gammon through the bars of the cage, as the butcher emerged onto the viewing platform. But Ned had miscalculated. Even Jem would have found it impossible to descend the Monument's crest without a rope; though the golden urn beneath the orb was furnished with many footholds, the grey dome beneath *that* was just a smooth, stone curve, damp and slippery.

Ned wondered if anyone on the ground would hear his voice if he shouted for help. Probably not, he thought. Not with the wind blowing so hard.

Then he caught sight of John Gammon's shiny scalp, moving anti-clockwise around the viewing platform. And he jerked his own head back.

Any moment now, the butcher was going to work out where Ned and Alfred were hiding.

'Sit on that!' Ned mouthed at Alfred, pointing at the lid. Only their weight would block Gammon from joining them. But Alfred shook his head. He retrieved his spear and carefully shifted position, his face taut, his eyes bulging. Soon he was poised to strike at whatever came erupting out of the orb.

Ned could only pray that Alfred's spear would hit the butcher before the butcher had a chance to fire.

Bang! Clang! Thump! All at once Ned felt the orb vibrating beneath him. He was convinced that Gammon must have gone back inside and spotted the ladder. But that ladder would be impossible to climb one-handed. Gammon would have to clamp his pistol between his teeth, or stick it in his belt.

Perhaps Alfred should try to spear him *before* he reached the top?

Clang! Thud! There was definitely someone in the shaft beneath them. Ned motioned to Alfred – a flipping motion, followed by a jabbing one. 'Now!' he was trying to say. 'Do it now!' But he couldn't speak because he didn't want the butcher to hear him.

Alfred licked his lips. He'd lost his hat somewhere, and his thick, greying hair was whipping about furiously in the cold wind. His coat was flapping like a flag on a ship's mast. His dark eyes in his white face looked like coals in the snow.

Ned had never seen Alfred frightened before, but the bogler was frightened now – so frightened that he didn't appear to have grasped the message that Ned was trying to convey: namely, that the broad-shouldered butcher would be at a disadvantage in such a narrow shaft, with his revolver clenched between his teeth and his eyes briefly dazzled by the unaccustomed light. Ned was explaining all this with hand-movements when he suddenly heard a muffled scream.

'*A-A-A-AGH . . . !*'

The orb stopped shaking. Silence fell. Even the wind dropped for a moment, as Ned and Alfred stared at each other. They waited and waited.

Finally Alfred croaked, 'Did he fall?'

'I dunno.' As Alfred stretched his hand towards the lid, Ned added, 'It might be a trick. He might be *pretending* he fell.'

Alfred froze, and seemed to be lost in thought. But after a while he came to a decision. First he adjusted his grip on his spear. Then he indicated, with a complicated gesture, that he wanted Ned to remove the lid at top speed. Ned saw at once what Alfred was planning to do. He was planning to catch Gammon by surprise, throwing the spear down the shaft before the butcher could fire his gun.

It was their only option, now.

Alfred held up three fingers. 'On the count o' three,' he mouthed. 'One. Two . . . *three!*'

Ned flung back the lid. Alfred hurled his spear. But no explosion of gunpowder followed. There wasn't even a roar of pain. All Ned could hear was the sound of the spear clinking against hard surfaces as it tumbled down the core of the Monument.

Once again, Ned and Alfred gazed at each other. It was several seconds before they slowly, reluctantly, peered down the shaft. Ned saw that one corner of the iron ladder had pulled away from the wall. He also saw a coil of stairs receding into the distance below him, making a perfect spiral pattern. But in the very centre of this spiral was a black dot.

And in the centre of the dot was a spreadeagled shape, white and blue against the dark limestone.

29

BIRDIE'S DEBUT

'I say!' Mr Harewood exclaimed. 'Where have you *been*? The overture's just begun – we shan't be allowed to go in if we don't hurry!'

He was standing in the vestibule of the Theatre Royal, which was almost deserted. Dazzled by all the gilt-framed mirrors and polished marble, Ned hadn't spotted him at first.

'I've your tickets with me,' the engineer continued, eyeing Alfred's stained and shabby clothes. Mr Harewood himself looked resplendent in a black tailcoat, white tie and white gloves. His hair was slicked back and his bruises were barely visible in the flattering glow of the chandeliers. 'You should have joined us in Bloomsbury before coming here, Mr Bunce,' he said, hustling Ned and Alfred into yet another vestibule, which was two storeys high, with a domed roof. 'Gilfoyle brought his spare evening clothes for you to wear. And Miss Eames was very anxious when you didn't arrive . . .'

'We was delayed.' Alfred spoke gruffly. After hours and hours spent in the station house on Bishopsgate Street, he and Ned had been allowed to leave only after the police officers there had communicated with their colleagues at Smithfield. Thanks to Sergeant Pike's efforts, the Bishopsgate police had at last been persuaded that Alfred's story was true – that he *hadn't* murdered John Gammon. But still the bogler and his apprentice had been kept in a small room, making sworn statements and answering questions, until long after sunset.

Upon finally being released, Ned and Alfred had found themselves with only half an hour to spare. So they had rushed back to Orange Court, dropped off Alfred's bogling sack, washed their faces at breakneck speed, and hurried to the Theatre Royal without exchanging more than a few rushed comments about practical things like cab fares.

As a result, Ned didn't really know how Alfred

was feeling. He himself was at the end of his tether. Being chased to the top of the Monument had been bad enough, but what followed had been even worse. Ned would never forget the horror of banging on the Monument door, shouting for help, with John Gammon's shattered body lying at his feet. Though a passer-by had finally heard Ned's pleas, and had gone to fetch a policeman, there had been a delay of at least an hour between the moment Ned had reached the ground floor and the moment when the policeman, after searching in vain for Mr Copperthwaite, had finally broken down the door.

And there had been other horrors as well. The horror of being accused of murder, for instance. The horror of seeing Alfred's spear destroyed. The horror of knowing, as he sat in the station house, that he – Ned Roach, one of Birdie McAdam's best friends – was probably going to miss her debut performance.

But he *hadn't* missed Birdie's performance. He and Alfred had made it just in time. And as they followed Mr Harewood up the stairs to the Grand Circle, Ned decided that he was going to concentrate on Birdie's performance, and not let anything else distract him from it. He wasn't going to dwell on the bloody scene at the Monument, or the loss of

Alfred's livelihood, or the fact that he himself looked completely out of place in the luxurious theatre, with his damp, dirty jacket and scuffed boots.

This was Birdie's evening, and he wasn't about to spoil it for her. Neither was Alfred. 'We'll tell no one about this. Not tonight,' he'd informed Ned, on their way to Drury Lane. 'Tomorrow we'll pass on the news, but I ain't about to discuss John Gammon in a box at the theatre.'

'We'll be sitting in a box?' Ned had asked dully.

'Aye. Miss Eames arranged it so. Ten shillings and sixpence, she paid. And wouldn't take nowt from me.'

It was the lowest box on the right-hand side of the stage. When Ned followed Mr Harewood over the threshold, he found himself in something rather like a jewellery box, encased in gilt and lined with velvet. Glittering in the centre of all the plush and gold fringe was Miss Eames, who turned sharply at Mr Harewood's entrance. She was wearing a gown of glossy grey satin, trimmed with crystal beads. There were feathers in her hair and diamonds in her ears.

She looked magnificent.

'Mr Bunce!' she hissed, glaring at the bogler. 'Where on earth have you *been*?'

'I'm sorry, Miss,' Alfred mumbled. 'We was delayed.'

'Hush, dear – don't make a scene,' Mrs Heppinstall said. She was sitting by her niece, wrapped in a dark fur. On Miss Eames's other side was Mr Gilfoyle, beautifully groomed in his black-and-white evening clothes. Mr Wardle was nowhere to be seen, but since there were only three vacant seats left, Ned assumed that the Inspector of Sewers had decided not to come after all.

'What happened at the Custom House, Mr Bunce?' Mr Gilfoyle asked in an undertone. But before Alfred could reply, Miss Eames said, 'Shh!', and the overture concluded in a burst of applause.

Then the curtain rose – and Ned was transported into fairyland.

He had never been to a theatre. He'd never even been to a penny gaff. So he was completely unprepared for the dazzling world that unfolded before him: the bright landscapes, the billowing seas, the gleaming battlements and coloured lights, the music, the trumpets, the clouds, the animals. He forgot all about flash-boxes and smoke-pots; he barely remembered that King Arthur was Frederick Vokes, or noticed that Jem was dancing in the ballet corps, small and nimble in a page's costume. Instead, swept up in the action, Ned let all thoughts of the *real* Theatre Royal vanish from his mind – along with everything that had happened to him that day.

When a giant's head appeared over the castle wall, Ned gasped. When the giant ate Tom Thumb, Ned squeaked. He clapped when Tom Thumb jumped out of the giant's mouth, then cheered when a huge bird seized Tom in its mighty talons. Like everyone else in the audience, Ned marvelled at Rosina's dancing. He laughed at the antics of a pantomime horse – the same horse he'd once seen shuffling along a backstage corridor. He applauded the singing of one young actor who, according to Mr Harewood, was 'straight out of the music hall'.

But when Birdie sang, Ned couldn't help crying. Perhaps his terrible day had left him feeling vulnerable. Perhaps he cried because at least two of the songs she sang were sad ones, all about motherless children and cold winter snows. Or perhaps he was moved because she looked so beautiful, standing there in a cloud of white gauze, with her hair gleaming and her eyes flashing and her astonishing voice ringing out like church bells.

Hearing the storm of applause that greeted every

one of her songs, Ned thought to himself, *She'll be going to places where I can't follow. There'll be no more bogling for Birdie.* Then he remembered that there would be no more bogling for *him*, either. Not unless Alfred could replace his broken spear.

Not if the bogles kept dropping dead all over London.

During the interval, he stayed in his seat, ashamed of his red eyes and shabby clothes. Alfred also remained seated. It was Mr Harewood who went to fetch ice cream, and Mr Gilfoyle who briefly escorted the ladies out to 'take the air'. For several minutes Alfred and Ned were left alone together. But Alfred would talk only of Birdie, and Ned decided to follow his lead.

When the others returned, the lights were already dimming again. Mr Gilfoyle, however, managed to ask what had happened at the Custom House.

'We wasn't needed,' Alfred replied shortly. 'On account o' the bogle were dead already.'

'Indeed?' said Mr Gilfoyle. 'How very odd.'

'Aye. 'Twere odd, right enough. For the coves working there killed it.' Hearing Mr Gilfoyle gasp, Alfred quickly added, 'With a poker. And a cutlass.'

'But surely that isn't possible, Mr Bunce?' Miss Eames protested. 'Surely those men must be lying?'

Alfred shrugged. 'There's a deal o' sickly bogles about. We saw one dead under Fresh Wharf. The bogle at the Custom House might have bin ailing.'

'And the Monument job?' asked Mr Harewood. 'Did you have time for that?'

Alfred and Ned avoided each other's eyes as Alfred took a deep breath. 'We didn't find no bogle at the Monument,' the bogler muttered. And that was all he said, to Ned's relief – for the curtain was rising.

Although the second half of the pantomime was even more magnificent than the first, Ned was distracted by troublesome thoughts. He couldn't seem to concentrate on Tom Thumb's adventures. It was only towards the end of the performance that he once again found himself caught up in the spectacle, as showers of sparkling fairy-dust descended on King Arthur's court. Birdie sang her last song during the grand finale; as a fairy princess, she bestowed her blessings on the whole cast with a wand that jingled like bells whenever its starry tip touched anything. The scene ended with a rousing chorus, two booming silver cannons that disgorged more fairy-dust, and a lot of well-timed acrobatics from the ballet corps. Jem did several backflips across the stage. Frederick Vokes kicked his legs straight up over his own head. Rosina floated through the air on a wire, like thistledown.

Then, as the cast members were taking their bows, Frederick made an unexpected announcement.

As the king of England, he declared, he felt justified in saluting the newest member of their troupe: Birdie McAdam, the Go-Devil girl. 'The voice that once lured monsters from their lairs is now luring the public into our noble auditorium!' he exclaimed. 'And *I* can take the credit for that, ladies and gentlemen! For when I first saw Birdie confronting a bogle, I thought to myself: this child deserves a far bigger audience than a monster in a basement! And now she has one, does she not? She has an audience that truly *appreciates* her extraordinary talent!'

His voice was drowned out by an enthusiastic roar, as the costumed performers around Birdie began to clap and grin. Up in her box, Miss Eames cried, '*Bravo!*', and soon others were following her example. Glancing sideways, Ned saw that Alfred was wiping his nose on the back of his sleeve, his face hidden from view.

When the applause finally died down, Birdie began to speak. She had been smiling and blushing, and executing graceful little curtseys. But all at once her smile vanished. With her head held high, and her clear voice pitched even higher, she declared, 'Thank you, yer majesty. I am so very grateful to you and yer court!' There was another burst of clapping and cheering, as Birdie waved her wand at the cast gathered behind her. 'However, we all of us owe an even *bigger* debt of gratitude to someone else,' she continued. 'To someone who's bin working away, killing the monsters as lurk beneath this city, without expecting no reward nor recognition.' In the sudden hush that fell over the theatre, Birdie's silvery tones became slightly strained. 'The truth is, I never faced down no bogles,' she finished, a little unsteadily. 'The man who did *that* was Mr Alfred Bunce. And I want to thank him for everything . . . for everything he's done.'

Her voice cracked on a sob, allowing Frederick Vokes to take over. 'Yes, indeed, ladies and gentlemen!' he cried. 'You must all have read about Mr Alfred Bunce, the famous bogler, whose name has adorned many of our most respected newspapers in recent days! Well, last Monday, Mr Bunce destroyed a bogle in the bowels of this very theatre! And what's more, he is *in the audience tonight!*' As a wild cheer erupted, the actor swivelled around to face Miss Eames's box. 'Stand up, Mr Bunce – do! Allow the people of London to express their heartfelt gratitude for the work you've done in saving so many precious young lives!'

Ned began to clap furiously. Miss Eames and Mr Gilfoyle had already turned in their seats; they, too, were clapping. So was Mr Harewood, and Mrs Heppinstall, and the entire cast of *Tom Thumb*. It dawned on Ned, as Alfred rose to his feet, that the bogler really *was* famous, now. Everyone in the theatre seemed to know who he was. Why, everyone in *London* seemed to know who he was! And more than that – they seemed to appreciate him.

Suddenly, watching Alfred turn a stunned face to the crowd, Ned was struck by a strange, illogical, but quite brilliant notion.

He knew why the city's bogles were dying.

AN EMERGENCY MEETING

'There have been reports from all over London,' said Mr Harewood. 'Shadwell. Limehouse. Millbank – even Pentonville. People are finding dead bogles everywhere.' He plucked a flimsy sheet of paper from the table in front of him. 'Why, I've just received this request to remove a dead bogle from the Charing Cross Hotel! I can't imagine how the manager discovered my name. No doubt he's acquainted with someone at the Board of Works.'

He gazed at the company assembled in Mrs Heppinstall's dining room. To his right sat Miss Eames, wearing a sober expression and charcoal-coloured clothes. Beside her, Birdie looked a little paler than usual. Ned had been surprised to see her with ruffled hair and purple smudges under her eyes. The night before, at the theatre, she had seemed immortal – like a fairy or an angel. It had been a shock to realise, on arriving at Mrs Heppinstall's house, that Birdie was still a girl who spilled jam on her bodice and complained bitterly about taking baths.

The chair next to Birdie was occupied by Mr Wardle. Though reluctant to attend an emergency committee meeting on a Sunday, he had finally agreed when urged to do so by his own children. For he *had* been at the theatre the previous night, along with his entire family. And now his two daughters were keen that Birdie should sign their programmes. 'I knew I wouldn't have a moment's peace until I came,' Mr Wardle had confided to the rest of the committee. 'So here I am.'

Opposite Mr Wardle sat Jem Barbary, yawning and sighing and rubbing his eyes. He had been dragged out of bed at noon, but still wasn't properly awake, in Ned's opinion. Upon being informed that John Gammon was no longer a threat, Jem hadn't seemed terribly excited. He hadn't even displayed much interest in the mystery of the dying bogles. 'If yer spear's broke, it's as well all them bogles is wasting away,' had been his only comment, after hearing Alfred's account of recent events. 'But you're not to worry about paying the rent, Mr Bunce. For I'm to be in the next show, or so Mr Vokes says – and *he* had it from the manager's secretary.'

Mr Gilfoyle had positioned himself opposite Mr Harewood. The naturalist had just finished reading aloud the minutes of the last meeting. Now he sat with his brow furrowed, the very picture of concentration – though his gaze did keep slipping towards Miss Eames, Ned noticed.

Ned himself was seated beside Alfred. The bogler was in a morose mood. He'd spent most of the day hunched by the fire in his garret, sipping brandy and ignoring the sound of church bells. When Mr Harewood had arrived on his doorstep, with the news that a committee meeting had been scheduled for that very evening, Alfred had declared himself 'not fit for the company o' ladies'.

'I've seen worse,' the engineer had retorted, evaluating Alfred's condition with a practised eye. 'A little coffee and some fresh air will do wonders.'

But Alfred had shaken his head. 'You don't need *me* no more. I ain't got nowt to contribute.'

Seeing Mr Harewood's mystified look, Ned had

reluctantly spoken up. 'Mr Bunce lost his spear. It smashed.'

'*Smashed*?'

'On the floor o' the Monument.' Ned had gone on to describe this tragedy, while Jem had tended the fire, and Alfred had puffed at his pipe. But Ned's story hadn't swayed Mr Harewood one little bit.

'I understand how such a death must weigh on you, Mr Bunce,' the engineer had said, 'no matter how wicked the fellow was, or how deserving of punishment. It does credit to your conscience that you should suffer so. However, your conscience must also tell you that as an officer of the Committee for the Regulation of Subterranean Anomalies, you have a duty to attend every meeting, unless some sort of infirmity prevents it. Indeed, the loss of your spear is one reason why you *must* attend, since it will be the leading topic of conversation, I feel sure.'

But Mr Harewood was mistaken. The first topic raised in Mrs Heppinstall's dining room was the mystery of London's dying bogles. And after Mr Harewood had passed around the letter from the Charing Cross Hotel, Mr Gilfoyle remarked thoughtfully, 'These deaths seem to be occurring all over the city. There doesn't seem to be a concentration in any particular spot.'

'If there was poison in the sewers, we'd be seeing dead rats as well,' Mr Wardle volunteered. 'And *that* hasn't happened.'

'Could someone else be killing the bogles?' asked Miss Eames. 'You said last night, Mr Bunce, that a bogle had been killed by a customs-house officer. Perhaps other people are doing the same thing, and leaving the corpses.'

Alfred didn't reply. It was Mr Harewood who said, 'Even so, that doesn't tell us why these creatures are suddenly so vulnerable. Once upon a time, they were impervious to everything but Mr Bunce's spear. Unless I'm mistaken, Mr Bunce?'

'You ain't mistaken,' growled Alfred.

'Are you *quite* sure?' Mr Gilfoyle spoke hesitantly. He cleared his throat before adding, 'Out of interest, Mr Bunce, have you ever tried to kill a bogle with a . . . what was it? A poker? Or a cutlass? Or anything besides your own spear?'

As Alfred glared at the naturalist, Mr Harewood said quickly, 'On Thursday, Raz. He used *our* spear, remember? And it didn't work.'

'True. Yes, of course.'

During the brief silence that followed, Mr Gilfoyle nodded thoughtfully. Jem yawned and Mr Wardle shifted in his seat. Then, before Ned could open his mouth, Birdie remarked, 'Mebbe dead bogles were allus lying about, but people ignored 'em. Mebbe everyone knows what to look for now, on account o' the newspapers.'

Miss Eames gave a start. 'Why, yes!' she exclaimed. 'That *could* be the case, could it not? Perhaps nothing has changed except the public's understanding.'

'But Mr Bunce were in the newspapers last summer,' Jem reminded her, 'and no one started seeing dead bogles back *then*.'

'Back then he weren't hired by the Sewers Office,' Ned weighed in. Glancing around at all the blank faces, he realised that he would have to explain an idea that was very hard to put into words – an idea that had first struck him the night before, at the Theatre Royal. So he took a deep breath and said carefully, 'Back then, Mr Bunce were just an East End bogler, and folk thought him either a downy cove or a madman. Nowadays they believe he works for the government, like a sewer flusher. So they think bogling is like street-cleaning.' Ned paused, but there was no response; just the same old puzzled frowns and pursed lips. Seeing this, he tried another tack. 'Mebbe Birdie got it right when she said bogles was magic,' he went on. 'Mebbe bogles *was* magic, once, when people believed they was. But that ain't so, no more. To most London folk, bogles can't be magic if the Sewers Office has taken over their management. For the Sewers Office don't deal in magic, any more'n the Post Office would be sending telegraph boys to work on broomsticks. I'll wager most Londoners looked at the newspapers, these past few days, and thought, "Why, bogles is just common vermin! They ain't magic creatures with strange powers, after all!" And when that happened, the bogles might have changed. For mebbe bogles cannot live without our common belief to sustain 'em.'

There was a long, long silence. Finally Miss Eames began to nod, as Mr Harewood and Mr Wardle looked at each other with raised eyebrows. Even Mr Gilfoyle seemed struck by Ned's reasoning.

'By Jove,' he murmured, 'that's an interesting theory. And a logical one, too, though ... well, the whole notion of *magical beasts* doesn't sit well with me ...'

He trailed off. Ned, meanwhile, had coloured at the sight of Birdie's approving smile. 'Why, that *must* be the answer!' she exclaimed. 'How clever of you, Ned! But I always said you were as sharp as glass.'

'It seems as good an explanation as any, for all that it goes against the grain,' Mr Harewood conceded. 'What do *you* think, Mr Bunce?'

'I think, if it's true, it's a mercy.' Alfred sat with his arms folded, staring at the tablecloth. 'For with no spear left, I've no chance against any bogle as ain't dead.'

There was a shocked silence, then a babble of anxious questions. No spear? What did that mean? What had happened? Luckily, Mr Harewood was able to describe the encounter at the Monument, because Ned himself couldn't have done so. Even hearing about it made Ned feel sick.

Birdie's sudden pallor, and Miss Eames's horrified gasp, only served to remind him how narrowly he had escaped with his life.

'Oh, Mr *Bunce!*' cried Birdie. 'Why didn't you tell us?'

'We wasn't about to ruin yer special night, lass.'

'But yer spear! Yer precious spear!' Tears began to spill from Birdie's eyes. 'How can you be a bogler without *that*?'

'I ain't a bogler no more,' Alfred said flatly. 'And

won't need to be, neither, if Ned here is right about them bogles.'

'But you *are* a bogler! And you allus will be ...' Birdie's voice cracked on a sob as Alfred's grim face softened.

'Don't let it fret you, lass, for it don't fret me,' he said. 'I'm getting too old to be a bogler. And the flypaper trade ain't so bad.' Without warning, he turned to Ned, his voice growing gruffer by the second. 'The one thing as weighs on me,' he confessed, 'is the promise I made to you, lad. For I said you'd have me spear when I'd done bogling, but now ...' He sighed. 'Now there ain't no spear to have, nor no livelihood with it. I'm sorry, Ned. 'Tis a cruel blow, and not one you deserve. For you're as good a boy as ever I met, with a hard life behind you.'

Ned didn't know what to say. Had *this*, then, been the cause of Alfred's gloom? Was he worried about Ned's future, rather than his own? The very idea made Ned feel so guilty that he almost choked on the lump in his throat. For the prospect of becoming a bogler had always filled him with something close to despair ...

All at once Mr Harewood coughed and leaned forward.

'You've no cause to fret about Ned's prospects,'

he assured the bogler, with a touch of embarrassment. 'Only yesterday I was discussing with Gilfoyle how we might further the boy's education. For I believe he has a very bright future as an engineer if he were properly schooled. Isn't that so, Razzy?'

Mr Gilfoyle gave a nod, adding, 'Christ's Hospital school takes charity boys, as does the Charterhouse school. With our support, I'm sure he'd find a place.'

'And I could teach him his letters before he enrolled!' Miss Eames offered. The smile that she bestowed on Mr Harewood was so warm and admiring that it made him flush. 'What an excellent notion, Mr Harewood! I do *so* approve!'

'Providing the boy agrees, of course.' Mr Harewood turned to Ned. 'Would you like to learn mathematics? I'm convinced that you would excel at it – in fact I'm sure you'd be a better student than *I* ever was! Eh, Gilfoyle?'

Ned didn't hear Mr Gilfoyle's answer. There was a buzzing in his ears and a whirling in his head. He kept opening and shutting his mouth, too stunned to speak. Such generosity hardly seemed possible. Why, Mr Harewood hardly knew him! And the others . . . what claim did he have on *them*, that they should care about his future?

Jem was grinning; he winked as he caught Ned's eye. *Better you than me,* his expression seemed to say. Birdie was clapping her hands as she bounced around in her seat. 'Oh, Ned is so clever, he'll learn to read much more quickly than *I* ever did!' she chirruped, beaming and nodding and blinking back tears.

Alfred was staring at the tabletop. But when Ned looked at him, he glanced up and offered Ned one of his rare, gentle, lopsided smiles.

'It'd be a weight off all our minds, lad, if you was set on such a course,' he murmured. 'For I'd die content, knowing all you children had fine lives ahead of you.' Seeing Ned's bottom lip tremble, he frowned. 'What's the matter? Don't you want to be an engineer?'

'Of *course* I do!' Ned blurted out. Then he started to cry, overwhelmed by such unexpected kindness.

Luckily, Mr Harewood seemed to understand that Ned was happy, not sad. 'Good!' the engineer said in a bluff and jovial manner. 'That's settled, then. And in light of what Mr Bunce has just told us, we should ask ourselves: do we need this committee any longer? For if there are no more bogles, and no more boglers, and no more boglers' boys . . .'

'Then there ain't no need for a boglers' guild!' Jem concluded briskly. His hand shot into the air. 'All those in favour o' making this our *last ever* committee meeting, raise yer hand!'

There was no immediate response. Slowly, however, other hands began to join Jem's, until at last Mr Harewood said, 'The "ayes" have it.'

'Just in time for supper,' said Jem. And he was out the door, calling for toasted tea-cakes, before Ned even had a chance to blow his nose.

EPILOGUE

A horse and trap pulled up outside a two-storeyed house with very small windows. The driver was a weathered-looking man whose carter's smock was splashed with mud. Beside him sat a beautiful young lady in a buff-coloured travelling coat. She wore an elegant bonnet over a froth of golden curls, and the ruffled gown beneath her coat was exactly the same shade of blue as her eyes.

On the seat behind her were two young men, one of whom jumped down onto the road as soon as the wheels of the trap stopped turning. Small and limber, he had a dandyish look about him, thanks to his bright silk waistcoat and yellow gloves. His jet-black hair had been carefully oiled, and his moustache curled up at the ends.

As he helped the young lady out of the carriage, his friend climbed down too. This second young man was much taller than his companion. Brown-eyed and broad-shouldered, he had a handsome, clean-shaven face and a slow way of moving. His clothes were plain and sensible, though his missing canine tooth gave him a slightly rakish air. He dropped a few coins into the driver's outstretched hand.

'Come back in two hours,' he said.

'Three,' the young lady corrected. 'Please, Ned, we can always catch a later train.'

'Yes, but your show . . .'

'Oh, *bother* my show!' The young lady tossed her head and marched towards the grey stone house, which was set back from the road, behind a garden full of sweet peas. Ned glanced at the black-haired young man, who rolled his eyes and said, 'Artistic temperament.'

'There'll be the devil to pay if she misses her cue,' Ned replied. 'It nearly happened last week.'

'You're too soft, old boy. You should put your foot down. Ain't that what husbands are for?'

Ned coloured. 'You may recall, Jem, that we're not married yet.'

'Which is exactly my point. Didn't I say you should put your foot down? Or she'll be off touring America before you've had a chance to tie the knot, and where will that leave you?' Jem shook his head in an impatient fashion, then turned to the driver. 'Come back in two hours,' he instructed. 'And not a minute later, mind, for I don't want to be waiting about on a country lane like a drunken ploughman.'

The driver clicked his tongue and flicked his reins. As the wheels of the trap began to move, Ned and Jem approached the front door of the house, which was framed by a climbing rose. 'Two hours, Birdie!' Jem declared. 'I'm dining with a business acquaintance in London, and can't afford to keep him waiting.'

Birdie snorted. 'A business acquaintance?' she echoed, tapping on the door. 'I daresay you mean a shady fellow who imports cheap rotgut and bottles it as port wine.'

'Nothing of the sort,' Jem rejoined. 'He's in artificial hair.'

'*Artificial hair?*'

'There's a fortune to be made in artificial hair, ladies' fashions being what they are,' Jem insisted.

'That's what you said about artificial whalebone,' Birdie reminded him.

'Artificial whalebone will come into its own, you mark my words. With the cost of baleen increasing, and corsets more popular than ever—' Jem broke off suddenly, as the door in front of him swung open. 'Good morning, Mr Bunce!' he exclaimed, doffing his hat. 'Or should I say good afternoon? One becomes quite muddled about the time, when one sets off at the crack of dawn . . .'

Birdie had already flung herself at the old man on the threshold, who was thin and bent and silver-haired. He staggered as she threw her arms around his neck, but quickly recovered, returning her embrace as he smiled at the two young men.

'You've chosen a fine day for it,' he muttered, his voice low and rough. 'Come in, lass. Come in, all o' you. I've oatcakes for yer tea.'

Sure enough, there were soft Derbyshire oatcakes waiting on a table by the kitchen fire, along with cheese, milk and butter. A kettle was boiling on the hob. Jem immediately tucked in, but before sitting down, Birdie made a quick tour of the room, peering into cupboards and sniffing at jars as she untied the strings of her bonnet.

'I don't recognise this,' she said, fingering a china slop bowl. 'Was this Mother May's?'

'Aye. I found it in the roof, catching drips,' Alfred replied.

'But the roof isn't leaking, is it?' Jem looked up from his oatcake with a frown. 'We just paid for thatching!'

'Nay, lad, the roof's sound enough,' Alfred assured him.

'And the cracked pane upstairs?' asked Ned. 'Did the glazier come?'

'He did.'

'That old crone can't have spent a penny on this place in thirty years,' Jem grumbled. 'Generous of her to let it fall apart and then leave it to someone else to repair!'

'I ain't complaining,' was Alfred's response. And Birdie said impatiently, 'Don't be so stupid, Jem – of *course* it was generous of her, even though I'd prefer to see Mr Bunce living closer to London. I really don't think you should be staying here another winter, Mr Bunce. Not with that dreadful cough. *Won't* you reconsider?'

Birdie fixed Alfred with the melting look that had won hearts all over England. But he remained impervious.

'I'm right as I am,' was his answer. 'Derbyshire suits me. I've friends here now.'

'Like the glazier, I suppose. And the thatcher.' Jem was talking through a mouthful of oatcake. 'I'll wager they're always delighted to hear from *you*, Mr Bunce.'

'Which is Jem's little joke,' Ned suddenly remarked. He had removed the kettle from the hob, and was preparing to pour the tea. 'We none of us begrudge a penny that we've spent on this house – do we, Jem?'

He raised an eyebrow at Jem, who cried indignantly, 'Of course not!'

'Besides, I don't know why *you're* complaining,' Birdie added, her gaze on Jem. 'It was Ned who paid the thatcher, not you.'

'Because my shipment was delayed!' Jem's accent grew broader as his temper flared. 'And I paid the plasterer, didn't I?'

'Now, don't you bicker. You know I don't like it.' Alfred spoke sharply, and though his voice was weak and a little breathless, his sombre, reproving gaze had its usual effect. All three of his visitors immediately fell silent. 'It's yer news I want to hear,' he continued. 'How is Mrs Harewood? And the children?'

'Edith's a little tired, but both her children are well again.' Birdie's face brightened. 'Did I mention that Ned will be building a bridge with Mr Harewood?'

'Oh, aye?' Alfred turned his slow smile on Ned. 'That's a feather in yer cap, I daresay.'

'It most certainly is!' Birdie answered before Ned could. 'Though the bridge will be in Scotland, which is wretched news. I don't know how I'm to bear it, staying in London without Ned.'

'You went to Paris without him,' Jem interposed.

'For six weeks! Ned will be in Scotland for months and months . . .'

As Birdie prattled on, with occasional inter-ruptions from Jem and Ned, Alfred listened quietly. He heard about Jem's latest business venture, and Birdie's clashes with her leading man, and Ned's design for a new kind of steam hammer. There was a brief discussion of Mr Gilfoyle's latest book. ('Chapter three is all about bogles,' Birdie revealed, 'but it draws no useful conclusions – does it, Ned? Because no one has even *glimpsed* a bogle for years and years, unless you count the Loch Ness monster, so of course poor Mr Gilfoyle can only speculate.') Then Birdie described Mr Wardle's daughter's wedding, which had been 'very handsome', and confessed that her own wedding plans would have to be postponed, thanks to the job in Scotland. 'But of course you'll be giving me away, Mr Bunce,' she said airily. 'And Edith will be my matron of honour, and her youngest will be my flower girl—'

'Her youngest will be a matron too, if you don't hurry up,' Jem remarked, whereupon he and Birdie began to argue again. They only stopped when they heard the sound of a horse and trap rattling down the road outside.

'Oh, dear! So soon?' Birdie lamented. 'It seems no more than a few minutes since we arrived!'

'Time runs away when you're here,' Alfred agreed, rising stiffly as Birdie jumped to her feet. 'But I know how busy you are. T'were good o' you all to come.'

'So you're well, then?' Ned asked the question he'd already asked three times. 'Nothing's been troubling you?'

'I've no complaints,' said Alfred.

'And you're not lonely?' Birdie couldn't suppress a little shudder as she glanced out the window at a view of dark woods and empty fields. 'I'm sure you must miss London. How could you not?'

'I miss some o' the folk in it,' Alfred replied. 'That's all.'

'You don't miss bogling?' Ned fixed Alfred with a calm and steady look, which Alfred received with a half-smile.

'No more'n you do, lad.' He laid his hand briefly on Ned's arm. 'You take care, now. Don't fret too much ower things you can't mend.'

'I shan't,' Ned promised, as Birdie once more flung herself at Alfred.

'Goodbye, Mr Bunce!' she cried, peppering his face with kisses. 'We'll return as soon as we can – next month, if not next week. And you *must* visit us in London.'

'I'll come for the wedding,' Alfred promised.

He followed his three visitors outside, then stood watching as they climbed into the hired trap. Jem glanced at his pocket watch almost before the driver had cracked his whip, but Birdie kept waving and shouting as the trap rolled away down the road.

'Goodbye, Mr Bunce!' she bawled, as loudly as a hazelnut seller at Covent Garden Market. 'Wrap up warm! And don't go out in the evenings!'

Beside her, Ned lifted his hand just once. Nevertheless, it was his gaze that held Alfred's until the vehicle finally disappeared behind a blackthorn hedge.

Alfred stayed by his gate for some time after his visitors had left, staring off into the distance. It was the cry of a rook that seemed to rouse him from his trance. With a little shake of his head, he turned and went back to the kitchen, where he fetched water from the pump and washed all the dirty crockery. Only after he'd finished his chores did he don an old green coat, tuck his pipe into his pocket, slap a wide-brimmed hat onto his head, and set out across the fields.

It took him half an hour to reach the heart of the woods nearby. Here, in a rocky cleft overgrown with ferns, a stream had pooled beneath a small, damp cave. Alfred settled onto a moss-covered slope opposite this cave, with his back against the trunk of an ash tree. He then took out his pipe, stuffed it with tobacco, and lit up.

As the shadows slowly lengthened, and the birds began their evening rounds, Alfred sat puffing away. Finally he said, 'The children came from London, today. I gave 'em tea. You never seen finer young 'uns – all growed up and not a scar on 'em, for all their troubles. They done me proud.'

No one answered. But deep in the cave above the pool, something sighed and rustled.

'D'you know what Birdie said?' Alfred continued. 'She said as how Mr Gilfoyle mentioned bogles in his new book. So you ain't gone, and you ain't forgotten.' As he paused, the listening silence was broken only by the gurgle of water and the swish of wind-tossed leaves. At last Alfred gave a snort. 'You're just old,' he murmured. 'Old and sick and left ower from times past. But I ain't about to ferret you out. We're both of us too old for that.' He cocked his head, watching the mouth of the cave intently. 'It seems to me a man shouldn't have no enemies at the end of his life, no more'n he should at the beginning. So if you stay in there, and I stay out here believing in you, we'll rub along well enough – for all we ain't neither of us too chatty.'

Still there was no reply. Yet Alfred stayed where he was, quietly smoking, until the pool was engulfed in shadow.

Only when dusk fell did he finally extinguish his pipe, struggle to his feet, and slowly make his way home.

GLOSSARY

BEAK *a magistrate*

BLUNT *money*

BONCE *head*

CHINK *money*

CLAMMED *hungry*

COCKS O' THE GAME *pickpockets*

COVE *a man*

CRACKSMAN'S CROW *a housebreaker's lookout*

CUT YER STICK *run*

DARKEY *evening*

DOLLYMOP *a street woman (insult)*

DOWNY *cunning*

FLAM *lie*

FLASH HOUSE *a criminals' rendezvous*

FOGLES *silk handkerchiefs*

FOOTPAD *a robber or highwayman who operated on foot instead of on a horse*

GLOCKY *half-witted*

HEAVY WET *port wine*

HOIST *to steal or shoplift*

HOOK IT *move it*

HUM *deceit*

KEN *house; know (Scottish)*

KICKSIES *trousers*

LAG *a convict*

LEG IT *run*

LUSH *to drink; a drunkard*

NIBBED *arrested*

NICKEY *half-witted*

NOBBLER *a thug*

PEACH *to inform*

PEELER *policeman*

PIGGLE *fiddle with or pick at*

PRIG *to steal*

RAMMEL *rubbish*

READER *pocket book*

SAIR *sore*

SLAP-UP SPARK *dandy*

SPEELER *cheater*

SPRING HIM *free him*

STAGGED US *saw us*

STUMP UP *to pay*

SWAG *booty*

SWELL *an elegant gentleman*

TICKER *watch*

WELL TOGG'D *well dressed*

WITTLE *worry*

ABOUT THE AUTHOR

Catherine Jinks was born in Brisbane in 1963 and grew up in Sydney and Papua New Guinea. She studied medieval history at university and her love of reading led her to become an author. Her books for children, teenagers and adults have been published all over the world, and have won numerous awards.

Catherine lives in the Blue Mountains in New South Wales with her husband, journalist Peter Dockrill, and their daughter Hannah.

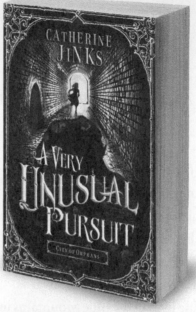

CITY *of* ORPHANS
BOOK 1

Monsters have been infesting London's dark places for centuries, eating any child who gets too close. That's why ten-year-old Birdie McAdam works for Alfred Bunce, the bogler. With her beautiful voice and dainty looks, Birdie is the bait that draws bogles from their lairs so that Alfred can kill them.

One life-changing day, Alfred and Birdie are approached by two very different women. Sarah Pickles runs a local gang of pickpockets, three of whom have disappeared. Edith Eames is an educated lady who's studying the mythical beasts of English folklore. Both of them threaten the only life Birdie has ever known.

But Birdie soon realises she needs Miss Eames's help, to save her master, defeat Sarah Pickles, and vanquish an altogether nastier villain.

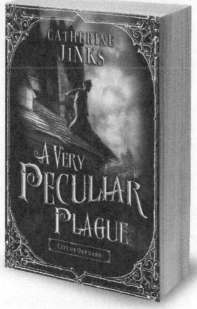

CITY *of* ORPHANS
BOOK 2

Eleven-year-old Jem Barbary spent his early life picking pockets for a canny old crook named Sarah Pickles. Now she's betrayed him, and Jem wants revenge. He also wants to work for Alfred Bunce the bogler, who kills the child-eating monsters that lurk in the city's cellars and sewers. But Alfred is keen to give up bogling, since he almost lost his last apprentice, Birdie.

When numerous children start disappearing around Newgate Prison, Alfred and Jem do join forces, waging an underground war. They even seek help from Birdie, dragging her away from the safe and comfortable home she's found with Miss Edith Eames. Together they learn that there's only one thing more terrifying than facing a whole plague of bogles – and that's facing some of the sinister people from Jem's past ...

Praise for the *City of Orphans* series

'A riveting read with some truly terrifying moments.'
AUSTRALIAN BOOKSELLER & PUBLISHER

'Jinks creates her setting and characters with clarity
and realism ... thoroughly entertaining ...
a fascinating new series.' THE SUN-HERALD

'Has a Dickensian feel ... and dark shades of Lemony
Snicket and Philip Pullman ... an unusually vivid historical
adventure.' THE SYDNEY MORNING HERALD

'Top-notch storytelling from Jinks ... full of wit,
a colorful cast of rogues, and delectable slang.'
PUBLISHERS WEEKLY

'A period melodrama replete with colorful characters,
narrow squeaks and explosions of ectoplasmic goo.'
KIRKUS REVIEWS

'With period detail, Dickensian charm, a brave heroine
and lots of suspense, this novel could make fantasy lovers
out of historical fiction fans, and vice versa.'
THE HUFFINGTON POST

'Dark, muddy and beautifully evoked with a cast of
characters reminiscent of a Dickens novel!'
ABC CANBERRA

'A lively, engaging story with an endearing protagonist
at its center.' SCHOOL LIBRARY JOURNAL

'Jinks is an assured storyteller ... Birdie is a bright,
stalwart heroine whose limitless font of haunting ballads
tinges the story with melancholy.' HORN BOOK